Raw Silk

Katherine sat on the edge of the fountain and put her face in her hands. She just couldn't bear it all; the beauty and the strangeness. She didn't belong here; she wasn't safe here, where she was prey to decadent polygamous princes and seductive irresistible sadists. She looked up to see Prince Somtow approaching.

'You don't need me, Somtow,' she said. 'Go back to your beautiful wife.'

'I do need you,' he said, as he seated himself next to her. 'I have waited so long for someone like you. Someone who combines intelligence and loveliness with a sex drive that matches my own.'

Katherine tore her gaze away from him. 'I can't be the other woman,' she said. 'In Thailand that may be acceptable, but I'm not Thai.' But even as she spoke the words, she knew that she had never known a lover so devoted to her pleasure. She knew this wasn't the end of things, and that they would only get more complicated, and more intense.

Raw Silk

LISABET SARAI

Black Lace novels are sexual fantasies.
In real life, make sure you practise safe sex.

First published in 1999 by
Black Lace
Thames Wharf Studios,
Rainville Road, London W6 9HT

Typeset by SetSystems Ltd, Saffron Walden, Essex
Printed and bound by Mackays of Chatham PLC

ISBN 0 352 33336 7

Contents

To KTR,
my partner and co-conspirator
and
GCS,
my master, mentor and muse

Chapter One
Bangkok Moon

*B*reathe ... Moist, ripe, heavy, laced with the scents of jasmine, garlic, diesel fuel, the tropical air was strange but welcome after the stale atmosphere of the airplane cabin. Kate O'Neill stepped off the jetway and filled her lungs gratefully. Even in business class, the twenty-hour flight had been gruelling. Kate ran her fingers through her tangled auburn curls and tried to smooth the wrinkles from her practical cotton skirt as she joined the crowds queuing at Immigration.

She felt a bit dazed. Only a month ago, she had answered the advertisement in the *Boston Globe*, and now here she was, half a world away, surrounded by foreign faces, buoyed by the musical rise and fall of Thai and a half-dozen other Asian languages.

It was nearly midnight, noontime in Boston. David would be headed out to lunch soon, perhaps to their favourite falafel place in Harvard Square. She remembered telling him of her decision to take the job, as they sat there nursing their espressos. His stricken face, the tears welling in his brown eyes; it was painful to recall.

Why had she chosen this course, so sudden and so radical? She was happy in her work, a senior engineer at a relaxed, progressive software company. Her family, her friends, her Back Bay condo, her dance classes, her

1

volunteer work, all tied her to New England. And then there was David, her lover of nearly three years, since they had met in graduate school. David was bright, funny, creative, gentle, strong. He shared her love of the outdoors, her interest in film, her enjoyment of exotic cuisines. David was her best friend as well as her partner in the bedroom.

A clear image of David came to her: lush, wavy brown hair; compact, wiry body; deft hands; and eager manhood. On their last night, he had sunk to his knees before her, weeping, begging her to reconsider. Then, the next morning, he had taken her unexpectedly in the airport parking garage.

Partially hidden by the open trunk of the car, he began by kissing her, hard, backing her up against a concrete support pillar. As their tongues entwined, he raised her skirt, pushed aside the fabric of her panties, and stroked her clitoris, lightly at first, then with greater force. Even as she worried about their exposed position, she could not help but respond, rubbing against his hand as he inserted one, two, then three fingers into her, all the while continuing to stroke with his thumb. His whole hand was inside her underwear, stretching the elastic, as she bore down, trying to work him even deeper into her.

Then, without warning, he stopped. Gently, he turned her around to face the pillar. He pushed her skirt up to her waist and pulled her knickers down around her knees. Kate had been only too willing to spread her legs wide, holding on to the rough concrete with both hands. A car drove past, seeking a parking spot, as David eased his cock into her hungry depths.

'Next, please.' She started, embarrassed, as a young man in uniform beckoned her forward to the counter. As he examined her passport, for what seemed like an inordinately long time, she wondered whether she had made a mistake, leaving David and her home for this land of strangers. David, though always enthusiastic, was not usually so daring and inventive, but perhaps he was changing. Her vague dissatisfaction and the sharp pang of wanderlust that had seized her when she first spotted the advertisement – were these realistic justifications for committing herself to a year in a foreign culture?

Finally, the inspector stamped her passport, with great ceremony, half a dozen times. Then the serious youth surprised her by breaking into a brilliant smile. 'Welcome to Thailand, Miss O'Neill. I hope you enjoy your stay here.'

Kate smiled back. 'Thank you.' She suddenly knew that she had chosen well. However this year turned out, it would be an adventure, a welcome variation in her well-ordered life.

She followed the stream of people to the baggage carousel and retrieved her luggage without incident. Trailing the cart behind her, she emerged from the international arrival area, into the confusion of the general concourse.

The area outside the gates swarmed with noisy humanity, faces everywhere, waving hands, shouting voices. Here and there, signs on sticks bobbed above the crowd, with hotel logos or the names of individuals. Kate scanned the scene nervously. She located the placard inscribed 'Katherine O'Neill', just as its bearer, a balding Thai with a drooping black moustache, noticed her. He pushed his way to the front of the crowd.

'Miss O'Neill?' The man grinned at her as she nodded, his lively black eyes taking her in at a glance: her petite frame, unruly curls, rumpled clothing. 'Welcome to Bangkok – City of Angels!'

'I am Chaiwat, Mr Harrison's driver. Mr Harrison has sent his own car, to take you to your house. Please follow me.'

Without waiting for her reply, he took charge of the luggage cart and started through the crowd toward the exit. Kate struggled to keep up, watching his back recede, worried at having lost control of her bags, trying to make progress through the press of bodies without seeming impolite.

Chaiwat was waiting for her on the kerb, still grinning. 'Stay here, please. I will go for the car.' He disappeared into the humid night.

Kate leant wearily against her largest suitcase. She had never met Edward Harrison, the Managing Director of DigiThai Ltd, her new employer, although they had spoken several times by telephone. Clearly, he was considerate, to offer her the services of his personal car and driver. Of course, he was an American (from Chicago, she recalled), and no doubt understood from personal experience how exhausted she would be after the trans-Pacific flight.

A sleek white Mercedes sedan slid up to the kerb and, almost before it stopped, it seemed, energetic Chaiwat was loading her cases into the trunk. He held open the back door, and she sank down on to the leather-upholstered seat with a grateful sigh. She drifted in and out of a half-sleep as Chaiwat drove out of the airport and turned on to the highway towards the city.

From under heavy eyelids, she watched the roadside sights fly by. Garish neon signs, in English, Thai and Chinese, lit up the night with the names of multinational corporations. Gleaming modern buildings two dozen storeys high alternated with stunted blocks of grimy concrete, weak fluorescent light visible through their open windows. Every now and again, she would glimpse the peaked, layered roofs and delicate spires of a Buddhist temple, rising incongruously from the middle of a residential or industrial district.

The full moon rendered the scene even more alien. High above the horizon by now, it lent a silvery sheen to the buildings, while creating sharp black shadows between and behind them. Brighter than any manmade illumination, it reminded Kate of an old-fashioned flashbulb. Each tableau seemed frozen in meticulous detail, captured by the moon like a surrealistic snapshot.

The car was silent, seeming to float over the road. The

4

slight hiss of the air conditioning soothed her. Kate tried to stay alert, to pay attention to her new surroundings, but drowsiness was irresistible.

She found her mind drawn back to David and the scene in the parking garage. The recollection, on the edge of sleep, was vivid, almost a hallucination. She could feel his hands, grasping her hips, positioning her for his thrusts. Despite their exposure, he did not hurry. His cock stretched her deliciously as he slid in, practically in slow motion, as if he were savouring every centimetre. He was deep inside her, but only for a moment before he started to withdraw. It was as if he were trying to memorise her body, imprint it upon his senses; he lingered at each stage, focused on each motion, constriction, texture.

Her own body was afire, but her urgency did not seem to communicate itself to him. Her nipples, hard as little pebbles, brushed against the smooth cotton of her blouse, raising a little gasp that she tried to suppress. David made no sound, breathed deeply but smoothly, in rhythm with his strokes, while she found herself panting, smothering her moans. She writhed, rubbing her bottom against him. The rough curls of his pubic hair against her bare skin made her wild.

She reached behind her and grasped the base of his penis with one hand. The other hand found its way between her own legs, working its way among the slick folds to find her aching clitoris. She squeezed David and massaged herself, both hands moving together. David responded, drawn out of his reverie, catching fire from her. He began thrusting harder, faster, deeper, just as she craved. Now he was panting too. She had to stop her self-caresses in order to hold the concrete support in front of her with both hands. Otherwise, the force of his thrusts would have knocked her over.

David made an animal noise, deep in his throat. He dug his nails into her flesh, pulling the mounds of her buttocks apart to have better access to the juicy cleft of her sex. Kate arched her back, opening herself wider, aching for total penetration. Again and again David plunged into her, riding her with a ferocity he had never shown before.

She loved this position, the feral quality of being taken from behind. She loved the danger, too, she admitted to herself, the chance of being discovered with her panties down and her private parts glistening with moisture. The thought of this, of how they would look to some passer-by, was the final stroke. That image, added to the furious friction of David's cock, the tingling in her nipples, the brush of his pubic hair on her thighs, his fingernails marking her arse, finally pushed her to edge and beyond.

David felt her spasms, and matched them. He collapsed forward on to her, both of them leant against the pillar. As their breathing gradually slowed to normal, David caressed her breasts, left tiny, precise kisses at the back of her neck.

Kate started, suddenly alert. Her real environment reasserted itself, the supple leather beneath her, the artificially refreshing breeze from the air-conditioning vents. She realised that Chaiwat was watching her in the rear-view mirror, at the same time as she found she had both hands in between her legs. Her sex ached with imagined or new hunger; she could not tell which. Casually, she moved her hands to her sides, sat up a bit straighter, tried to ignore the grin she saw reflected towards her.

The car had left the highway now, and was cruising through nearly deserted city boulevards. Then Chaiwat turned sharply right and began winding through a maze of narrow lanes, lined with stucco and cement walls broken by an occasional wrought-iron gate. Finally, he brought the Mercedes to a halt in front of one such gate, got out and rang a bell. The grille slid open. Chaiwat was already back in the driver's seat guiding the car into the compound.

'Here we are, miss. Your house. Mr Harrison hopes that you will find it satisfactory.'

Kate extricated herself from the car's comfortable embrace. The house was small, almost a cottage, but had two storeys, and was surrounded by lush gardens. A huge tree with gnarled, contorted limbs stood before the building, bearing drooping masses of vines and creepers. She breathed deep, savouring the sweetness of flowers she could not name. The humid air caressed the bare skin on her arms. She heard the chittering of insects and, softly, the music of flowing water. There must be a pool or fountain, she thought, smiling to herself. She noted a balcony on the second floor, overlooking the garden.

The front door was open; a feminine figure was silhouetted in the light. As Kate approached, the woman glided forward to meet her; she was barefoot, the bright colours of her sarong vivid even in the semi-darkness. The woman placed her palms together at breast level and bowed slightly, bringing her fingertips to her brow. 'Welcome, madame. I am Ae, your maid. Please be at home.'

'Hello, Ae. I am pleased to meet you,' Kate began, but the young woman had already picked up one of the bags that Chaiwat had unloaded and was carrying it into the house.

Kate followed, marvelling at the maid's grace, even when she was lugging a heavy suitcase. The woman's jet-black hair hung down her back to her waist. Her diminutive stature made Kate, barely five feet tall herself, feel huge by comparison. Ae turned back to make sure Kate was following, an innocent, joy-filled smile on her lovely features. 'Please remove your shoes,' she reminded Kate.

Kate left her slip-off pumps in the foyer and entered the living room: polished teak floors under her feet; whitewashed walls; floor-to-ceiling drapes across sliding doors that led to the garden; simple, comfortable-looking furniture of some blond wood; a spiral staircase of wrought iron in the corner, leading to the second floor. Kate surveyed her new abode with pleasure.

There was a well-equipped kitchen and dining alcove, plus a breakfast bar with rattan stools. On the counter stood an enormous basket of exotic fruit, elaborately decorated with ribbons and coloured foil. She read the card. It was another welcoming message, signed 'Warmest wishes, Edward Harrison'.

Once more Kate wondered about her new boss. He seemed very concerned about her comfort and welfare. Well, she would meet him soon enough. It was Saturday (Sunday, by now, she corrected herself) and she planned to start work on Monday.

Ae glided down the stairs and stood quietly, waiting to be acknowledged. 'Your bags are upstairs in the bedroom, madame, and there are towels laid out in the bathroom for your shower. Can I do anything more for you tonight?'

The notions of a shower and a bed were overwhelmingly appealing. 'No, thank you, Ae.' She turned to thank Chaiwat and say good night, but the driver was nowhere to be seen. A strange man, she thought, remembering his almost lustful stare in the mirror.

'Then good night, madame.' The lovely creature made another half-bow, which Kate recognised from her reading as the traditional *wai* of respect. 'If you need anything, please call. My room is just outside the back door.'

'Good night, Ae.' Kate watched the maid check the lock, then close the door firmly. Were all Thai women so exquisite? Looking at Ae, Kate felt an odd pressure in her chest, like a sob trapped, tears unshed. Like catching a glimpse of a deer motionless along the roadside, or finding a single, fragile lady's-slipper half buried in the moss of the forest floor.

Kate shook her head to clear it, and slowly pulled herself up the stairs to the bedroom. Soon hot water was streaming over her, deliciously sluicing away the grime of her journey and easing her aching muscles. As she rubbed herself dry, she couldn't help but approve of her own body. Her creamy skin spoke of her Irish

8

background, her muscular thighs and calves of her years of ballet and modern dance classes. Her breasts were not large, but they had a pleasing symmetry, with plump nipples that stayed erect regardless of her state of arousal. Her hips and buttocks were surprisingly full, contrasting with the general impression of petiteness and delicacy she conveyed to the casual observer.

She brushed the towel lightly over the reddish curls below her navel, and felt a faint electric thrill, an echo of her earlier desire. With a sigh, she turned out the light, climbed into bed, pulled a sheet over her nakedness (she generally slept in the nude, a habit she had acquired while in college) and tried to relax.

The room stayed bright with moonlight filtering in through the translucent curtains. The sliding door to the balcony was open. Through the screen the gentle breeze brought the garden scents into the room.

Despite her exhaustion, Kate found it difficult to sleep. After all, it was the middle of the day back in her normal time zone. The moon made patterns on her closed eyelids; she tried the strategy of focusing on them, watching them ebb and flow like wavelets on a beach. She began to drift along with the moon-tides a little.

Then, she heard a sound, or thought she did, a human sound like a cry or moan. Silently she rose and went over to the balcony door, peering between the curtains. Was there someone there, perhaps hidden in the deep shadows under the twining tree? Then she heard the noise again, from the left, the far corner of the garden where the moon shone full on an intricate sculpture of a Thai temple.

At first she couldn't see anything. Then, as her eyes adjusted to the brightness, she discerned two figures below the temple on its pedestal. A man and a woman, in a fervent embrace.

It was Ae, Kate realised, recognising the multi-coloured sarong. Her companion's face was in shadow, hidden in the luxurious mass of her hair. He stood behind her, encircling her with his arms, his right hand massaging her breast while his left was cupped firmly over her pubis. Ae writhed in his grasp, clearly welcoming his touch.

Kate watched, holding her breath, as the right hand unbuttoned the maid's blouse one slow button at a time. Simultaneously, the left hand loosed the twists in the cloth that held the sarong around her waist. The fabric fell to the ground, revealing the girl's shapely thighs and buttocks.

The man's right hand now grasped her right nipple, delicately rolling it between finger and thumb. The left hand travelled languidly up the front of her body to the other breast, capturing the other nipple in a symmetric caress. The maid arched her back in pleasure, pressing her buttocks against her partner's body. Another soft moan escaped her lips.

Now the man gently released Ae's breasts, and turned her towards him. The moon lit up his face, and Kate recognised Chaiwat's drooping moustache and ironic grin. Somehow, she was not surprised.

He was not particularly tall, but he appeared to tower over the tiny figure of the maid. He bent to kiss her, full on the lips, then stripped off his trousers and shirt with amazing speed.

Kate continued to watch the naked couple. Chaiwat lifted Ae with both hands and settled her on to his ready cock. Kate felt a stirring between her own thighs as the maid wrapped her legs around Chaiwat's waist. The driver held his partner firmly by the buttocks, and began to rock her up and down, slowly at first, with time for one long breath between each thrust. Meanwhile, he used his tongue on Ae's breasts, circling one nipple and then the other in the same deliberate rhythm.

Hidden behind the curtains, Kate let her fingers linger on her own breasts, teasing, barely touching, imagining the sensations the maid was experiencing. She leaned against the doorframe and gave herself up to her own pleasure, her hands travelling familiar pathways across her own flesh.

Ae gripped Chaiwat's shoulders. In the brilliant white light, Kate thought she could see indentations where the maid's nails pressed into his skin. Chaiwat countered this, taking a plump nipple into his mouth and lightly applying his teeth. Ae gave a little yelp.

Kate pinched her own nipple as hard as she could. Waves of sensation, too delicious to be pain, spread from that focus down to her sex. With her thumb and forefinger she pulled on her clitoris, imagining the wiry driver's hands on her arse. She felt the moon washing over her; her smooth skin was luminous, damp with the heat and with her excitement.

Kate turned her eyes again to the scene below her. Ae had Chaiwat locked firmly between her thighs. His thrusts came faster now, and Ae was making soft whimpering sounds each time he drove his cock into her. The rhythm quickened still more. Kate stroked herself in time, her breath becoming quick and shallow as climax grew closer.

Suddenly Ae cried out sharply. Kate opened her eyes just before she reached her own peak, to see the maid arched backward, long hair falling around her in a dark cascade. Moonlight burnt the scene into Kate's memory: entwined limbs and gleaming flesh, fragrant shadows and silken tresses.

City of Angels, indeed. As Kate surrendered herself to the irresistible waves of orgasm, one small part of her mind noted that Chaiwat had been looking up, grinning obscenely, directly at her bedroom window.

Chapter Two
The Prince

*T*he first week flew by in a blur. Jet lag muddled Kate's thoughts and perceptions as she tried to assimilate the fascinating and mystifying details of her new surroundings.

Despite her persistent drowsiness, Kate managed to get herself into a taxi and over to the Silom Road offices of DigiThai Ltd on Monday morning. The company leased a suite on the tenth floor of a modern office building. Kate announced herself to the receptionist, a friendly young woman with stylishly short hair who introduced herself as Anchana.

'Please sit down, Miss O'Neill. Mr Harrison will be with you in just a moment.' Anchana's English was nearly perfect, with only a slight accent.

Kate admired the understated décor of the anteroom: Scandinavian-style teak furniture upholstered in raw silk, multicoloured weavings framed on the walls, a single spray of white orchids in a simple celadon vase on Anchana's teak and glass desk. Kate's new company, it appeared, was far from struggling.

'Katherine!' The hearty voice matched the man who emerged from the door behind Anchana's desk. Edward Harrison was large, grizzled, bear-like. He wore gold-rimmed glasses, a matching Rolex watch, several rings and a perfectly-tailored grey suit. He beamed at her and shook her hand enthusiastically. 'We didn't expect to see you today. I had assumed that you would take several days off to recover.'

Kate returned the vigorous handshake and the smile. 'I was eager to get started, Mr Harrison. Also, I thought that perhaps being busy would help me to forget how sleepy I feel!'

'Please, call me Edward. Well, we are delighted that you are here.' He surveyed her, in her trim navy skirt and blazer, and heels, with obvious approval. 'You are even better than I had hoped.'

This struck Kate as a very odd remark. However, Harrison continued without giving her time to dwell on it.

'Anchana will show you your office, introduce you to everyone and help you get settled. Later this morning, why don't you drop by and we'll have more opportunity to get acquainted.'

DigiThai, it turned out, consisted of about a dozen individuals. Aside from Kate and Edward Harrison, all were Thai. The company developed and sold off-the-shelf and customised multi-media systems: computers, graphics displays, video-recording and display equipment and, of course, the software. This was where Kate apparently fitted in. She had been hired as the technical manager, to enhance and expand the company's software offerings.

The sales and marketing team consisted of two earnest young men with slicked-back hair and dark suits. They grinned broadly when introduced, belying their studied self-presentation as businesslike and serious. The company also included Ruengroj ('call me Roj'), a commercial artist and photographer with faded blue jeans and black ponytail, several hardware engineers (white business shirts, dark pants, no neckties), and a three-person software engineering team, all recent graduates from prestigious King Mongkut Institute of Technology.

Despite their common background, the software engineers were diverse. First, there was Wang, a plump, cheerful man of Chinese descent who favoured loud shirts and cowboy boots. In contrast, Suvit was skinny and shy with a voice so soft Kate could hardly understand him, despite his good English. Finally, there was Malawee, a woman perhaps five years Kate's junior, with straight shoulder-length hair and wire-frame glasses. Aside from the receptionist, and Kate herself, Malawee was the only other female in the company.

It was Malawee who helped Kate become acquainted with her new surroundings. Initially reserved, the Thai woman became much more open and friendly when Kate made it clear that she considered Malawee a colleague, not a subordinate.

Malawee helped Kate set up an account on the network, configure her email and access the existing software libraries. She spent several hours introducing Kate to the company's products and capabilities before leaving Kate in her office to explore more deeply on her own.

Edward Harrison provided Kate with a business orientation.

'As I told you when we spoke on the phone,' he boomed, 'we are targeting the entertainment and advertising industries here in Thailand. These sectors are growing rapidly, and they are extremely keen on digital technology.' He gestured at a graph tacked to the wall behind his desk. 'There have been thirteen new cable-television channels launched here during the last six months. Two cyberclubs opened in Bangkok, complete with virtual-reality booths and long-distance video-conferencing. Half a dozen new Internet service providers have registered with the authorities.'

'Meanwhile, Thai advertising agencies are booking clients from Singapore, Hong Kong, even Australia, all of whom want technically sophisticated visual effects. As you may have noticed –' he beamed at her over the rims of his glasses '– the Thais frequently exhibit an amazingly refined aesthetic sense.'

This remark reminded Kate of her beautiful house and garden, and her equally exquisite maid. Ae had given no indication, the next morning, that anything unusual had occurred. She appeared as guileless, innocent and composed as she had when greeting Kate the night before. While eating a late breakfast, Kate had watched Ae sweeping and tidying in continued amazement at the maid's grace. Was this really the same woman she had spied on in the garden and who had writhed and groaned in the arms of her salacious lover?

During that first week, Kate saw no further signs of Chaiwat, and she began to wonder whether, dazed with fatigue and missing her own lover, she might have imagined the moonlight scene. She was busy enough with her new life and responsibilities, though, that she did not have time to dwell on the possibility.

By Friday Kate found she was regaining her customary alertness. No longer did her head feel as if it were stuffed with cotton wool. She could stay awake past 9 p.m., and had stopped finding herself in bed, wide-eyed and unsleeping, in the early hours of the morning.

Friday, around noon, as Kate was leaving to get some lunch and do a few errands, Edward Harrison called out to her.

'Katherine! Do you have a few minutes? There is someone I'd like you to meet.' He held open the door and ushered her into his plushly appointed office. A Thai man, seated among the silk cushions of the carved sofa, rose gracefully as she entered.

Katherine made no outward sign, but she inwardly caught her breath. This was one of the most handsome men she had ever seen. Thick, wavy black hair framed a pale, smooth, symmetrical face. The features were delicate, almost feminine, and the full lips jarred slightly with the man's attentive, serious demeanour, but the strong chin and straight nose conveyed a sense of

15

natural authority. The man's eyes were large, dark, almond-shaped, with a distinct twinkle that Kate found immediately appealing.

She still found it difficult to determine the age of the Thais, but Katherine guessed that he was in his early thirties. He moved with the kind of fluid control that she associated with dancers, or athletes. The man was dressed impeccably, if a bit conservatively, in a charcoal-grey suit of beautiful Italian wool. A flash of gold from his cuffs caught her eye.

'Katherine, this is Khunying Somtow Rajchitraprasong, our Thai partner in DigiThai. Khunying Somtow, Miss Katherine O'Neill.'

The smile brewing in the man's eyes burst on to his face as he took Katherine's hand. 'A great pleasure, Miss Katherine,' he said, bowing slightly. 'I have been looking forward to meeting you ever since Edward told me that you were coming. How are you enjoying your stay in Thailand?'

Kate returned the handshake. The man's skin was cool, dry, remarkably pleasing to the touch. 'Khunying Somtow, the honour is mine.' She relinquished his hand almost reluctantly. 'Since I've been here only a few days, I've seen very little. But I'm most impressed by what I have seen so far.'

'Perhaps I will be able to show you more of the real Thailand, Miss Katherine.' When Somtow Rajchitraprasong smiled, the whole room lit up. 'Edward, I have taken enough of your valuable time, and Miss Katherine's. I must go now.' Turning back to Katherine, he bowed a second time. 'Once again, a pleasure.'

Edward Harrison cleared his throat. 'Katherine, would you mind walking Khunying Somtow to the elevator? Anchana is still not back from lunch.'

'Of course. I was on my way out in any case.' The Thai man stood aside politely for her to exit the office, then held the door of the suite for her. She tried to ignore her raging heartbeat as they waited for the elevator.

'Edward tells me that you are very accomplished as a software engineer, that you have several patents.'

Katherine blushed, uncharacteristically. 'Well, I can't take complete credit; I was just the leader of the development team.'

'Even so. I am sure that you will be a tremendous asset to DigiThai.'

'Well, of course I will do my best.' The elevator arrived and they stepped into the empty cabin.

'And also, I understand that you are a dancer.'

Katherine froze. Why would Edward have communicated this tidbit of her life's history to this man who was, in effect, her Thai boss? She tried to answer lightly. 'It's just a hobby, although I do enjoy it very much.'

Somtow looked at her directly, clearly evaluating and appreciating her body. Somehow, his honest gaze was more flattering than insulting. 'I can see that you would, Miss Katherine.' He held her eyes for a moment then smiled as the elevator reached the ground floor and the door slid open.

As they reached the street door, Kate held out her hand.

'Well, goodbye. I hope to see you again sometime.'

'Why not now?' Somtow smiled. 'Would you do me the honour of joining me for lunch?'

Flustered, Katherine shook her head. 'I'm sorry, but I have several pressing errands. Also, I must be back in time for a meeting at two-thirty.'

'So diligent!' Kate thought she heard a touch of laughter in his cultured voice. 'In that case, would you come to dinner? At my home, tomorrow evening?' For a moment, she felt as though someone had cut the elevator cables; her stomach plummeted and she was out of breath. 'Please, Katherine. It will be a first opportunity for me to show you something of our Thai ways.'

Katherine was confused. This was her boss's partner, clearly a man of wealth, power and influence. Was it proper for her to see him socially? At the same time, she found him extremely appealing: his lively good humour and slightly old-fashioned manners as well as his laughing eyes and lithe body.

'Well . . .' she began.

'Please. Here is my card.' He offered it with both hands, and she took it automatically. 'My home address is on the left; on the back you will find it written in Thai for your taxi driver.' Katherine turned the square of cardboard, admired the archaic, flowing characters. 'Would eight o'clock be convenient?'

'Ah – yes, yes of course. Eight o'clock would be fine.' She still felt dazed.

'Wonderful. I will look forward to seeing you.' He took her hand in both of his. 'Until then, Miss Katherine, I will take my leave of you.'

As Kate awkwardly bid him farewell in turn, out of the corner of her eye she saw Anchana re-entering the building. The young woman's eyes were wide with surprise.

When she returned from lunch, Anchana beckoned to her. 'Do you know who you were talking to?' the receptionist asked in an excited, hushed tone.

'Of course,' said Kate. 'Khunying Somtow is the Thai partner of Digital Enterprises Limited. Mr Harrison introduced us this morning.'

Anchana could hardly contain herself. 'But, that's not all! He is a Khunying – a member of the Royal Family. What you would call in English a prince. He will probably never be King, but his family has a high place, very high.'

A prince! And he had invited her to dinner. Now Kate felt twice as nervous.

The taxi took Katherine into an unfamiliar part of the city. She sat in the back seat, her hands folded in her lap, trying to distract herself by observing the sights around her: sidewalk noodle carts surrounded by rickety metal tables and stools, gleaming display windows showing off designer clothing and imported cars, vacant lots fenced in corrugated tin, red and orange tiles on the layered roofs of the occasional temple.

She had spent half the day worrying about what to wear. How formal should she be? Should she wear heels, or were sandals sufficient? Her basic black sheath with its short hemline and her pearls? The flowing blue batik she had found in the little shop around the corner from her house? Should she wear a suit, given that Khunying Somtow was a business acquaintance? She wanted to look attractive, she admitted to herself, but not overly seductive; she did not want to send the wrong message. But what message did she really want to send, she asked herself privately.

She had settled for simplicity: an ankle-length, sleeveless dress of forest-green Thai silk and black patent sandals. Her good pearls set off the scooped neckline of the gown. The luscious green of the silk made her hair blaze all the more brightly; the slit skirt allowed her to walk comfortably and provided an occasional glimpse of her well-muscled thigh.

In a moment of rebelliousness that she was beginning to regret, she had decided to forgo wearing a brassiere. It was too hot, she told herself, too uncomfortable. Now, as the cab pulled in through a set of elaborate wrought-iron gates, Katherine could feel her bare nipples brush against the light silk. She gave a little shiver. What had she been thinking? Well, it was too late now.

The taxi had stopped in a circular driveway, in front of massive double doors of carved wood. As Katherine paid the fare, the doors were opened by a regal woman in a purple sarong and close-fitting gold-embroidered blouse. A sash with an intricate pattern of purple and gold crossed her breast and was held at one shoulder with a brooch like a sunburst. Her hair was piled high on her head, held in place by combs with matching sunburst designs.

The woman made a graceful *wai* then spoke in accented English.

'Miss Katherine, you are welcome to the Khunying's

home. Please leave your shoes here and follow me. Dinner will be served in the *sala* in the garden.'

Katherine found herself in a semi-circular entrance hall. She slipped out of her sandals and savoured the cool smoothness of the polished terrazzo floor under her bare feet. The maid led her through a set of French windows to a long corridor floored with teak parquet. A subdued light came from intermittent electric sconces designed to look like candle lanterns. The corridor was lined with etched glass doors, all closed. Occasionally, she and her guide would pass a painting, a piece of sculpture, or a porcelain vase, artfully lighted so that it seemed to glow from within. Katherine particularly noted a seated Buddha image of white marble, no more than six inches high but wrought in exquisite detail.

Eventually, the corridor ended in another set of French windows. The maid threw these open, and Katherine nearly swooned at the rich floral scents that flowed from the garden beyond. She stepped from the mysterious corridor into the sweet, humid night.

Katherine found herself on a winding path paved with smooth pebbles that tickled her bare feet. Occasional torches provided enough light to see the tangled vines, towering ferns and vivid blossoms that surrounded her as she walked. From ahead, she heard the sound of flowing water and, faintly, the haunting notes of a solo flute. The path twisted around the trunk of a massive tree, and she saw before her a pavilion of unpainted wood with a steep-pitched roof like one of the temples.

The *sala* was perched on stilts in the middle of a pool. A rough set of stairs, arching over the water, led up to the platform. Her heart echoing in her ears, she slowly mounted the steps and entered the enchanting building.

Dozens of flickering candles in earthenware jars lit the porch-like platform. Bright pillows were strewn over the wooden floor, around a low table. Khunying Somtow sat cross-legged on one of the cushions, a bamboo flute poised at his lips.

For a moment he did not notice her, and she could admire him. He wore a high-necked shirt and loose pants of white satin. His dark hair shone like jet in contrast. His eyes were half-closed, and a look of peaceful concentration graced his handsome features.

Some slight sound, or movement of the air, made him look up. His expression of repose was replaced with animation.

'Miss Katherine! Welcome. I did not hear you arrive. Please, come in, sit down.' He rose in one fluid motion, took her hand, and led her to a bank of cushions piled up against the wooden rail that surrounded the pavilion. 'I ask your pardon for my amateurish playing.'

'Oh no, it was lovely! Though it was very different from anything I have heard before.'

'No, I do not have the time to give my music the devotion it deserves. Classical music requires discipline. I am no more than a dilettante, as I am in so many other things.' He sighed a little, then smiled. 'But it gives me pleasure to play, and that is perhaps enough.'

He gazed at her for a moment, with the same frankness that she had noted in the elevator. 'I am so glad that you have come. May I offer you some wine?'

'Yes, please,' said Kate, already relaxing a bit in response to his easy charm. He filled a crystal glass from a bottle that even she recognised as expensive, then picked up his own half-full goblet from the floor next to his cushion.

'To new friendship,' he said, touching glasses and looking into her eyes.

Katherine held his gaze for a few moments. She felt herself beginning to blush again and was irritated at her own weakness. 'To new experiences, in a new land,' she countered evenly.

The wine was delicious, with a slight chill even though the night was warm.

'So,' said Somtow, reclining a little against the cushions, 'after a week, what are your impressions of my country?'

21

'Beautiful, but confusing.' Katherine took another sip, felt the wine coursing through her and loosening her tongue. 'Full of contrasts. In some ways, the Thais are so modern, with their skyscrapers, their computers, and their cellular phones. Then, only yesterday, I was walking through the market near my house. Piles of vegetables, fruit, flowers, balanced on those circular woven baskets. Raw meat laid out in the open on beds of ice. The vendors squatting behind their wares in sarongs and straw hats. I thought, this probably looked the same fifty years ago.'

'Oh, yes,' Somtow smiled. 'We are a people of ancient traditions, but we have always been open to outside influences.' Almost languidly, he leaned forward to refill her glass. 'Do you know about Ayuthaya?'

'The old capital, upriver, that was destroyed by the Burmese?' Katherine was glad she had done some research in the month before her departure.

'Ayuthaya was a marvel – a city of glittering temples and palaces, the purest expression of the Thai spirit. The court at Ayuthaya welcomed ambassadors from all over Europe, eager to learn about their culture, trade in their riches, enjoy their pleasures.'

Somtow drank the last of his wine. 'I would be honoured if you would allow me to show you Ayuthaya as it is today. The tumbled heaps of brick and overgrown pagodas still have a certain majesty.'

Katherine looked into his dark eyes. 'That would be wonderful. I cannot think of anyone I would rather have as my guide.'

A slight sound drew their attention to the stairs, where they saw the purple-garbed woman carrying a tray filled with a bewildering assortment of food. She knelt by the table and placed the various dishes before them.

'Thank you, Orapin.' The woman rose, bowed without speaking, and left as quietly as she had come.

'Did you signal her somehow?' asked Katherine.

'Orapin knows me very well, and can often anticipate

22

my wishes. We have been together since childhood; her mother served my father.'

'Come, try some of these. I ordered my favourite delicacies for you.' Somtow gestured towards the food; rich, tart aromas rose making Katherine's mouth water. She reached for one of the appetisers Somtow was indicating, whole prawns in some red sauce. The shrimp was succulent, sweet and spicy. Somtow smiled as she licked her fingers, then stretched out his elegant hand to pick up one of the crustaceans for himself.

A flicker of candlelight caught on the gold band around his middle finger. Kate suddenly felt a chill.

'You are married?' she asked.

'Of course,' he said.

'And do you have children?'

He smiled proudly. 'Oh yes. My daughter is twelve and wants to be an engineer. My son is seven.' All at once, he grasped that she was concerned. 'My wife is on holiday in Hua Hin, playing golf. One of the few passions we do not share. The children are visiting their grandmother for the weekend.'

Kate shifted uncomfortably on the soft cushions. 'Still . . .'

'You are wondering whether it is appropriate, for me to be entertaining you, alone in this secluded garden, when I am a married man?'

She nodded, mute in her discomfort.

'Ah, Katherine!' He leant close to her, and she could smell a hint of sandalwood on his skin. 'We Thais see things differently, perhaps, than you in the West.' He reached towards her with one long, graceful finger, and brushed her earlobe. Her pearl earring shivered as a tingle ran down her spine.

'In Thailand, we have a long tradition of polygamy.' The finger traced a line down the side of her neck, barely touching her skin. 'The position of the *mea noi* – the mistress or "little wife" – is understood and respected. By everyone.' Now he was just grazing her collarbone with his touch.

'Nongseurat, my wife, knows that I invited you here this evening. She knows that I have been most eager for your arrival.'

Somtow held her eyes for a moment. His pale face was slightly flushed. Katherine felt weak, unable to speak or argue. He bent over her, and took her left nipple into his mouth through the thin silk of her dress. His lips were dry, but his hot breath made the fabric slightly damp. The nipple swelled and blossomed under his attention.

Katherine sank back into the pillows. Somtow moved his mouth to the other nipple now, leaving the first one throbbing, aching to be touched. Katherine closed her eyes, abandoning herself and her notions of morality.

Without losing contact with her for a moment, Somtow began a trail of kisses down the length of her body, between her breasts, across her belly. He lingered just below her navel, kissing softly, breathing deeply. The silky layer that separated him from her bare flesh seemed to heighten the sensation, as if each touch had a faint, sweet echo.

Finally, he reached her sex. Now he probed with his tongue through the silk of her dress and her light underwear, pushing the slithery fabric up between the folds, into the crevices. Katherine moaned softly and took his head in her hands, her fingers entangled in his thick, soft hair. Forgetting any sense of propriety, she urged his tongue deeper into her, arched her pelvis toward his eager mouth.

As his tongue continued his explorations, Katherine felt his cool hand upon her bare thigh. He reached up through the side slit of her dress, teasing her skin with just the slightest touch of a single finger as his hand travelled upward. He hooked the finger into the waistband of her bikini panties. His mouth left her pubis only for the briefest moment, as he pulled her undergarment down her thighs and out of his way.

Katherine moaned with pleasure, moving her own hands to her nipples which hummed and tingled. Somtow looked up at her for a moment; his dark eyes sparkled when he saw the look of abandon on her face.

He paused in his ministrations. With incredible swiftness and grace he drew her shift up over her head. Almost before she realised it, Katherine was lying naked before him on the cushions, wearing only her pearls, as he gazed at her intently.

'So beautiful,' he murmured. A fingertip touched her nipple, almost reverently, sending a delicious chill through her. His other hand brushed lightly over the auburn curls between her legs. 'Katherine, you are magnificent.' She felt his finger parting her lips, entering her hungry sex. A second finger gently and rhythmically massaged her clitoris. She lay back, closed her eyes, swam in the rich flow of sensations as he continued to pleasure her. Behind the dark of her eyelids, she imagined his glowing eyes, his half-parted lips, the fluid movements of his muscles under his silken trousers.

Somtow did not hurry. Katherine felt no pressure; she allowed the tension to build gradually as she became more and more sensitive, more and more aroused. Her sex was wet, open, waiting. She was very close to climax.

Then she felt new sensations: warmth, hardness, satin-smooth skin. She opened her eyes to find Somtow over her, his cock already half inside her. Somehow he had managed to remove his garments without interrupting his attentions or distracting her from her own pleasure.

He saw that her eyes were open and suddenly looked concerned. 'May I?' he asked, quite seriously. Though she smiled at the obviousness of the answer, she also realised that if she said no, he would immediately withdraw. 'Yes,' she said huskily. 'Yes, please.' She reached towards his shoulders and pulled him down on to her, into her.

They fitted together perfectly, two pieces of a puzzle, lock and key; yet there was also the shock of unfamiliarity. Katherine ran her hands over his back, across his buttocks, savouring the strangeness of his nearly hair-less body. He was so unlike David, who had lovely curls on his chest and back, and a wiry tangle of pubic hair. This man's skin was silky, smooth, sensuous, like the petals of a flower.

Katherine had a sudden desire to taste him. She ran her tongue delicately over the skin on his chest, then took his nipple between her lips. He moaned and twisted his pelvis against her. He tasted of salt, musk, something floral, and again, there was that faint hint of sandalwood, unfamiliar and exciting.

As he moved in her, faster, harder, something blos-somed fiercely in her heart – wild, exotic, foreign, free. A scream of pleasure burst from her throat as she felt her flesh blooming in answer. Beyond her own voice and the pounding of her heart, she heard Somtow crying out in Thai. And somehow, beyond that, she thought she could discern the quiet voice of the foun-tain, speaking the gentle secrets of the night.

She was floating, tingling all over, little electric sparks still flaring between her legs. Somtow kissed her linger-ingly on the lips, murmuring endearments. 'Ah, Kath-erine, sweet Katherine. Forgive me for being forward, but you are so lovely, and so delightfully sensual.' He supported himself on his elbows so that his weight did not oppress her. 'Too often, it seems, you Americans get trapped by your notions that sex is something shameful. You cannot seem to let go and just enjoy this gift.'

Katherine wondered, briefly, how many American women he had charmed and tried to seduce to have formed this opinion. He nuzzled again at her nipples, tickling a little. She squirmed and laughed softly. 'I hope I have somewhat redeemed my countrywomen in your eyes, Khunying Somtow.'

'Indeed!' He smiled. 'But I am such a poor host. Here I have invited you to dinner and hardly a bite has passed your lovely lips.'

He reached behind one of the cushions, and retrieved two sarongs, one of which he offered to her. He showed her how a Thai woman would secure it above her breasts, taking the opportunity to caress her as he did so.

'It suits you well,' he said. 'But I suspect that would be true of any costume.'

She noted that he had the sarongs ready and waiting. 'Did you plan this?' she asked, not sure whether she liked the implication.

'I did not plan,' he said, giving her one of his winning smiles. 'But I will admit I did hope this would come to pass.'

'Come, have something to eat. I hope that you enjoy spicy food.'

'Definitely,' Katherine replied with a smile. 'At home they say that it's because of my red hair.'

Somtow ran his fingers affectionately through her curls. 'I see. So perhaps red hair is associated also with hot blood? Try this, then.'

He offered her a plate of raw papaya salad. She recognised this as one of the spiciest dishes available from Thai restaurants at home, but was not prepared for the stunning effects this version had on her tongue.

'Goodness!' she said, taking a spoonful of the coconut rice that normally accompanied the dish to dampen the fires in her mouth. 'I thought I could handle hot food!' They both laughed.

Somtow opened another bottle of wine and refilled their glasses. They continued to nibble on the exotic delicacies he had provided, sitting half-naked on the cushions in the balmy night.

Katherine found her gaze drawn again and again to his smooth, muscular chest. The folds of the sarong around his waist hid his penis from her eyes. She wondered what he would do if she reached down to touch him as she longed to do.

Somtow was talking about Thai cuisine, the two thousand royal dishes and the hundreds of other, 'country-style' recipes. Suddenly, it seemed, he noticed her looking at his body. She blushed a little. He said nothing, but reached across the table to pick up a bowl of raw chillis.

'Did you know, Katherine, that Thai chillis are considered to be among the hottest in the world?' He picked up a bright green pod between his thumb and forefinger and raised it to his mouth. Instead of eating it, however, he ran the pepper across his lips, almost as if applying lipstick. Then he leant forward and kissed Katherine lightly.

The chilli oil made her own lips tingle and burn. 'Mmm,' she murmured as she returned the kiss with enthusiasm. She felt him untying her sarong, and then his lips were on her nipples again, first the left, then the right.

She was not prepared for the sensations that assaulted her as the pungent oil touched her skin. Her nipples were still hard, sensitised from her recent arousal. They burnt and throbbed, almost painful, as Somtow deliberately anointed them with the remnants of the pepper. The near-pain was overwhelmed by the pleasure, though, as a delicious warmth radiated out across her breasts.

'Oh . . .' she sighed, closing her eyes and savouring the heat. 'That is incredible.'

A light touch between her legs caused her to open her eyes. Somtow had another chilli in his fingers, brilliant red this time. With one hand, he parted her lower lips gently. Then, holding her open, he began to stroke the rigid little pepper against her equally rigid clitoris.

The effects were explosive. Sensitive though her nipples might be, the delicate tissues of her sex were much more so. Her labia swelled and ached; she rubbed herself against the fingers that held her open. The little knob of flesh directly in contact with the pepper pulsed and flamed. Part of her thought she could not bear it (and she knew he would stop immediately if she asked). Still, another part of her craved even more of this hot pleasure/pain. She groaned.

Somtow made some soft sound in answer. Looking at

him, she saw that he had crushed the pepper between his fingertips. Now he was rubbing the red pulp over his penis, up and down its stiff length, over the bulbous top. Katherine understood, suddenly, that his cock must be burning with the same almost unbearable intensity as her labia and clit. He looked into her eyes, without a word, and she knew he saw her consent as he plunged his fire-laden member into her cunt.

Katherine gasped and dug her nails into his shoulders. Intense sensation nearly overwhelmed her. She was still wet from their previous coupling. He moved easily within her secret cavities, spreading the incendiary chilli oil inside and out.

Her labia, clit, and sex all blazed with the odd, delicious pain. His cock was a flaming candle, searing her flesh. She felt raw, saw crimson, spread her legs wider so that he could ignite her deeper still.

Then she felt him withdraw, momentarily. Deliberately, he touched the head of his penis to the tight knot of her anus. He did not push or try to enter, merely let the fiery unguent work upon delicate flesh around that most private of places.

This finally loosed the conflagration within her. Katherine cried aloud, writhed and moaned. Then, in the midst of her climax, she felt cooling liquid filling her, streaming down her thighs. She opened her eyes. Somtow held the wine bottle and was deliberately pouring the remaining contents into her, an almost childish delight on his face.

'Ah, my Katherine!' He leant over and began to drink the wine from her flesh, lapping the ruby drops from her thighs. 'Excellent wine, but the taste can only be improved by mixing in your delicious liqueur.'

Katherine lay back and allowed him to clean her with his eager tongue. She marvelled at his sensitivity, his inventiveness, and his generosity. She noted that his cock was still fiercely erect, though she felt wonderfully satisfied.

'Somtow,' she said. 'You are so considerate – you forget your own pleasure.'

'Oh, no,' he said, 'I cannot imagine any greater delight than pleasing you.'

'Nevertheless,' she said, 'if you will allow me . . .' She raised herself up on her hands and knees in front of him. A little hesitant, she touched her tongue to the tip of his penis. Most of the chilli oil had rubbed off; there was only a mild tingling. But now she tasted the salty, slightly bitter flavour of her own sex, new and exciting.

She wrapped her lips around his swollen member. He moaned softly as she took him deep into her mouth then little by little released him. He relaxed back into the pile of cushions and closed his eyes. She bent lower, raising her hips, spiralling her tongue down his silky rod.

Unlike many men, he allowed her to set the pace. She started slowly, teasing him, sucking hard, then withdrawing so that her lips just grazed the glans. Gradually, she picked up the rhythm. With each stroke she felt him swell larger in her mouth. Now he was breathing heavily, in time with her as she slithered her mouth up and down. At the base she sometimes paused to give a quick lick to his balls. He groaned and writhed beneath her.

He was getting close to orgasm. Katherine could feel it. All at once, she was very aware of her own body, her naked buttocks elevated and exposed, her breasts swinging with the exertion of her strokes. Her mind presented her with a vivid, intensely arousing image of how she must look, lavishing such indecent attention on his engorged member.

She felt a warm breeze stir against the skin on her inner thighs, as though someone moved nearby. Her face buried in Somtow's crotch, she had the sudden conviction that they were being watched. The thought was disturbing, and thrilling. With one hand she grasped the base of her princely lover's cock, squeezing hard. She thrust the other between her legs, pinching her clit between thumb and forefinger.

The rod of flesh in her mouth contracted, then swelled and overflowed. Somtow cried out in Thai. She tasted his warm, acrid fluid on her tongue; some spilt out of her half-open lips. As she swallowed, she sank her fingers deep down between her lower lips, forgetting everything but the pleasure unfolding there.

It seemed that she lost consciousness for a moment, drifted off into some separate realm of sensation. The next thing she was aware of was the tip of Somtow's tongue. He was running it delicately around her mouth, lapping up the drops of spunk that lingered there.

Katherine was too blissfully exhausted to be surprised. She lay against him, her head on his shoulder. He stroked her tangled hair gently, his eyes closed, relaxed and sated.

They stayed in that position, their naked bodies entwined, for what seemed like an age. When Orapin glided up the steps and began quietly to remove the dishes, Katherine hardly noticed.

Chapter Three
The Grotto

Monday morning found Katherine distracted, confused and guilty. Somtow had driven her home himself, in the wee hours of Sunday morning; she had rebuffed his repeated invitations to stay the night, feeling uncomfortable sleeping in the bed that he normally shared with his wife.

When she thought back to his sensuous, passionate lovemaking, she felt familiar warmth between her legs. But then she remembered his wife, and David, too. Somtow told her that his wife understood and approved. Meanwhile she and David had never made any pledges of exclusivity, though in fact (or at least, to her knowledge) neither of them had indulged in any outside sexual activity since they first became lovers. Until now, Katherine reminded herself. She wondered, briefly, how David was consoling himself in her absence.

She turned her attention back to the information on her computer monitor, willing herself to pay attention to her work. She focused on the screen, pushing away any other thought almost angrily.

She was so intent on her tasks that she didn't hear Malawee approach. She started at the Thai woman's respectful voice.

'Miss Katherine, Mr Harrison asked me to see if you were available. He is meeting with a client and would like you to join him.'

'Of course,' said Katherine, stifling a surge of frustration as she followed Malawee to the conference room.

She knocked, then opened the door. Edward Harrison sat at the far end of the polished table, a look of annoyance on his face. Sitting beside him was a man of unusual appearance – disquieting, thought Katherine, then questioned the relevance of her reaction.

The man was European or American. He was dressed casually, entirely in black: black shirt with a stand-up collar, and tight black jeans. He had long, straight hair, also black, pulled back in a ponytail with an ornate silver barrette. Katherine thought she saw a flash of silver at his throat; his long fingers, clasped before him on the table, were similarly adorned with silver.

His face was tanned, almost weathered, shaped in strong planes: broad forehead, high cheekbones, resolute chin. His mouth at the moment framed a smile, but Katherine thought that she caught a twist of irony in his expression.

As she entered, he turned his attention to her, and she saw his eyes: shocking, unexpected blue under heavy black brows. Intense, piercing, and completely without restraint, any sense of politeness or etiquette. He continued to hold her gaze with his for an awkward moment. Then Edward broke in, clearing his throat.

'Ah, Katherine. Thank you for taking the time to join us. We have need of your technical expertise.'

'Of course, Edward,' she said softly, seating herself several chairs away from the man in black. She was aware that he was still staring at her and still smiling.

'Katherine, this is Gregory Marshall, one of our clients.' The man in black rose and bowed, a polite gesture, yet somehow unconvincing. Katherine realised that he was very tall, well over six feet. 'Mr Marshall, Katherine O'Neill, our new director of software development.'

'My pleasure,' said the man, perfectly civilly. So why did Katherine feel he was mocking her?

'Mr Marshall is the proprietor of one of the foremost establishments in Pat Pong.'

'The red-light district?' Katherine blurted out, then nearly bit her tongue in embarrassment.

'The entertainment district,' countered the man in black smoothly. 'The Grotto is just a go-go bar, offering the same types of entertainment available at many places in the city. However, I am trying to make it more distinctive, more creative, more – interesting. That's where DigiThai comes in.'

'Yes,' said Edward Harrison, trying to recapture the conversational initiative. 'Six months ago we designed and installed a custom multimedia system for Mr Marshall's bar, The Grotto. Video-walls and cameras, a simulated aquarium with computer-graphic inhabitants, acoustically driven digital kaleidoscopes – very elaborate.'

'And very successful,' said Gregory Marshall, with a broad smile that bared his straight white teeth. 'I am very happy with your work. It's just that now I want to go further.'

'Mr Marshall has some novel ideas, but as I have been telling him they are barely feasible technically. And certainly not for the money that we have been discussing.'

Always attracted by a technical challenge, Kate found herself interested. 'What do you have in mind, Mr Marshall?' she asked, mustering her most professional tone of voice.

'Well, now . . .' The man's voice was melodious, controlled, expressive. The voice of an actor, thought Katherine. He riveted her with his gaze again. She stared back at him, proudly, rebelliously, not willing to be cowed. Eventually, he continued his sentence without looking away from her.

'Three-dimensional imagery is what I am looking for. Something like the holograms one sees in science fiction movies. My girls are already fantastic, but I'd like to project more fantastic images still, images from people's dreams and nightmares – mysterious, evocative, disturbing, erotic. Furthermore, I would like to somehow link these images to the music, so that my customers will see projected before their eyes reflections or echoes of the emotions aroused by the beat and the melody.'

Katherine was silent for a moment, gathering her thoughts. Gregory Marshall watched her attentively. Finally, she spoke, choosing her words carefully.

'Three-dimensional imagery on a two-dimensional screen has now become inexpensive and commonplace. Projected 3D, though, still requires costly hardware and custom software – the sort of thing only available to Disney or Spielberg.'

She paused and took a deep breath before continuing. 'I have some familiarity with this area. I did some related research when I was in graduate school.'

'Would you be willing to work on this for me?' interrupted Marshall, clearly excited. 'I believe that I can make you understand exactly what I want.' He paused dramatically. 'What do you say, Kate?'

Part of her bristled at the liberties he took, using her name so familiarly on such short acquaintance. Part of her warmed in response to that very familiarity, the tone of persuasive intimacy. Meanwhile, she was undeniably eager for the opportunity to pursue her ideas on the problem. As for the chance to work for Gregory Marshall – well, that notion filled her with equal measures of excitement and dread. She could not deny that despite his brashness and poor manners she found him intriguing.

'That decision is for Mr Harrison to make, Mr Marshall.' Katherine responded as coolly as she could. 'If the two of you can resolve the financial issues, I would be very happy to continue my researches in this area. However, we cannot promise you success; the work is at too early a stage for that.'

'I want no promises from you – now,' said the man in

black softly. 'And I am patient.' As his eyes bore down on her, Kate felt suddenly confused. Thankfully, he shifted his attention back to Harrison once again.

'Edward, let me consider my financial position and get back to you on this. I'll call you in the next day or two, and make you an offer.'

'Meanwhile, Miss O'Neill –' the extra emphasis on the honorific was unmistakable '– I hope that you will think about our conversation.' He stood up, apparently ready to leave. Kate and Harrison rose also. Gregory Marshall shook her boss's hand briefly, then reached for Kate's. He towered over her.

'I enjoyed meeting you, and I look forward to working with you.' He paused, but Kate found herself unable to respond. His skin felt hot, as if he had a fever. Kate herself felt a little faint.

'Come visit The Grotto sometime soon. I'll give you the grand tour. Until then, goodbye.'

Kate stood aside, clearing a path to the door so that he could leave. There was plenty of room, though Marshall was a big man. Still, as he passed her, he brushed his body against hers, and worse, she could swear that she felt her backside pinched hard through her linen skirt. Before she could protest or call out, he was gone.

She sank back down into her chair, indignant, marvelling at the man's impudence. How outrageous! She wondered if she should mention the incident to Edward. However, her boss was already grumbling about their recent visitor.

'That man! He's impossible. I never know how to deal with him; he always seems to get the better of me. I hope you didn't find him too offensive, Katherine.'

'Oh, I'm used to dealing with obnoxious boors,' she said lightly. 'The world is full of men who think that women's only appropriate place in software is as models for the scantily clad heroines in computer games.'

'He knows how to bargain, though,' Harrison continued. 'Probably the result of his background. His father was American and his mother was Australian, but he grew up in Thailand. I've always suspected that his father was involved in intelligence work, during the Viet Nam War. In any case, he is fluent in Thai, and has a Thai's facility for getting as much as he can for as little money as possible.'

Kate considered this. She didn't see much influence of Thai culture or aesthetics on Gregory Marshall. How different his behaviour was from the considerate, refined, and gracious manner of Somtow Rajchitraprasong! Gregory Marshall was raw, crude, unfinished, full of uncontrolled energy, with few traces of the civilised demeanour she had come to associate with Thais.

That wasn't quite true, though. He did have control; he exercised control over himself, and over others. He used his voice, his eyes, his stature, to intimidate and influence. Looking back over the brief meeting, she recalled nuances, inflections and gestures that he had used to steer the discussion in the direction that he wanted, or to arouse particular emotions in his audience. She remembered her notion that he had a theatrical background.

She turned her attention back to her superior.

'By the way, Katherine, you definitely shouldn't take him up on his invitation to visit The Grotto. It wouldn't be appropriate for you to be seen there. I will not have you jeopardising the reputation of DigiThai.'

Katherine found herself irritated. She was an adult; she would make her own decisions about what she did in her private life.

'If you will excuse me, Edward, I've got to get back to work.' She stood up resolutely. 'I will be thinking about the problem Mr Marshall has posed us, just in case he manages to make a financial proposal that meets your requirements.

'You realise, I hope, that if we did succeed in developing a relatively inexpensive technology for projected

3D, the sales potential would be tremendous. Not just here in Thailand, but worldwide.'

'Excellent, Katherine, excellent!' Harrison was smiling again. 'It would of course be a coup for DigiThai to develop this kind of new technology. So go ahead and work on it, when you get the chance.'

When Katherine returned to her computer, she discovered that she had incoming email from an address she didn't recognise. She double-clicked on the message icon to read the text.

Kate,
I heartily enjoyed our first encounter.
I hope that you did, too.
I am waiting for you.
Gregory

Kate was amazed. The man had left their offices no more than fifteen minutes ago. How had he sent the message so quickly? For that matter, how did he know her email address? She had deliberately chosen an obscure pseudonym (dancer@digithai.co.th) to avoid the floods of junk mail that usually followed setting up a new account.

The arrogant and mocking tone of the message made her fume. His on-line persona was certainly in keeping with his face-to-face personality, she thought. She moved to click on the delete icon, then changed her mind, saving the message in a new folder labelled '3D'.

Kate found it harder than ever to concentrate on her work. She kept thinking that she heard Gregory Marshall's soft, provocative voice in her ear. Damn him. She chided herself for her own lack of control and resolutely pushed all images of him from her mind. Still, it was already dark outside by the time she was fully engaged again in the problems that had been occupying her before the meeting.

She was just getting ready to leave the office when

her computer beeped, notifying her of incoming mail. This time the originating address was familiar.

Kate,
Night is falling.
Time to act on your darkest desires.
I know what you need.
Come to me.
Gregory

Kate swallowed hard. She read the missive again, finding it disturbing. The tone was different from his previous message, she realised: less humorous, more seductive. Still, there was that same annoying self-confidence, bordering on conceit. He was so sure of himself.

Brusquely, she flipped the switch to turn off her computer. To hell with him, she thought. What did he know? She shouldn't waste her energy on him.

When Katherine arrived home, she found a gorgeous bouquet waiting on her breakfast bar. Sprays of orchids, in shades from cream to rich purple, tumbled in profusion from a basket of deep-green foliage. Katherine sighed in relief and delight as she read the card.

The flowers were from Somtow. In an elegant, slightly old-fashioned hand, he thanked her for her company the previous weekend. He asked if she would do him the honour of joining him on a trip upriver the following Saturday to visit the ruins of Ayuthaya.

Katherine's spirits rose at the prospect. In contrast with Gregory Marshall, Somtow seemed even more appealing. Not wanting to risk telephoning, she penned a note of acceptance, trying to convey the warmth and excitement she felt.

'Ae?' she called, wanting the maid to mail the letter.

'Yes, madame?' The maid appeared almost immediately; she must have been in the next room, though Katherine had not heard her.

'Would you please mail this tomorrow morning, when you go to the market?'

'Of course, madame. Will there be anything else?'

'No, thank you, Ae.'

'Beautiful flowers, madame,' the young woman commented. She stood smiling sweetly, her hands clasped in front of her. She seemed to expect Katherine to give her more information.

'From a new friend,' replied Katherine. She was reluctant to share more details with the woman. After an awkward moment of silence, Ae took the letter and left the room. Katherine sat back and allowed herself to daydream about her Thai lover.

When Kate arrived at DigiThai the next morning, she found another message from Gregory Marshall.

Kate,
Why deny yourself?
Do not deny me.
I am the one you seek.
Gregory

The nerve, thought Kate. Still, the message brought a little self-satisfaction. Let him beg, she thought smugly; let him pretend that he can control me. She set to work with a lighter heart.

He sent another email around noon and still another as she was getting ready to leave.

Kate,
I know you.
I see you.
Kneeling before me.
Trembling beneath me.
Do not keep me waiting.
Gregory

This time she caught a hint of anger or impatience in his style. It scared her, a bit. She considered whether she should reply to the message, to tell him to leave her alone, but decided that would just add fuel to his strange fire.

The pattern continued; the messages became more intense. On Wednesday night she received the longest and most explicit yet. She read it over several times, with an odd, hollow feeling in the pit of her stomach.

Kate,
Believe – believe in me, and in your own dreams.
For I will make them real.
I am the one, the master.
Give me your nakedness, your naked heart.
As you open yourself to me, so I will satisfy your lust.
Come.
Gregory

There was no message waiting Thursday morning. Kate found that she was dismayed and disappointed, but she did not allow herself to examine the feelings too closely.

Around noon, Edward Harrison knocked on her door. 'I just got off the phone with Gregory Marshall,' he told her. 'We've reached an agreement on the projected 3D project.' She heard satisfaction in his voice. 'The arrangement should be quite lucrative for DigiThai, even if the project is not a success. So, I'd like you to give this top priority from now on.'

Katherine's stomach did a flip at the sound of Marshall's name. 'Of course, Edward,' she said. 'I'm eager to get started.'

'Keep me posted on your progress,' he said. 'And do not, under any circumstances, talk to Marshall about your work, if he should call for information. That man is a snake; I wouldn't trust anything he says.'

Katherine nodded, distinctly uncomfortable at this assessment. As an antidote to her discomfort, she threw herself into her work. She spent the afternoon reviewing her notes on the 3D problem, checking references, and thinking hard.

Immersed in her researches, she did not notice the passage of time. It was past eight o'clock when she finally looked up, realised that it was dark and that all her co-workers had left long ago.

She was pleased at what she had accomplished. As she stood up and stretched luxuriously, working the kinks out of her muscles, she recalled that she hadn't heard from Marshall all day. Maybe he'd given up on her? He didn't seem to be the type to relinquish a conquest so quickly. Perhaps now that he was subsidising her research work he felt that it was inappropriate to have a social relationship? That certainly seemed unlikely; rarely had she met anyone who seemed less concerned with propriety. Could it be that he had experienced some emergency or disaster which was distracting him from his attempts at on-line seduction? Katherine suddenly felt concerned.

The Pat Pong district was only a few miles away, at the other end of Silom Road. Maybe she should get a cab and drop by The Grotto, just to check on him. He was, after all, a client; his well-being was important to DigiThai, especially since this recent deal.

Even Kate didn't find these arguments convincing. Still, in a few minutes she found herself at the corner of Pat Pong One Road, standing there slightly bewildered in her tailored suit and heels, trying to decide what to do next.

The side street was crowded and noisy, with a carnival atmosphere. Vendors hawking fake Rolex watches and novelty cigarette lighters vied with loud rock and roll that poured from curtained doorways. Garish neon signs identified dozens of bars and clubs: 'SuperStar', 'King's Castle', 'Sexy Night', 'Butterfly'. Kate tried to look comfortable strolling down the lane, as girls called out to her from the entrances. 'Come inside, please.

Take a look. No cover charge. One beer, fifty *baht*. Come inside, madame.'

Her path was suddenly barred by a stocky dwarf of a man. He leered at her. 'Free show, madame. Free show upstairs.' He held out a laminated card listing the various acts. 'Pussy ping-pong ball show. Pussy banana show. Man woman sex show. Come upstairs.'

'Excuse me,' said Kate brusquely, pushing past him. She walked doggedly on, her heart pounding madly. She felt vulnerable, and highly visible, in her stylishly short skirt and high-heeled shoes. She tried to remember whether she had seen any other western women since she had entered the street. She felt the eyes of both the Thai and the western men following her.

Then, a little way down the block, she saw the turquoise lights advertising The Grotto. Below the sign, just outside the dark-draped doorway, stood Gregory Marshall, talking to a striking Thai woman.

An odd relief washed over Kate. She hastened towards the couple. As if sensing her approach, Marshall looked up. She could swear that she saw a genuine smile of welcome on his face as she arrived in front of him.

'Kate! What a pleasant surprise! I did not expect you – tonight.' He made a slight movement, as if he were about to bend down and kiss her, then caught himself. He did not touch her, though Kate thought she could feel the heat emanating from his black-clad frame.

Instead, he turned to the Thai woman next to him and put his arm around her shoulder. 'Noi, this is Kate, from DigiThai. The one I told you about.'

'Kate, allow me to present Noi, my partner in The Grotto. Noi works as my *mamasan*, keeping the girls safe, and keeping them in line.' He kissed Noi briefly but deeply on the mouth. 'I don't know what I would do without her.'

Kate felt a tightening in her chest. Jealousy, anger, and embarrassment struggled within her. Noi was remarkable, there was no doubt of that. She stood much taller than the average Thai, topping Kate by at least half a foot. A silk headband of bright red circled her brow, keeping her unruly black hair out of her eyes. Like her partner, she was dressed in black. Her slender, athletic body was perfectly suited to the leather miniskirt, spandex tank top, and laced-up spike-heeled boots. Her high cheekbones and almond eyes suggested a Mongol princess. Her full, smiling lips reminded Kate of Gregory's; behind the smile was a twist of something devilish.

Noi reached out and took Kate's hand. 'I am delighted to meet you at last,' she said. She seemed sincere. Kate wondered uncomfortably what Gregory had told the woman about her.

Gregory casually laid his hand on Noi's shoulder. 'Noi, would you mind showing Kate around? Kate, I have a few things that I must attend to. I will join you shortly.'

'Of course. Come with me, Kate,' said Noi, not relinquishing her hand. She pulled Kate through the curtains. Inside, all was lit in red. A steep stairway rose before them. Faint music drifted down the stairs. Kate smelt jasmine incense, and just a hint of male sweat.

At the top of the stairs was another door, padded with red leather. Noi pushed it open and nudged Kate through into a kaleidoscope of colour and sound.

The room was generally dark, stretching into an unseen distance. But here and there the ceiling pulsed with light, in rainbow hues. To her left, a wall of video screens flickered and danced with vivid images. On this side of the door, the music swelled and broke like waves. Kate could feel the vibrations of the bass in her stomach.

An elevated platform outlined in lights rose in the centre of the room. Female forms in various degrees of undress swayed and writhed on the stage. The swirling, seething lights painted their flesh in unnatural colours.

Benches and round tables lined the room. These were crowded, with mostly western men. Each of these men,

Kate saw, was surrounded by a bevy of Thai girls, laughing, chattering, sitting on their laps, cuddling and flirting.

'Sit here,' instructed Noi, indicating one of the few empty benches. Kate tried to ignore the curious stares of the customers on either side of her. The *mamasan* settled in next to Kate, her bare thigh pressing against Kate's. Kate shifted position nervously; Noi followed suit, keeping their skin in contact.

'You are very beautiful,' said Noi unceremoniously. 'Gregory did not exaggerate.'

Kate felt her cheeks burn. She didn't reply.

'You are just in time for the live show. That will begin in just a few minutes. In the meantime, what do you think of our dancers?'

Kate turned her attention to the stage. Half a dozen Thai women were dancing. All were lovely, but Kate was struck by how different they were, in appearance and demeanour. A curly-haired, compact woman wearing only a sequined G-string and patent-leather boots did energetic bumps and grinds, a lascivious grin on her lips. An innocent-looking girl in a pink tank suit moved slowly and gracefully, serious and dreamy, face half-hidden in her long hair. One woman wore torn stockings and chains around her waist, her eyes hidden behind a glittery silver mask. A willowy creature, bare-breasted under her lace chemise, danced sinuously in rhythm with the music, ripples starting in her pelvis and moving fluidly up her spine.

Kate swallowed. It was warm in the bar. Noi's thigh was hot against hers. The sensuous dancers and their erotic costumes made her feel a bit faint.

'The dancer in lace is particularly good,' she said, trying to make conversation. 'Sexy and feminine at the same time.'

Noi laughed. 'You mean Lek? She is a *katoey* – a lady-man!'

'Lady-man? You mean a transvestite?'

Noi nodded. 'Yes. We have many lady-man dancers. Customers come, buy them drinks, and never realise!'

Kate looked again at the delicate features and rounded limbs of the dancer. She still could not believe it. The dancer caught her glance and gave her a radiant, slightly sad smile.

'Why are some of the women dancing topless and some not?' she asked Noi.

'It is up to them,' said the *mamasan*. 'If they bare their breasts, they make more money. But no one will force them to do it. And it is up to them whether they go with a customer.'

'What if the customer insists?'

'Then I take care of it,' said Noi, giving Kate's hand a hard squeeze. Kate suspected that Noi could be formidable when she chose.

The music stopped and the dancers left the stage. Lek donned a short kimono, then came over to Noi and Kate's table.

'Hello, madame,' she said, holding out her hand to Kate. Kate took it, marvelling at the softness of the skin, the perfectly manicured fingernails. 'Do you like my dancing?'

'Yes, Lek.' Kate could not help but smile. 'I like it very much.'

The *katoey* seemed overjoyed. 'Thank you, madame, you are very kind.' She leant over, and kissed Kate's cheek, then spoke to Noi. 'You take care of her, OK, *mamasan*?'

'Oh yes, Lek,' said Noi. 'I will take care of her.'

The lights dimmed. For a moment the bar was almost quiet, the low murmuring of customers and bar girls the only sound. The sense of anticipation was palpable.

Then spotlights illuminated two doors at opposite corners of the room. Simultaneously, there was new music, something slow and sultry. A saxophone wailed. Two figures appeared in the pools of brightness, a man and a woman. The light tracked them as they walked towards the central platform. They mounted the steps

46

perfectly in time and faced each other on the stage as the two spotlights merged into one.

The young man had a shaved head and a sensitive, expressive face. Slowly and gracefully, he let his kimono fall to his feet, revealing a lithe, muscled body and a stunning erection. Kate felt her cunt tighten at the delicious sight. Noi's hand was resting on Kate's thigh now, stroking her lightly.

Kate recognised the woman as the curly-haired vamp who had been dancing earlier. However, her teasing, sluttish manner was gone. Instead she stood before her partner, gazing up at him in passionate adoration.

In time to the music, the youth took the woman in his arms, bent her backward and tenderly kissed the hollow of her throat. She let her head fall back in ecstasy. Holding her with one arm around her waist, the man deftly untied her kimono. It slipped off her body in a shimmer of satin, baring to the spotlights her swelling breasts, sweet brown nipples and downy pubis.

The young man ran his free hand lingeringly over her flesh. Still supporting her with his right arm, he used his left hand to part the lips of her sex. He entered her in one swift motion. Her body convulsed in response.

Kate could see every detail as he began his thrusts. His cock disappeared as the woman took him all the way into her. Kate could see the way she was stretched and filled; her own cunt dampened as she imagined herself in the woman's place.

A feather-light touch on her pubic area sent a delicious shock up her spine. Noi's hand was between Kate's legs now, her thumb pressing delicately against Kate's clitoris. Kate did not move, and neither did Noi. The thumb just rested there, a statement, a challenge. Kate felt herself harden in response to the pressure, knew that Noi could feel that her panties were wet. She hardly breathed.

On stage, the couple moved gracefully from one position to another, always connected, always in rhythm with the music. Now the woman's back was to her partner, her legs around his waist, her hands on the floor, as he drove his erection even deeper than before. He pulled out nearly all the way after each thrust so that his audience could appreciate the length and thickness of his cock. The woman's hair fell in tangles over her face. She clenched her thighs around his body and arched her back.

Noi increased very slightly the pressure of her thumb. Kate struggled to hold still. She was sweating, and panting a little. The urge to grind herself against the other woman's hand was nearly irresistible. Her composure and self-control were fast dissolving.

The couple moved, danced, assumed a dozen different poses. Now the woman was backed up against a pole in the centre of the stage. Her hands over her head, she held on tightly as her lover delved more deeply than ever into her flesh. Her eyes were closed, her lips half-open; she might have been moaning, drowned out by the song, which was now surging to a climax.

Then the song ended, and abruptly so did the show. The young man removed his still-erect shaft and helped his partner to a standing position. They both bowed to the audience, the man incongruously holding his hands over his genitals as if to hide them.

At the same moment, Noi removed her hand. Kate almost cried out in frustration. Her clitoris throbbed, swollen and sensitive. She looked up at Noi, trying to read her face, but the Thai woman's attention was focused on the other side of the room. Following that gaze, Kate saw Gregory Marshall coming towards them.

She shifted uncomfortably on the velvet-upholstered bench, feeling dampness on her thighs and the heat of a blush on her face.

'Well, Kate,' said Gregory heartily. 'How did you like the show?'

'Very – interesting,' she responded. She was surprised at how calm her voice sounded. 'Not the sort of thing one tends to see in the States.'

'Indeed!' She heard the familiar hint of mockery in

his well-modulated voice. 'You'll find that Thailand is different in many respects.

'In any case, now I can give you my full attention. I apologise for leaving you so long in Noi's hands.' Kate could swear she saw the two of them exchange an amused glance. Marshall reached out his hand to help her up from the bench. This was the first time he had touched her that evening. Her flesh burnt at the contact. 'Come with me. I'll continue with the promised tour.'

He led her across the crowded room, dodging the bar girls who scurried about serving drinks and the new set of dancers heading for the stage. Opening a door in the corner, he nudged her gently through. 'Up the stairs.' She felt him close behind her as she mounted another steep stairway, close enough to pinch her bottom. However, he kept his hands to himself.

The stairs opened on to a red-lit hallway lined with closed doors. The music was muffled here, but she could still sense the vibrations of the beat through the floor. She thought she heard muted voices and laughter. She understood, suddenly, that these rooms were intended for customers who wanted to take their favourite bar girl or dancer 'out of the bar'.

'Here we are,' said Gregory, throwing open one of the doors. She hesitated. 'Go on, Kate,' he said quietly. 'We both know that this is what you came for.'

The room was small, but not cramped. Most of the floor area was occupied by a king-size bed with an ornate rattan headboard. A matching rattan armchair stood in a corner. Through the open window, high up on the wall, Kate heard the street sounds of Pat Pong, the vendors and the raucous music. Flashing neon painted patterns on the wall.

Kate felt paralysed. She stood by the side of the bed, staring at her hands, feeling incongruous in her business clothes, her heart pounding crazily.

Gregory followed her into the room, closed the door and relaxed into the armchair.

'Strip,' he said.

'What?' Kate looked at him, almost in panic.

'You heard me,' he said softly. 'Strip for me.'

Not understanding why, not believing what she was doing, she began to obey. Her fitted jacket was already unbuttoned; she slipped it off and let it fall to the floor. With one hand, she undid the buttons on her grey-silk blouse; with the other, she unzipped her skirt.

Gregory sat motionless, his shining eyes following her every move.

She shrugged the blouse off her shoulders and stepped out the skirt. Her bra unhooked in front. Almost defiantly, she paused a moment, looking back at him before she unfastened it and dropped it on to the pile.

Her nipples were painfully hard; she knew that her arousal would be obvious to Gregory. She felt confused, embarrassed, but oddly proud. Her nakedness was nothing to be ashamed of.

She began to remove her bikini briefs, her only remaining garment other than her heels.

'No, wait,' said Gregory. 'Leave those on – for the moment.' He rose from the chair and walked slowly around her, measuring, evaluating, savouring. He towered over her; he was very close, but still he did not touch her. Kate found herself looking at his hands, willing him to use them on her body, but to no effect.

He stood behind her now. His breath stirred the hairs on her neck as he bent close to her ear. 'Now,' he said, almost whispering. 'I want you to masturbate for me. Through your panties. Show me what a sweet, hot little slut you really are.'

He seated himself again, so that he could watch her. 'You may close your eyes, if you like,' he said. 'This time.'

Part of Kate's mind rebelled, horrified. Nevertheless, as if in a dream, Kate began to caress herself. She brushed one hand lightly over her taut nipples, relishing simultaneously the tingling in her palm and the tremors in her sex. Her other hand moved slowly down to her pubis and rested there, her two middle fingers pressing against the swollen knob of flesh hidden by her underwear.

At first she just thrummed her fingers rhythmically, barely moving, savouring the building tension. Her motions were discreet, controlled, hardly visible. Before long, though, this was not enough. She began to rub herself more roughly, pinching and kneading her clit between her finger and thumb. Her breath came in little gasps. She brought her other hand down between her legs and tried to penetrate herself through the damp cloth, frustrated by the resistance it offered.

Through it all, behind closed eyelids, she was acutely aware of Gregory Marshall's gaze. It felt tangible, concrete; she could tell when his eyes were resting on her breasts, her thighs, her busy hands. The weight of his attention inflamed her still more. She moaned softly as she ground one fist into her sex.

Marshall spoke. 'You may touch yourself inside your clothing, if you wish.' There was that edge of mockery again. Clearly he knew how excited she was, how she craved more direct stimulation. She dared to open her eyes.

He was sitting forward in his chair, drinking her in eagerly. His blue eyes flamed with eager lust. But his voice remained almost dispassionate, totally controlled. 'You know you don't need to be shy with me, Kate. Go on, do it.'

She did not hesitate further. Stretching the waistband of her briefs, she slithered her fingers through her pubic curls to touch the slippery knob of flesh at the heart of her sex. At the same time, she pushed aside the fabric covering her crotch and thrust three fingers deep into her cunt.

Now she twisted and pounded her clitoris, sensation building on sensation. Her other hand thrust in and out, fingers spread wide. She was very close to climax. She tried to ignore her audience, to lose herself entirely in the explosion of her senses. Instead, she found herself fantasising, imagining his coarse face above her, thinking about what it would be like to have his cock inside her instead of her fingers.

She began a low keening, feeling her orgasm just out of reach. Then she heard his voice, his tone sharp. 'Stop. Right now.'

She wouldn't have thought it possible to obey. Yet somehow, for some reason, she did. She opened her eyes and looked at him blankly, breathing heavily, both her hands still inside her panties.

'Good,' he said softly. 'Very good. It's not time for you to come yet.'

'Take them off,' he ordered. Kate removed her hands, shimmied the damp garment down her thighs to her ankles and stepped out of it. Suddenly, incongruously, she felt incredibly exposed. Her sex gaped hungrily, her lower lips swollen and red.

'On your knees now.'

Once again she felt a flare of resistance. Part of her, though, wanted to follow his direction. She felt a strange pleasure as she sank to a kneeling position across from him. She looked at the floor, not daring his eyes.

'Pick up the panties in your mouth. Using just your mouth. Then bring them to me.'

Awkwardly, still in her high-heeled shoes, she bent down and took the discarded briefs in her teeth. Her nostrils filled with her own musky scent and she felt a new surge of lust.

Somehow knowing that this was what he wanted, Kate put her hands down and crawled the short distance to the chair where her tormentor lounged comfortably. With her arse in the air, she felt even more vulnerable, and more aroused. He sat up, thighs apart, and gestured to her to come closer. Finally, she was at his feet, between his spread legs. She sat up, leaning back on her heels, offering him the garment in the manner of a family pet offering the newspaper.

Gregory gave a little laugh, of delight more than mockery. He took the panties and held them to his face, inhaling deeply the womanly perfume with which they were soaked. 'Wonderful!' he said. 'Even better than I had hoped.'

He leant forward, cupped her chin in his hands, and searched her face. 'Are you all right?' he asked, quite serious. Kate nodded, revelling in the fact that finally he was touching her. She focused her attention on him, silently begging him to handle her breasts, to stroke her arse. But instead he sat back in his chair, still regarding her gravely.

'Shall we continue, then, my little Kate?' he asked.

'Yes,' Kate whispered, not knowing to what she was agreeing. 'Yes.'

Marshall rose from his chair and stood towering over her, almost straddling her. He took another sampling of her scent and smiled down at her. The mocking tone returned. 'Undo my fly, then,' he said. 'And give me your mouth.'

Kate tried to be gentle and careful unfastening his jeans. Tight under normal circumstances, his erection stretched them to the point that the zip would hardly operate. Every time her hands brushed that taut organ through the denim, a shiver ran through her own flesh.

When Marshall's cock finally became visible, she stifled a gasp. His member was on the same scale as the rest of him. It pulsed with heat, as if this were the heart of his fevered self. She ran her tongue delicately down its length, tracing the raised veins, tasting salt and bitterness.

'Open yourself,' he said. As she did so, he slid his cock into her mouth, slowly, steadily. 'Wider,' he murmured. 'I want you to take all of me, every centimetre.' He pulled back slightly, then pushed in further.

Kate fought rising panic as she felt herself choking.

'Relax, Kate. Open to me, receive me, honour me.' His voice, husky with lust, reassured her. Waves of warmth flowed through her limbs as she allowed her facial muscles to go limp and let go of the constriction in her throat. He pushed even deeper; she willed herself to open more. Then she realised her chin was against his

53

pubes, that in fact his entire shaft was inside her mouth. Pride surged through her, even as he began thrusting, out and then all the way to the root once again.

His rock-hard flesh battered her lips, yet somehow the pain did not reach her. She marvelled at the silky skin that covered that hardness. As he slammed his hips against her, the rough denim of his jeans grazed her nipples, which were just as hard, sending electric spasms through her body. Kneeling, legs apart, she felt her own juices running down the inside of her thighs. Her clit throbbed in rhythm with his thrusts. Somehow Kate knew she didn't have permission to touch herself.

His motions quickened. Kate felt a premonitory contraction in the rod of flesh that had taken over her mouth. Exultation filled her. Let him come, she prayed to herself; let me taste him, swallow him, serve him. She closed her eyes and focused on becoming the perfect receptacle.

As always, he did not do as she hoped. Clearly just on the brink of orgasm, he stopped. He slid out of her mouth. Kate stared at him, her mouth still open, disappointment flooding through her.

'Now, Kate,' he laughed. 'You mustn't be greedy! I'll decide when you taste my come.' He leant closer. 'Don't worry, though. You will.'

Kate looked down at the floor, embarrassed by her own need, chagrined at how well he discerned her desires.

'Time for the next scene,' said Marshall lightly. Before she knew what was happening, he had swooped down and picked her up. Her shoes fell off with a clatter, but Kate hardly noticed. She relished the strength in his arms, the iron muscles rippling beneath his shirt.

He carried her over to the bed and laid her down on her back. 'Lift your arms above your head,' he commanded. As she complied, her hand brushed against something dangling from the headboard. She turned to look at the braided ropes of red silk fastened to the rattan spokes and suddenly understood why Gregory had disappeared when she first arrived. A few things to attend to, he had said. So he had left her with his lady co-conspirator, trusting his comrade and the performance to inflame Kate's senses and imagination while he came and installed these bonds.

Gregory watched the comprehension dawning in her eyes. 'Yes, Kate. I prepared these for you. Only for you.'

He leant closer. 'I want to tie you here, hand and foot, so that you will be more completely at my disposal. I believe that you want that, too. But you must tell me so. I will not do this without your permission.'

Kate was silent. She had never been so unsure in her life. Fear, suspicion, shame, and distrust warred with curiosity and desire. In his arms she felt both sheltered and helpless, and she longed for those feelings again. Yet he was essentially a stranger, she reminded herself, a stranger with a shady profession and an unsavoury reputation.

When she looked at him, though, she saw concern and attentiveness in his eyes, even though his cock still pulsed hugely from his fly. This sight sent a delicious weakness through her limbs. I must be crazy, she thought to herself, as she nodded her assent.

'Do it,' she murmured, and did not trust herself to say any more.

With expert skill, he bound her wrists with the silken braids. 'Silk is a marvellous substance,' he commented. 'So soft, but incredibly strong. Like you, my little Kate. I know you can endure much, Kate. Much more than you would believe.'

Kate shivered, wondering exactly what he meant. He was working on her ankles now, in a businesslike fashion, leaving her knees bent and open so that her sex was spread wide. Every time he touched her, heat travelled through her to that burning centre, still sensitive and hungry from her earlier ministrations. She squirmed a bit, involuntarily pushing her pelvis towards him.

'Be still,' he said sharply. 'Be patient. You must learn to wait.'

Finally, she was bound, restrained from all but the tiniest movements. She found she was panting. Gregory stood at the foot of the bed admiring her, or his handiwork.

'Excellent. Just as I imagined.'

He began to remove his clothes. Her eyes followed his every gesture. When he dropped his shirt to the floor, Kate sucked in her breath. Marshall's left arm, from shoulder to wrist, was elaborately and beautifully tattooed. A pattern of multicoloured flames writhed over his flesh, scarlet, green and turquoise. A trick of the flashing neon, or perhaps simply the motion of his muscles, made the flames dance across his flesh as if they were consuming him. A similar flame flickered in his blue eyes as he pulled off his trousers.

He mounted the bed and straddled her with his thighs. His engorged penis hovered above her body. Despite herself, she writhed below him. In response, he leant over and pinched both her nipples, hard enough that she cried out.

'Still, I said! You are mine now, mine to do with as I wish. I will fuck you, or not fuck you, as I please.'

'But,' he added, smiling, 'I do please.'

The bonds already held her wide open. Her sex was already drenched with arousal. Never taking his eyes off hers, he sank his cock into her, into depths she had not known existed.

She had never felt anything like it. It was fire and knives, hot and sharp, a blazing sun in her cunt. She was filled, stretched, split open, it seemed, pinned to the bed by his rod of velvety steel.

For a long moment, he stayed there inside her, his gaze riveted to hers. She felt him throb and swell as if he was willing himself to grow larger still. She tightened her muscles around him, but otherwise tried to remain motionless, even as her flesh ached to thrash and thrust herself against him. She kept her eyes open, held captive

56

by the weight of his gaze. She knew her own lust showed clearly on her face; she did not care.

He pulled away, to the edge of her lower lips, and she bit her tongue so as not to cry out with the loss. Then he came crashing back into her, hard, deeper than before. The flames surged. He withdrew and thrust again and again, always harder, almost brutal. Kate found that the edge of pain only sharpened the pleasure, made it stronger and more complex. And she saw no cruelty in his face, only a kind of fierce delight.

She strained against her bonds now, fists clenched, still struggling to follow his prescription of stillness as he fucked her, as the knot of sensation within her sex drew tighter and tighter. Yet somehow climax seemed far away, even as she climbed to higher and higher levels of arousal.

She whimpered a little. Gregory's eyes bore down on her. Then she swore she heard his voice, though his lips did not move. 'You are mine, Kate, mine. Admit it to yourself and to me. Let go, give yourself to me. Let me give you the satisfaction you crave.'

She looked at the man looming above her, felt him probing her with his cock and his mind. Something in her loosened. Her hands opened and she let the ropes support her arms and legs. She relaxed her inner muscles, allowed herself to be opened and stretched even further. Gregory responded by grinding his cock into her, filling all that she offered to him.

Then she felt the wave coming, as if from far off. A thundering crest of pleasure swept over her, casting her mind and body adrift. As her consciousness slipped away, she caught a final glimpse of Gregory's face, with its expression of mad triumph.

He was dressed when she came back to her senses, though she could still see the flames graven on his skin, peeking from beneath his rolled-up sleeve. He had pulled the chair to edge of the bed and sat there, watching her. She could have sworn there was a look of worry on his face, but it evaporated when she smiled at him.

'Ah, Kate,' he said lightly. 'I'm glad you're back. I think that's enough, for tonight. Don't you agree?'

Kate felt dazed. She didn't know how to respond. However, the question must have been rhetorical because Marshall began to untie her ankles, then her wrists. Still she lay there, deliciously exhausted, languishing in the perfect passivity of her climax.

'Get up. Get dressed now. I will get you a cab to take you home.'

As if in a trance, Kate followed his instructions. She refastened her bra over her still-aching breasts, zipped up her skirt, buttoned her blouse up to its high neck. She looked around for her panties, and saw that Gregory held them in his hand.

'I'll keep these, if you don't mind,' he said with a mischievous grin. 'To remind me of you. Until the next time.' Kate felt the starched fabric of her skirt brushing against her bare arse, and smiled back, rather weakly.

Marshall stood before her now. He bent down and kissed her deeply, his tongue as probing as his cock had been. She found herself responding with equal passion, the taste of him re-igniting the fires in her still-damp sex.

'You did well, Kate, very well,' he said, almost tenderly. 'You were born to this. You may not understand, yet; you may not believe. But I will teach you.'

'Do you want that?' he asked, pulling away so he could see her face.

Kate blushed and lowered her eyes. 'I don't know,' she said. 'I'm confused.'

Gregory raised her face to his. 'Think about it. Think about me.'

'And if you decide that this is what you want, here is your first assignment. Since you are leaving your panties with me, I want you to go to work tomorrow without any. No underwear, or stockings. And every time you sit down, let the sensations in your flesh remind you of me, of us, of who and what you are.'

Kate, too lost in embarrassment, didn't answer. But she knew, somehow, that she would obey him, tomorrow and in the future.

Chapter Four
Reclining Buddha

Kate slept deeply and woke late. She lay in bed, her brain still foggy, some half-formed thought tickling the back of her mind. Merely some dream image, perhaps, but it left a sweet taste in her mouth and a feeling of voluptuous relaxation in all her limbs. She stretched like a cat, spreading her fingers towards the sun-dappled ceiling.

Then recollection slammed into her: the bar, the bonds, her shame, her passion. Gregory Marshall, with his damned knowing smile and granite cock. She blushed and shook her head, as if to clear away the mists of her temporary insanity. How could she have done such things, behaved in such a way? She felt angry and ashamed at her own weakness.

Yet even as she berated herself, she also felt aroused. She studied her wrists. The silken ropes had left no marks, but she could still feel their rough caress on her skin. Her hand strayed to the warmth between her legs. She discovered that she was wet, almost as if she had just left Marshall's presence. One finger only she allowed to rest on her clit, but even that was enough to make her squirm.

Stop this, she told herself sternly. It was nearly ten o'clock. She was late enough for work as it was.

Briskly, she rose, showered, began to dress. As she reached for her panties, she suddenly remembered Gregory's instructions. Go bare-bottomed to work! Did she dare? He would never know, so why should she follow his orders?

Still, she hesitated. He had given her what she wanted, ultimately, what she needed: sexual release such as she had never known before. If he made this request, should she not honour it? Wasn't that part of keeping the bargain?

What bargain? she wondered. What promises had been made? She remembered Gregory's tattooed inferno and smiled to herself at the quaint notion that she might have sold her soul.

Finally, she chose her longest skirt, a paisley silk that flowed to mid-calf, and a white pique blouse. She tip-toed down the spiral stairs, not wanting to encounter Ae and her questions. At the door, Kate slipped on her sandals, grabbed her handbag and briefcase, and closed the door softly behind her.

As she waited on the sidewalk for the bus, the light breeze blew her skirt against her legs, between her thighs. The smooth, cool fabric brushed against her skin, as the wind seemed to whisper, 'Remember . . .'

When she reached her office, she was disappointed to find no word from Marshall. There was, however, a long, chatty email from David. He had spent a weekend in Maine with some friends, hiking and eating lobster. There was a new Mexican restaurant on Mass. Avenue that was excellent. He had managed to get tickets to see the Bolshoi Ballet next month; he was sorry she couldn't join him.

The tone of his note was light and cheerful. In the last paragraph, though, he became more serious.

You realise, of course, that I miss you terribly, Kate. Every night seems longer than the last. I lie awake, staring at the ceiling, imagining you in the bright

61

sun of the tropics, remembering your smile, your
taste, the auburn curls at the back of your neck . . .

When can I telephone you? I need to hear your
voice, at least . . .

Kate felt helpless and guilty. She had hardly given a
thought to David since she arrived. Of course she had
been busy getting settled and adjusting to her new job
and surroundings. And busy being fucked, she
reminded herself harshly. By two different men.

She sighed to herself and began to compose a
response, trying to sound warm and reassuring but at
the same time trying not to reveal her recent activities.
She suggested that he call her next Sunday morning, his
time, Sunday evening Bangkok time, and they could
have a long talk.

That duty concluded, Kate turned to her work. She
tried to concentrate, but she was jumpy and easily
distracted. Every time she heard footsteps in the hall,
she found herself looking up. Eventually she got up and
closed her office door, but this didn't help. In the quiet,
she could hear her own heart pounding. Whenever she
shifted position in her chair, she felt her bare buttocks
move against the slithery material of her skirt. When
Malawee came to ask her a question, Kate felt her cheeks
grow red. Even seated behind her desk, she felt exposed.

The telephone rang. Kate started, then grabbed it on
its second ring. When she heard Somtow's voice, warm
relief flooded over her. Yet at the back of her mind, she
realised, she had expected and hoped that it would be
Marshall.

'Hello, Katherine! How are you?'

'Oh, very well, Somtow. Busy.'

'I am sure you are being very productive.' Katherine
could imagine Somtow's gentle grin. 'Are you still available to join me in a trip up-river to Ayuthaya
tomorrow?'

'Oh, definitely. I'm really looking forward to it.' Katherine realised this was the truth. After her experience

with Marshall, Somtow's easy-going humour, impeccable manners, respectful attention, and honest lust, seemed exceptionally appealing. Her discomfort about his marital status was minor in comparison to the confusion she felt about Gregory Marshall.

'Wonderful. I will pick you up around nine o'clock, if that is convenient for you. My driver will take us to the summer palace at Bang Pa-in. From there we will travel by water.'

'Perfect. I'll be ready by nine.'

'You should wear something cool and comfortable,' said the Thai. 'But avoid very revealing clothing, since this would not be proper attire for visiting temples.' He paused. 'Much as I might enjoy seeing you in such attire, of course!'

They both laughed. 'Of course, I understand,' said Katherine. 'Till tomorrow, then.'

'Till tomorrow, my dear Katherine.'

Kate felt much better after the conversation. The Thai's sunny presence seemed to have scattered the shadows that gathered around the image of Gregory. She set to work with a new will, and actually began to make some progress.

Around five o'clock, she finished up and began to collect her things. She and Malawee had a date to go shopping after work. An evening in female company would be soothing and relaxing, she thought, after her recent escapades.

Just as Katherine was leaving her office, her computer beeped to notify her of new mail. She was unable to prevent herself from turning back to read the message. It was, of course, from Gregory.

Kate,
I am pleased that you followed my instructions.
I knew that you would.
Till next time . . .
G.

Katherine just shook her head and sighed. Was he merely guessing, or was he really so sure of his power over her? She didn't have the energy to think about it now.

Her doorbell rang at exactly nine the next morning. Katherine opened it to find Somtow on the threshold, a broad smile on his handsome face. She felt her own face light up in return.

'Good morning! I'll be right with you. Just let me get my bag.'

'Do not rush,' said Somtow. 'We have all day.'

Somtow was dressed casually, in beige twill trousers and a cotton knit shirt of vivid blue. The shirt was open at the neck, revealing the pale sheen of his skin. His hair shone jet black in contrast. He looked good enough to eat, thought Katherine, and then smiled internally at her choice of metaphor.

Katherine wore a long, loose skirt and matching tunic of white cotton gauze. Already the day was hot; only the slightest of breezes stirred the fabric as she and Somtow walked through the garden to his car.

Soon they were on the highway, speeding north toward Bang Pa-in.

'Bang Pa-in has been a royal retreat since the seventeen hundreds,' said Somtow. 'But most of the buildings that you will see today date from the late nineteenth and early twentieth centuries. It is a delightful mix of Thai, European and Chinese styles. Very eclectic.'

Typically Thai, thought Katherine. When the Thais admired something, they simply copied it, modified it, made it their own.

Somtow continued to provide her with background on Bang Pa-in and Ayuthaya. Katherine tried to listen, but she found herself distracted by his physical presence. He sat quite close to her, but not touching. He was relaxed yet animated, punctuating his comments with graceful gestures. He was irresistibly attractive.

Katherine had a strong urge to touch him. However,

she did not want to seem pushy or forward. She continued to nod and smile in response to his running commentary as she shifted slightly on the leather upholstery. Little by little she brought her body closer to him. Then she gradually parted her legs under her long skirt, so that finally her thigh was in contact with his.

The feel of his hard muscles against her raised an involuntary sigh of satisfaction, undoing her careful strategy of concealment, and stopping Somtow in midsentence. He searched her face, a half-smile on his full lips. She blushed and lowered her eyes.

'Ah, Katherine, forgive me for neglecting you!' His lips joined hers, his tongue darting into her opening mouth. Katherine melted into his arms, savouring the now-familiar taste of him. His hands roved over her body as he continued to kiss her, cupping her breasts through the thin fabric, brushing across her belly.

When she felt his fingers stray between her thighs, her first reaction was to spread her legs wide and let him explore her. Then she stiffened, remembering the driver in the front seat, without even a glass partition between them. He was an elderly Thai with a dignified, respectful manner – nothing at all like Chaiwat, Katherine had noted. Surely it would be improper, and would make the driver uncomfortable, if she and Somtow were to continue with this kind of open play.

Somtow sensed the change in her and broke the kiss, looking into her eyes. She said nothing, but inclined her head slightly towards the driver. Somtow smiled and nodded. 'Of course,' he said, sitting up. 'Now, what was I saying? Oh yes. The Burmese attacked Ayuthaya in seventeen sixty-seven, razing temples to the ground, melting down the Buddha images for their gold, and kidnapping many of the citizens.'

He continued his history lesson in an even tone. However, he did not remove his hand from Katherine's lap. As he talked, he burrowed his sensitive fingers into her moist cleft, teasing and thrumming the little button of flesh there. Kate tightened her muscles and tried to remain still, watching the driver in the front seat for signs that they were being observed. The sensations grew; she desperately wished that she were nude, that she could feel Somtow's fingers directly instead of through her clothing.

As if reading her mind, Somtow removed his hand. While discoursing on the significant influence of French and British cultures on Ayuthaya, he silently moved the hand along the leather towards her, until it was under her skirt. Next, Katherine felt his fingers slide along her thigh, and then inside her underwear. She held her breath. Finally, there he was, rolling her naked clit between his thumb and forefinger while his middle two fingers plunged in and out of her hungry cunt.

Katherine put her fist in her mouth, pretending to yawn but actually stifling a moan of pleasure. She spread her thighs wider, the skirt hiding all, and sank back a little more into the seat, offering Somtow even better access. His nimble fingers stroked and teased, now lingering just at the edge of her swollen lips, now buried deep inside her. She tried to remain quiet and keep her breath even, but the closer she came to climax the more difficult this became.

'Ayuthaya was named after Ayodhya, the fortress of Rama, in the Ramayana epic,' Somtow continued calmly. 'It means "unconquerable" or "unassailable".' As he made this remark, he suddenly pushed all four of his fingers hard into her well-lubricated sex, spreading her wide and bringing her over the edge. She stifled a cry as everything within her trembled and convulsed, the tension in her muscles making the pleasure more acute. Like aftershocks, little spasms continued to shake her as Somtow gently cupped her sex, the heel of his hand pressed lightly against her throbbing clit.

'This was not an auspicious or appropriate name, as it turned out,' said Somtow, looking at her with a twinkle in his eye. 'Though the Thais resisted the Burmese siege, Ayuthaya's riches and glories made her ripe for the taking.'

Katherine blushed, hearing in his words a metaphor for her own wantonness. He removed his fingers from her private parts and took hold of her hand, giving it a little squeeze. 'But I must be boring you with all these details,' he said. 'Description is no substitute for experience.' His tone was kind, his expression one of attentiveness and delight. Katherine understood that he did not condemn her for her lust; indeed, he revelled in it.

As Katherine's heart began to slow to its normal rate, the car also slowed to a stop before an ornate wrought-iron gate. 'Here we are, at our first stop,' said Somtow. 'The royal gardens of Bang Pa-in.'

He came around to her side of the car, opened the door and helped her out. Katherine took a deep breath, looking around her. Old trees draped with moss were scattered over a manicured lawn. Gravel paths bordered by rainbow-hued flowers wound invitingly off into the distance. It was cooler here than in the city. A pleasant breeze stirred her clothing, heightening her awareness of the dampness between her thighs.

Somtow gave instructions to his driver, then he steered Katherine down one of the paths. They strolled through the gardens in companionable silence, enjoying the clarity of the morning. Every now and again Somtow touched her, almost absently, a hand laid lightly on her buttocks, an arm around her shoulder. Katherine enjoyed the familiar ease of his touch. Despite their recent acquaintance, and the fact that she really did not know or understand him, she somehow felt comfortable and relaxed in his presence. They came around a bend in the path and Katherine gasped. They had emerged on to a marble platform on the edge of a small lake. The water was perfectly still, mirroring the brilliant blue of the sky.

In the middle of this shimmering expanse, seeming to float above the surface, stood an intricate, exquisitely proportioned Thai pavilion. Five tiers of red-and-green-tiled roof formed steep, overlapping eaves, climbing to a central spire. Ranks of gilded columns supported the roof. Sunlight flashed on the multicoloured chips of mirror that decorated the peaked panels above each entrance. The whole structure was delicate, airy, almost insubstantial, an imaginary palace from some fairy tale. The scene was made even more unreal by the other buildings Katherine saw on the opposite shore: an Italian-style villa with arches and domes, a Chinese pagoda, and a tower that reminded Katherine of a New England lighthouse.

'Remarkable, is it not?' Somtow smiled at her reaction. 'This pavilion is considered to be one of the finest examples of classic Thai architecture in the kingdom. Perhaps this gives you some idea of what Ayuthaya must have been like in its day: hectare after hectare of palaces, temples and pavilions, their graceful eaves sweeping towards the earth, their golden towers pointing to the sky.

'But come. Let us make our way down to the quay. I have hired a converted rice barge to take us upriver. I think that you will find life along the Chao Phya quite a contrast to this scene of royal eccentricity.'

The barge was waiting, a broad wooden craft with a central cabin and open decks on either end. A convex roof covered the whole length of the barge, shading the decks. They were met by a handsome youth with a shy smile who helped them across the gangplank and on to the forward deck.

Then he cast off from the mooring and disappeared to the stern. Katherine felt the barge vibrate as the engine started. Soon they were headed upstream, moving smoothly through the muddy water.

Katherine and Somtow lounged comfortably on the cushioned benches that lined the sides of the boat. A young woman in traditional dress appeared with refreshments: ice cold lemon juice and an array of tropical fruit. Somtow picked up a spear of pineapple, dipped it into a dish of white and red powder that sat in the middle of the fruit platter and offered it to Katherine. 'This is the typical way that Thais eat fruit,' he said. 'With salt and chilli. I know that it may sound odd to you, but try it.'

Katherine took a bite. The complex of sweetness, saltiness and spiciness was quite remarkable. She smiled appreciatively. 'That's fantastic,' she said. 'Like nothing I've ever tasted before. But whatever inspired you to try this in the first place?'

'Just our natural creativity,' said Somtow with a grin. 'Or perhaps our craving for new and exciting sensations.' He leant forward and kissed her, his taste adding to other flavours mingling on her tongue.

The roar of an unmuffled motor roused them from their embrace. A narrow boat with a high, sharp prow raced past them, leaving the barge rocking gently in its wake. 'A long-tail boat, as they are called,' said Somtow. 'A modern adaptation of the traditional dragon boats that plied the river in past centuries.' He kissed her again, lightly. 'Personally, I prefer a more leisurely pace.'

Katherine stood up and leant on the gunwale, taking in the myriad sights of the river. Stretches of verdant jungle alternated with rickety-looking wooden houses perched on stilts at the river's edge. Women in sarongs squatted on the porches of these shacks, doing laundry or cooking on charcoal braziers. The delicious smell of frying garlic came to her across the water.

She saw the slick heads of children, heard their shrill cries as they splashed each other. A flat-bottomed boat piled high with bananas passed their barge, propelled by a long pole in the hands of an elderly woman in a conical straw hat.

Then she caught sight of tiled roofs and gilded spires through the palm trees. It was a *wat*, a Buddhist temple, inaccessible except by water. A winding stairway led from the complex of buildings down to the shore. At water level sat a small pavilion with the typical peaked roof and upturned eaves. Katherine saw a young man draped in orange robes seated there, pensively watching the river flow by. The monk looked up as they passed.

Kate felt an ache in her chest. His beautiful, serious face, lit by the late-morning sun, was too perfect.

Immersed in the scenes on the riverside, Katherine started when she felt Somtow's hands on her hips. She twisted around to look at him.

'No,' he said. 'Please, just stay the way you are.' She obeyed, turning back to the river and leaning her elbows on the railing. She felt her skirt being drawn up until it was around her waist. Next, her knickers were pulled down until they were at her ankles.

'Perhaps I should just stop wearing any underwear,' Katherine remarked with a little laugh. Gregory's face flashed briefly in her mind's eye; she pushed the thought of him away.

'Perhaps that would be a good idea,' said Somtow, completely serious. He helped her step out of the garment.

'Now, spread your legs a bit, Katherine.'

'What about the young pilot, and the girl who brought us the fruit?'

'They know better than to bother us,' said Somtow. He was kneeling behind her. She felt his tongue, tracing a line up the inside of her thigh.

'In any case,' he said after a moment, 'you would not really mind if they were watching, would you?' He lingered in the crease where her thigh swelled into the fullness of her buttocks. Katherine let out an involuntary sigh, and opened her legs a little wider.

She didn't answer his question. Her imagination, though, supplied an image of the pilot and the serving girl, peeking out of the cabin at her bare backside liberally anointed with her lover's saliva. The thought brought a strange, forbidden thrill. She imagined the pilot unbuttoning the girl's top, while guiding her hand to his swollen cock. Somtow could see right through her, she realised, writhing as he swept his tongue along the length of her sex.

He licked her in broad strokes, front to back, starting at her clit and moving smoothly to the spot where her aching pussy-lips came together again. She arched her back to give him better access and closed her eyes, savouring the fantastic sensations he was giving her. She felt incredibly wet, from his saliva and her own juices. Sunlight reflected from the water danced on her closed eyelids. The low rumble of the barge's motor set up a sympathetic vibration in her limbs. She felt the roar of the engine deep within her cunt.

Then came a new, a different, feeling, like an electric shock. Somtow reached the back of her sex, but instead of beginning a new cycle he set his tongue to work on her anus.

His hands were on her cheeks, pulling them apart. He circled around the tight knot several times, then poked his tongue into the ring of muscle, probing and teasing.

Embarrassment swept over Katherine, that he should be exploring such a private spot. She almost asked him to stop. At the same time, she was unbelievably excited. Every time he delved into her hind hole, her cunt was seized with a new spasm of pleasure. She grasped her nipples, squeezing hard, and pushed her hips back, silently begging him to search her more deeply.

The intimate kisses stopped, and Katherine felt mingled relief and regret. Before she could analyse this, there was another change. Somtow's hard rod of flesh slid into her cunt. He pumped her steadily, rhythmic strokes that brought moans to her lips. She rocked in time with him, tightening her inner muscles each time he entered.

His hands were on her hips, guiding her on to his princely cock. Then Katherine realised she only felt one hand. The next moment, she burnt again with shame as Somtow slid his wet forefinger into her arsehole.

She felt sluttish, dirty, wild. He worked his finger in time with his cock, careful not to push too deep or too hard. Even that little bit of stretching in that sensitive area produced unbearably acute sensations. She twisted and writhed, forgetting everything except the dance between her legs. As another long-tail roared by she reached back and grabbed her own buttocks, holding them wide open, inviting Somtow to penetrate her more fully.

The sight of her, drenched in sweat, her fingernails digging into her own white flesh, seemed to drive Somtow on to orgasm. He plunged his cock and his finger into her, as deep as he could go. His fierce coming pulled her along with him. The breeze carried her cries over the water. A woman hanging her laundry on the bank looked up curiously.

Katherine clung to the rail, panting, her forehead on her hands. Her whole body was shaking. She felt Somtow put his arm around her shoulders, helping her back to a sitting position on the bench. She pulled her skirt modestly over her knees. Underneath, she felt herself open and wet, front and rear. Little electric thrills still chased through her sex, especially when Somtow brought his lips to hers.

'Katherine, you continue to amaze me,' he said softly. 'Thank you, for being you and for being with me.'

'It is you who are amazing,' Katherine answered. 'I have never met such a perfect gentleman, or such a dedicated lecher, in my life!'

Kate went off to the tiny bathroom in the cabin to splash some water on her face and clean up a bit. She had grabbed her underwear from deck on the way. She began to put it on, then she changed her mind and stuffed the garment into her shoulder bag. Just in case, she thought, with a mental shrug.

She emerged to find the barge pulling up at what was clearly a public boat ramp. As she and Somtow climbed the wooden stairs leading up the river bank, she felt the eyes of the pilot and the serving girl upon them. But perhaps it was just her imagination. She didn't dare turn around to see.

The bare, dusty area at the top of the steps was crowded with food vendors and *tuk tuks*, three-wheeled, open-air taxis that were basically a motorised adaptation

72

of a rickshaw. The drivers were aggressive, competitive, and friendly.

'*Tuk tuk*?' they called.

'One hundred baht for the day!'

'I can take you, show you all the sights, only eighty baht!'

'Come, madame, sir, let me take you in my *tuk tuk*!'

Somtow turned to Katherine. 'Shall we hire a *tuk tuk*, or walk? The ruins are fairly spread out, but you get a much better sense of the scale of Ayuthaya's former magnificence on foot.'

'Let's walk,' said Katherine, smiling at him.

'Fine. Then we will need some supplies.' He went over to one of the stalls and in short order had purchased a bottle of water, a bag of crispy fried bananas and two straw hats. Donning the hats, they set off down the road which bordered the river.

Before long, they reached a half-tumbledown brick wall, overrun with luxuriant vines. Fragments of stone sculpture were strewn around it: a graceful hand, the folds of a robe, part of a set of legs frozen in a full lotus position. Behind the wall, Katherine could see a precariously leaning tower and a set of broken columns, equally festooned with greenery.

'This was Wat Mahatat,' said Somtow. 'One of the grandest temples in the city. At one time its tower, or *prang*, was nearly fifty metres high.'

They wandered among the ruins, which had a kind of melancholy beauty. The day was getting hot, but there was still a breeze. The vines rustled softly, whispering of days long vanished.

As they continued, they came to a grassy expanse dominated by three huge *chedis*, conical towers that looked like upturned children's tops. 'The ashes of two royal princes and an abbot are buried within those monuments,' said Somtow. 'During the prime of the Ayuthaya, the *chedis* would have been gilded, and could have been seen, above the city walls, from a long way away. They are positioned to catch the last gleams of the setting sun.'

They stood at the foot of one of the *chedis*. Katherine looked up. Most of the stucco that had once covered the structure had worn away. She could see the precise brickwork used to create the tapering outline.

Next, they reached a temple that appeared to be intact. 'Wat Suwan Dararam,' said Somtow. 'This temple was built near the close of the Ayuthaya period; it was badly damaged, but now has been restored. Shall we go inside?'

'Oh, yes,' said Katherine. The shady interior looked very appealing.

'Leave your shoes on the steps,' said Somtow, doing so himself. As they entered, an elderly monk bowed in a respectful *wai*. Somtow put some money in the wooden box beside the man, and picked up two bundles of incense sticks.

The interior of the *wat* was fragrant with sandalwood. Woven straw mats covered the floor, their texture pleasant under Katherine's bare feet. Columns carved with mythical beasts supported the peaked ceiling; brightly painted frescoes decorated the walls.

An enormous bronze Buddha image sat at the far end of the sanctuary, surrounded by banks of candles, jars of flowers and many smaller images. Several orange-clad monks sat before the figure, chanting softly. Somtow approached the Buddha and knelt reverently. He lit his incense from one of the candles, holding it between his two palms. Then he repeatedly bowed, bringing his hands and the incense to his forehead.

Katherine watched him with some surprise. His eyes were closed. His lips moved slightly with some inaudible prayer or invocation. His devotion was clearly genuine.

She lit her own incense and stuck it in one of the bronze pots filled with sand that were provided for this purpose. Then she sat quietly, marvelling at the peace that pervaded the place, and at the transformation of her lover.

Eventually, Somtow opened his eyes. He looked at her and smiled, then took her hand and led her out of the temple. The sun was blinding as they emerged. The heat had intensified.

'I hope you were not bored,' said Somtow.

'Oh no,' said Katherine. 'It was lovely, very tranquil.'

'It is important to pay one's respects,' said Somtow seriously. 'Especially for me. I have such a need to make merit.'

Abruptly, his mood lightened. He grasped her hand again, smiling his infectious smile. 'Come, I have something else to show you.' He led her down the road and then turned on to a winding path through thickening vegetation. Suddenly they came to a clearing. There, surrounded by bricks and rubble, was a massive statue of the Buddha in a reclining pose.

As was traditional, the figure lay on its right side, the stone head resting on the right palm. Calm eyes contemplated them serenely. From the flame of knowledge rising out of his head, to the soles of his feet decorated with the eight-petal lotus, the statue must have been at least ten metres in length. Katherine gazed at the figure, impressed by its scale and its overwhelming air of quiet power. She lost track of Somtow for a moment. Then she heard a sound behind her.

She turned to see Somtow, totally naked, lying on the grass in the shade. Like the statue, he lay on his side, his ear resting on his hand. Unlike the Buddha image, though, his expression was one of mischievous invitation.

'Somtow,' Katherine exclaimed, 'you are completely outrageous! Don't you consider this disrespectful?'

'The Buddha rejected asceticism. He taught the middle way, moderation in all things.' Somtow grinned. 'I am just more moderate in some areas than others.'

Katherine shook her head in disbelief. Her Thai prince looked as irresistible as usual. His hair was a bit dishevelled, curling damply on his brow. His pale skin flowed with patterns of shadow as the sunlight filtered through the trees. His cock was hugely erect, glistening with a bit of premonitory moisture.

What the hell, she thought to herself. She pulled her tunic over head and stepped out of her skirt. The breeze was delicious on her bare skin.

As she approached, Somtow rolled on to his back. Taking his cue, she straddled him and slowly, teasingly, lowered herself on to his eager cock.

She was a little sore, she found, from their earlier escapade. The irritation gave a sharp edge to the pleasure of his entering. Her dancer's muscles allowed her to control her movements as she slid up and down on his stiff rod of flesh, building the tension as gradually as she could.

Somtow rocked his pelvis in time with her strokes, but otherwise remained still. He watched her as she rode him, harder now, grinding herself down on him, finding exactly the right position, the right angle, for her own satisfaction. Now he reached up and caressed her breasts gently, trapping the nipples between his first and second finger. Katherine responded by pinching his nipples, hard. His back arched, pushing his cock deeper into her.

'Katherine,' he moaned. She began a circular motion with her hips, spiralling her lubricated cunt up and down the length of his cock. 'Oh, Katherine!'

His eyes were closed. He grabbed her arse and began to pump her body, in and out, up and down. She relaxed a bit, allowed him to move her, control her, use her flesh to stimulate his own. Somehow this increased her own excitement. Katherine saw, in a moment of clarity, that this was what she liked best: to be fucked, used, taken over, turned into the vessel of someone else's pleasure.

Her tangled hair fell over her eyes. Somtow's cock split her wide, again and again. They breathed in unison, panting in time to his quickening thrusts. She swept her thumbs over her taut nipples, savouring the electric

76

spasms this produced in her sex. Her back arched; her backside in Somtow's firm grip, she let go entirely, let him probe her deepest cavities, let him swell and burst, exploding inside her.

And as she felt that explosion, her flesh sent up answering fireworks, a fiery cascade of the senses that left her breathless. Yes, she thought, yes, this is what matters, what I want, what I live for.

Later, as she lay naked and sweating on her lover's body, under the wise and tranquil gaze of the reclining Buddha, she felt no shame.

Chapter Five
Lessons in Leather

On Sunday, Katherine was sore. Her muscles ached; her sex was red and tender. Somehow, she didn't mind. Every little twinge reminded her of Somtow's lust, and her own abandon. She couldn't help smiling to herself as she ate her late breakfast.

Still, she was surprised at herself. She had always enjoyed sex, but lately, it seemed, she had gone over the edge. What was happening to her? Her body was alive in a new way; the slightest hint of the erotic, the merest suggestion of the salacious, was enough to make her damp and hungry. Meanwhile, her mind painted pictures that made her blush, starting with memories of what she had done and embroidering to create lurid fantasies of what she might have done – or might do.

It wasn't just Somtow, of course, but Gregory also. The alternation of brightness and shadow, respect and mockery, seduction and domination, had left her dizzy, reeling. Never before had she had two lovers at the same time – three, if you counted David. It made her feel a little crazy. Was she being rash, taking too many risks? Was she a slut, as Gregory had labelled her?

Katherine was confused, but searching her soul she honestly could not feel any regret. I have not lied to anyone, she thought, and I have not done anything wrong. I am glad for both of them, I admit it. I don't want to give up either of these strange, exciting liaisons.

Ae normally took Sunday off, so Katherine had the house to herself. She spent a leisurely day, listening to music, reading in the garden, taking a stroll around her neighbourhood. As evening drew near, she remembered that David had promised to call. She felt great trepidation. How could she tell him what was happening to her? On the other hand, how could she not be truthful?

Promptly at nine o'clock, the telephone rang. She picked it up nervously.

'Hello?'

'Katherine? It's David.' Two breaths. 'God, Kate, it's so good to hear your voice!'

'Yours, too,' said Kate, and she meant it. Her nervousness melted away at the familiar sound of his laugh and his Boston accent. 'Oh, David, it's so strange here! I love it, but I do miss home, and you. There is a kind of magic here, but sometimes I worry I've been bewitched.'

'Tell me about it,' he said, his voice warm, and kind. 'You can tell me, Kate. I'm your best friend.'

'Well . . .' She hesitated. 'Somehow, I'm constantly turned on, constantly horny.' There was silence on the other end of the line. She swallowed. 'In the few weeks since I've been here, I've had sex with two different men. It's as if I can't help myself.'

She waited, expecting tearful recriminations or angry jibes. When he finally spoke, though, he sounded calm, even gentle.

'Katherine, you are the most sensual woman I have ever known. Of course you have taken lovers. How could you not? I don't blame you at all. But I do miss you. You don't know how much I wish I could be there with you.'

He paused, then continued softly. 'I replay that scene in the parking garage again and again, Kate. You can't imagine how intoxicating you looked, with your skirt around your waist, your sweet cunt swallowing up every inch of my cock.'

'Yes,' said Kate. 'I can imagine. I do.' The familiar tingle started again, between her legs. She switched the telephone receiver to her left hand and began to massage her sex with her right, slowly, languidly, in time with her breath. 'David, I was overwhelmed by you. I could hardly believe you would do that to me, in such a public place!'

'I get a hard-on every time I think about it,' David whispered. 'So exposed. I think about how I should have closed the trunk and laid you face down on top of it, your ass in the air, as I ploughed your pussy. Then everyone could have appreciated the fine view . . .'

'So . . .' Kate was beginning to pant. 'Do you have a hard-on now?'

'What do you think?' David's voice was huskier.

'I know just what you look like,' she said. 'Your cock is getting longer and thicker by the minute. It's purple, throbbing, full of blood, the soft skin stretched tight over the swollen hardness beneath. Just feel how soft that skin is, David.'

'Meanwhile,' she continued, in a low, seductive voice, 'I'm lying on my silk-upholstered sofa. My robe is open. My nipples are as hard as your cock, throbbing too. I trail my fingers up the inside of my thigh, just barely touching. Now I'm burying my fingers in my bush, probing for my clit. I spread my legs wider, so I can touch myself more deeply.' She stopped for a moment, breathing heavily, momentarily overcome by the delicious feelings flooding her sex.

'My finger is in my pussy, now, as deep as I can go.' She heard David panting. 'It's not enough, though. I want your cock there, filling me up, touching every part of me inside. Nothing feels as good as your hard cock inside me.'

There was only breathing on the other end of the line. Kate was getting more and more excited. She struggled to keep control of her voice.

'Squirt some lubricant on to your palm, David,' she instructed. 'Get your hand nice and wet and slippery.

Now, take hold of yourself, move your hand up and down that lovely long length of cock. It feels so good, doesn't it? Imagine that's me, sitting on your cock, sliding you in and out.'

'Oh, Kate . . .' David was groaning.

'I'm very wet,' she said, and it was true. 'I'm going to come on you, David, all over you. You're so wonderfully deep inside me.'

She had both hands between her legs now, the phone pressed between her shoulder and her ear. Her left thumb and forefinger pinched and twisted her clit; all four fingers of the right hand were buried in the juicy folds of her pussy. 'David,' she moaned, 'I'm going to come. Come with me, David; fill me; fuck me, David, now; David, come now!'

Katherine closed her eyes and allowed the climax to take her. She heard David's cries and suddenly could see him, his jaw clenched, his compact, muscular body in spasms as the come spurted from the organ he held with both hands. She was suddenly filled with the desire to kiss him tenderly, to kneel before him, licking the sticky white fluid from his sweet flesh.

'Oh, David, I miss you,' she sighed. 'Forgive me for not appreciating you, for taking you for granted. You're wonderful, David.'

'No,' said David softly. 'You're the one who's wonderful.'

The conversation with David seemed to settle her. Katherine started the week determined to be more productive. She was calmer, less obsessed with the sexual, finally able to concentrate on her work. Every now and again a thought of Somtow, or of Gregory, would tickle the edge of her consciousness. She would push these thoughts resolutely away. Later, she thought, I'll indulge myself later.

Her resolution received a boost when Somtow called her Monday to tell her he was leaving for a business trip to Hong Kong. Apologetically, he indicated that he would be away for at least a week. 'I will contact you when I return,' he said. 'I hope that we will be able to get together then.' Katherine felt a little thrill, speculating on what he might have in mind for their next meeting. 'I will miss you, Katherine.'

'I will miss you, also,' she answered sincerely, but her regret was mixed with gratitude. She needed some time to recover, to sort out her feelings, and hopefully to make some progress on the projected 3D project.

Kate had not heard anything from Gregory since his email the previous Friday, and for now she hoped he would keep his silence. Their sexual encounter had strengthened her determination to demonstrate her professional expertise. She could, perhaps, accept the apparent fact that debasing herself before him, offering herself as his sex toy to manipulate and control, excited her beyond belief. But she could only bear his mockery, she felt, if she could earn his respect for her intelligence and technical skill.

It was a quiet week, and she worked hard. By Thursday afternoon, she actually had a prototype. She asked Ruengroj to help her set up the equipment in the conference room: a digital video projector, linked to her computer, and a cylindrical screen, constructed of finely woven mosquito netting stretched tightly around a frame.

The basic idea was simple. Humans see the world as solid and three-dimensional, but in fact depth, the third dimension, is an illusion constructed by the brain. Various types of information available in a scene allow the visual system to infer the relationships between objects, or parts of a single object. One of the most powerful cues is parallax, the differences in the motion of objects that are nearer versus those further away from the viewer.

Katherine had written software to artificially generate parallax cues. She could take a pre-existing or computer-animated video sequence and selectively change the motion of specific parts of the images, so that an observer would see the objects in the video clip as having depth. The free-standing screen would enhance the illusion by making it seem as though the motion was occurring in positive space, rather than in the space 'behind' a screen.

The algorithms required to identify sections to be modified, and the mathematics involved in computing the correct motion, were definitely complex. The principle, however, was straightforward. Roj finished attaching all the cables. The screen sat on the conference room table. Katherine signalled him to dim the lights, then turned on the projector and adjusted the focus.

A moving image took shape on the table: a female figure, a dancer, undulating in time to unheard music. Her body was gilded from head to toe. Her hair was gold, plastered against her head. Her eyes were closed. Her long fingernails trailed threads of gold through the air as she raised her arms in a gesture of entreaty.

Katherine had chosen to animate the credits sequence from an old James Bond movie, one of her favourites. She could hear the theme song playing in her head as she and Roj watched the dancer.

The effect was surprisingly convincing. Occasionally Katherine could detect some discontinuity in the movement, a slight jerkiness or an unnaturally swift change. Overall, though, the dancer appeared to be real, solid, her curvaceous figure inviting the eye. One could almost reach out and touch those rounded limbs, cup those swelling breasts.

The room suddenly went dark as the video clip ended. 'Whew!' said Ruengroj, whistling appreciatively. 'That was really something! She seemed so real! I am truly impressed, Katherine.'

Katherine realised that the imperfections she had noted were probably not apparent to her co-worker.

'Thanks!' she said. 'It still needs a lot of work. Plus there are many problems remaining to be tackled, such as how to deal with different points of view in the same image. Also, Mr Marshall wants to somehow synchronise the images with the mood of the music.' She could not help noticing how her heart beat a bit faster as she said his name. 'That will open up a whole new set of issues.'

'Nevertheless, this is a great start,' Roj continued, his enthusiasm unabated. 'Mr Harrison will be overjoyed at what you've accomplished in such a short time.'

Katherine was pleased with the praise. Back in her office, she set to work looking for the logic or calculation errors that had produced the few flaws she had noticed. Deep in concentration, she jumped when Edward Harrison knocked on her door frame.

'Katherine! Ruengroj tells me that you already have a working prototype of your projected 3D technology. I'm leaving town tonight, but I would really like demonstration early next week. Would that be OK?'

'Of course, Edward. Have a good trip.'

'I will,' said her boss heartily. Then he lowered his voice. 'By the way, don't say anything to Marshall about this yet. I want to make sure that we get everything that we deserve before we turn this over to him.'

'Oh, this is nowhere near ready to be delivered to the customer.' Katherine avoided saying his name. 'As I told Ruengroj, there are many issues and problems that I have just begun to look at.'

'Even so. Keep it quiet for now.'

'I will,' she replied, slightly irritated. He should be cautioning Roj to be more circumspect, not her.

Kate arrived at DigiThai the next morning full of energy. She was excited by the success of her initial demo and eager to move forward with the project.

The email message awaiting her scattered these expectations of productivity.

Kate,
If you have plans for this evening, cancel them.
Await my instructions.
G.

Damn him, thought Kate. She sat back in her chair, her heart pounding despite herself. How could he do this to her? Why did she let him?

She abruptly clicked the delete button and returned to her work. I can ignore him, and I will, she resolved. She half-succeeded in this resolution, finding two bugs in her software before she and Malawee left to have a quick lunch.

As they re-entered the office suite, Anchana called out to her. 'Miss Katherine, this package arrived for you while you were out.' It was a long, narrow box with the label of a local florist.

It couldn't be from Gregory, Katherine thought scornfully. He would never consider sending her flowers.

However, she was wrong. The box contained a single long-stemmed rose nestled among green ferns. The petals were just beginning to unfold. The blossom was a creamy white, with a delicate tracery of red veins. Kate had never seen such a curious pattern.

In addition to the rose, there was a heavy brass key and a sheet of writing parchment folded in half. Kate's hands trembled as she unfolded the note.

Montien Hotel, Room 1263. Eight o'clock.
Love,
G.

Only those few words, inscribed with black ink in a strong, open script. Kate was intrigued and troubled. She knew the Montien, a four-star hotel on Suriwong Road, quite close to Pat Pong. Edward Harrison had taken her there for a drink a few days after she arrived.

It was clear enough what Marshall wanted. Should she comply? Meet a man she hardly knew, in an anonymous hotel room, to participate in who knows what perverted activities?

Images of their previous encounter flooded her. She remembered looking up from her knees at his blazing eyes and hugely swollen cock. She recalled him laughing at her helpless lust as she masturbated at his command. She felt the ropes holding her down, holding her open, as he ravaged her sex. It was all the secret, shameful dreams, of rape and ravishment, use and abuse, that she had ever dreamt and denied.

Her nipples were hard and she knew she was damp. She almost wanted to cry at her own weakness. Yet still her excitement grew as she understood that she could not, would not, say no to him.

Then there was the sign off. Love. She didn't know how to read this. She could hear him say it, with that characteristic irony in his luscious voice. Surely he was mocking her, once again. Or perhaps he was asking a question, asking her to look within and answer: so what is love, after all, and what did it have to do with the way that their bodies and their minds connected?

The hotel lobby was bright and noisy with tourists. Kate felt conspicuous and embarrassed as she crossed to the elevators, as if she were already naked.

In the elevator, a western man and a Thai girl fondled each other, whispering and giggling. They left at the sixth floor. The ride to the twelfth seemed to take a long time. Everything was hushed, muffled. Her heels made no sound on the thick carpet. Her heart beat in her ears, absurdly loud.

Kate hesitated as she turned the key in the lock. Seized with sudden fear, she nearly turned and ran back down the hallway to the elevator. This was irrevocable. She knew that. In opening this door, she would open her well-ordered life to chaotic and irrational forces that she did not understand.

She remembered Gregory's words. 'You were born to this,' he had said, and, 'I will teach you.' She swallowed hard and turned the doorknob.

The room was dim, and apparently empty. She closed the door quietly behind her and looked around.

Spacious, luxurious, undistinguished – she might have been in a hotel anywhere. The only sound was the slight hiss of the air conditioning. A floor-to-ceiling window, with the curtains open, sparkled with the lights of the city. A comfortable-looking oversized arm-chair, a teak desk, a vanity with a tall mirror, a king-size bed with carved teak head and foot boards, these were the sum of the room's furnishings. The diffuse, rosy light came from a brass lamp on the desk. Someone had covered the shade with a scarf of red silk.

Kate noticed, on the desk, a narrow brass vase. It held a single rose, white traced with red, matching her own.

There was no one here now. But someone had been here.

She examined the wooden head and foot boards but found no ropes affixed there. Then she noticed the items arrayed on the quilted silk bedspread: five circles of leather, decorated with stainless steel. She picked one up, savoured the softness of the leather, ran her fingers around the attached metal ring. One of the circlets was larger; all were adorned with rings, perhaps an inch in diameter, and the larger circlet was decorated with steel studs as well.

Kate blushed, though there was no one to see her. She understood the purpose of these artifacts: wrist and ankle restraints, and a slave collar.

Though he had left no instructions, Gregory's intent was clear.

The bracelet of leather was lined with satin. It was held closed by sturdy snaps. Kate put it on her wrist. She was just curious to see how it felt.

Oddly, it was comfortable. It fitted her well. Kate hugged herself nervously, walked around the room, stared out at the traffic on Suriwong Road, returned to the bed.

Slowly, almost reluctantly, she began to remove her clothes. As in her previous encounter with Marshall, she felt that she was moving in a dream. Now he was exercising his will without even being present.

She seemed to be watching herself as she placed her folded garments on the bed and reached for the other wrist restraint. Now she bent and attached the leather anklets. Finally, she lifted her curls and snapped the collar around her neck.

She was naked, save for the leather adornments. Daring herself, she walked barefoot across the plush carpet to the mirror. What would Gregory see, she wondered, when he arrived? Was this a worthy offering?

Kate stood before the mirror, legs slightly apart, hands on her hips. She was breathing heavily; she could see her chest rise and fall. Her nipples were round and rigid, the size and shape of ripe olives. She imagined Gregory taking one in his mouth and shivered. The dark leather around her throat made her creamy skin seem even whiter. The studs on the collar were red with reflected light, as if this emblem of submission were encrusted with rubies.

She gazed at her face, trying to recognise herself. The expression was strange, desperate, wanton. Her chest hurt from the pounding of her heart.

A slight sound; and she saw the opening door reflected in the mirror. Gregory stepped in. Her knees went weak.

'Kate,' he said softly. Before she could turn, he was behind her at the mirror, his hands resting lightly upon her shoulders. He towered over her; her head barely reached his chest. 'You look very fetching, little Kate,' he said with that familiar hint of derision. She blushed, ashamed to have been caught admiring herself, arrayed in this paraphernalia.

Gregory bent and touched the tip of his tongue to the side of her neck just above the leather. It was scalding hot. Her sex burned in answer.

'I'm glad to see you prepared, Kate.' His hands were on her breasts now; he flicked painfully at the nipples with his thumbs. He ran his hands down her arms and grasped her leather-clad wrists in a vice-like grip. He turned her around. 'Are you prepared, Kate? Are you?'

Kate hung her head, unable meet his eyes. 'Look at

me,' Gregory said, almost in a whisper. Even his whisper held authority. She raised her eyes to him.

He was beautiful, like some wild, sleek animal. His long hair was loose tonight, framing those searing blue eyes. His mouth was half-open; Kate could see sharp teeth. Gregory was also clad in leather, tight black leather trousers and a waistcoat with studs that matched her collar, over a flowing black shirt.

'Are you ready for the next lesson, Kate?' His voice was serious, no trace of the usual ridicule.

Kate nodded weakly, her mind fogged with desire. 'I – I think so.'

'Do you trust me?' he asked. Kate searched her heart. 'Yes,' she said finally. 'I am not sure why I should, but yes.'

'Good girl,' he said, levity entering his voice once again. 'In that case, I have something else for you. Put your hands behind your head.'

As Kate obeyed, he reached into his pocket and drew out two items that sparkled in the red light. He held them up so she could see them better.

Kate was horrified. They were spring-loaded clamps, like the 'alligator clips' used to attach wires to battery terminals.

'They are quite stiff,' Gregory said, flexing one of them in his strong fingers. 'But then, they have to be, to be effective.'

Kate realised that her current position, with forearms raised and hands clasped at the nape of her neck, was intended to expose and elevate her breasts. 'Take a deep breath,' said Gregory. As she did, he caught her right nipple in the jaws of one of the clamps.

Kate gasped. Fierce pain shot through her. The clamp was lined with smooth leather, not serrated like an electrical clamp. It did not break the skin. But it squeezed the swollen knob of flesh and sent sharp stabs radiating through her body.

It was torture; Kate bit her lip, trying not to cry out. Somehow, though, by the time the pain reached her sex, it had become something different, equally sharp, but more pleasurable, a kind of hungry aching.

'Hungry,' said Gregory, as if he had read her mind. 'You are hungry for more. I can feel it.' He captured her left nipple in the other clamp. The pain grew, magnified tenfold rather than twofold.

Kate was sweating, trying to be still, to be quiet, to please him. The clamps hung off her flesh, heavy, clumsy. Her nipples felt huge, the size of eggs or golf balls. Tears gathered in the corners of her eyes.

Gregory surveyed her, an expression of satisfaction on his face. 'Yes. That's just right,' he said. 'They suit you very well.'

He knelt on one knee before her. 'Be still, now,' he said brusquely. With two fingers, he began probing her cunt, first deeply, then sliding his fingertips across her clit.

The heat that grew between her legs changed the sensation in her breasts. The pain flowing from her nipples was met and transformed by the pleasure radiating from her sex. Still excruciating, unbelievably intense, it nevertheless became something that she wanted. She stopped fighting against the pain and allowed it to wash over her, obliterating all her fear and her doubt and her shame. She closed her eyes; the accumulated tears spilt down her cheeks.

Something changed. She realised that Gregory had removed the clamps. Her breasts still throbbed with pain, her nipples screaming and tender. Opening her eyes, she saw that Gregory was still kneeling before her. He placed his lips around one aching red nodule and sucked gently. There was the heat again, but now it soothed rather than burned, blissful comfort like a warm hearth on a winter day. He switched his attentions to the other nipple, touching her only with his lips and tongue.

She wanted so badly for him to take her in his arms, cuddle her, comfort her, praise her. But she knew he wouldn't, or not at least when she wished it. He was the master, and it was his part to decide when to deliver pleasure, when to mete out pain. As he had told her that first night, she must learn to be patient.

Gregory stood up to his full height, grasped her wrists again, and brought her hands down from behind her head. 'Better now?' he asked. Kate nodded, still confused by her paradoxical reactions.

'Good. Come over here, then.' Still holding her wrists, he led her towards the window. He fished in the pocket of his waistcoat and brought out a length of ordinary hemp rope. 'This should do,' he said archly. He threaded one end of the rope through the ring attached to her wristlet. He tied the other end to a wrought-iron ring on the wall to the right of the window.

In her initial survey of the room, Kate had assumed that this ring was decorative, intended for tying back the curtains. Now she saw her error; the metal circle was far heavier and stronger than was necessary to hold the curtains. With mixed fascination and distaste, she understood that this was Gregory's special room, customised for his particular purposes by the hotel management. What other special features might he have requested? The room was so quiet; perhaps it had been soundproofed to muffle the cries and moans of his 'visitors'.

As the leather-attired giant tied her other wrist to the ring on the opposite wall, Kate wondered about the other women Gregory had lured to this room. (Or men. So far she had seen no indication that his dominant stance extended only to females. His manipulation of Edward Harrison suggested the contrary.) Who were they? How did they behave? How much pain, how much humiliation could they endure? More than she could, no doubt. Suddenly she felt woefully inadequate. She watched Marshall, finishing off a neat bowline and testing its strength. How could she ever satisfy him?

He caught her glance, read the distress in her eyes. 'Yes, Kate, I admit I have brought others here to my comfortable urban dungeon. But that should not concern you.'

She was bound now, arms stretched wide across the window alcove.

'Spread your legs a little more,' he ordered. 'You will find yourself more stable.'

He stood before her, hands on his hips. 'You are mine now, Kate, mine because I chose to make you mine. Mine because you chose to answer my call.' He brushed the hair back from her anxious eyes. 'Your role is to obey me, serve me, please me.' He paused, then continued softly. 'And you do, Kate, you do please me, even in your innocence and inexperience.'

'If there are others who also serve, what is that to you? You should be grateful to them, for giving your master pleasure.'

Kate felt her jealousy and despair melt away. He was right. As long as she could please him, what else mattered?

She heard him moving behind her, near the bed, then he stood before her again, something dark in his hands.

'I left this also on the bed, for you to examine and consider. But apparently you did not notice – or did not allow yourself to do so.'

He held out the article for her inspection. Kate swallowed the lump in her throat. The item in his hands was clearly some sort of leather whip.

'The technical term,' Gregory said, smiling, 'is cat-o'-nine-tails. You'll notice the many strands of leather radiating from the handle.' He grasped the handle, which was neatly encased in braided leather, in his left hand, running his right over the strands as if caressing a lover's hair. 'Each thong ends with a knot. When used correctly, the thongs apply a sharp heat, while the knots digging into the skin provide an extra sting.'

He dangled the whip above her shoulder, the knots just touching, then brushed it lightly across her breasts. The leather was amazingly soft, but as he dragged it across her still-swollen nipples, she felt the echo of the clamps on her flesh.

Now he was delicately tracing an upward path from her pubic fur, across her belly, sending delicious tremors up her spine and down her bound arms. Thus far, he was using the cat-o'-nine-tails as an instrument of pure pleasure.

He spoke again, without stopping his leather caresses. 'Have you ever been beaten by a lover, Kate?'

Kate shook her head and felt herself blush, though she did not understand why.

'Have you ever dreamt or fantasised about such a thing?' Gregory asked.

'No,' said Kate, indignant. 'Of course not.'

Gregory laughed. 'Of course not? Indeed! Perhaps you do not remember your dreams, Kate.' He leant close to her ear, whispering. 'The first time I laid eyes on you, Kate, I sensed that you craved the whip. I saw it in your eyes, in the way you moved, in your fierce, almost defiant independence. I felt your yearning to be mastered, to be set free.'

Kate hung her head and said nothing. Was what he said true? Did she really know so little of herself?

'I want to whip you, Kate, whip you well, to open your mind and your senses to the possibilities within you.'

He lifted her chin with the end of the whip so that her eyes met his.

'Will you do this for me, Kate? Do you dare to take this next step?'

His gaze was a spotlight, searching the depths of her soul. Kate felt fear and desire, rebellion (I'll show him what I dare!) and devotion (how could I not do whatever pleases him?). She found herself fascinated by the leather implement of punishment that he wielded with such familiarity. She was curious, disgusted and, as usual in Marshall's presence, unbelievably aroused.

Finally she answered. 'Yes,' she said softly. 'I dare. For you.' Her cheeks burned at admitting her weakness.

'Good,' he said. 'Once again, you do not disappoint me.' He circled around behind her. 'Now, relax. And breathe.'

The first stroke caught her by surprise. Confused by her mixed emotions and muddled by her lust, she had not been thinking about the pain. Each leather strand was a red-hot wire, searing the flesh of her buttocks. She bit her lip, trying not to cry out.

A precise *snap*, then a second stroke landed, a little lower, on the fullest part of her rump. 'Ouch!' Kate could feel the individual traces left by the knots, a dozen separate bites all over those swelling cheeks.

'Does that hurt, Kate?' said Gregory, with a little laugh. 'But I have just begun.' He swung the whip three times in rapid succession, crisscrossing her behind with sharp leather kisses. Then there was another snapping sound, and the thongs raked across the sensitive skin on the backs of her thighs.

Kate whimpered. Each stroke built on the pain of the previous one. Her whole rear reddened and stung as the man behind her methodically applied the whip to her arse, her thighs, and her shoulders. She twisted and writhed, trying in vain to avoid the lashes; the bonds held her tight.

Gregory used an uneven rhythm so that she couldn't anticipate the blows. There would be a pause of several breaths, then he would rain four or five quick strokes on her quivering flesh. Kate could no longer feel the individual strands of the whip – all had blended into a hot haze of pain, streaking up and down her body. Tears pricked in her eyes. She wished she could see her tormentor; perhaps that would give her courage.

Even as this thought came to her, he stopped. She felt his palms cupping her buttocks. Even against her inflamed skin, his touch was hot. Now she felt him sliding his fingers into her cunt, probing and massaging.

Kate knew that she was drenched with arousal, that the beating had left her sex more swollen and hungry than before. 'Just testing,' said Gregory with his characteristic mocking tone. 'I want to make sure that you're enjoying yourself.'

Kate was mortified. It was hard enough to admit to herself that the whipping had excited her; for him to know was too much to bear.

'I am not finished yet, my little slave.' He came around to face her. He was flushed and breathing deeply, yet his voice was totally controlled. 'I'm just getting a bit warm.' He stripped off the waistcoat and shirt as she watched with fascination. The sight of his lean, hard body made her weak with lust. She was glad for the ropes that held her upright.

'No, Kate, you're only half-done.' He raised the cat' over his shoulder and brought it down sharply across her right breast. The force of the blow horrified and thrilled her as she watched the muscles move under his skin. The sting of the lash was complicated by the ache in her still-sore nipples. A second stroke landed on her other breast.

Kate watched his face as he slashed the thongs over her belly and, with amazing precision, up and down the insides of her spread thighs. His full lips were pressed together, a hint of a smile behind intense concentration. His blue-diamond eyes darted over her body, measuring, evaluating the effects of each stroke and planning the next. He was a powerful machine, a pagan god, a lurid nightmare in black leather.

She floated now on the waves of pain, sensitised, tender, without thought. He would never stop, it seemed, and she didn't want him to. Vaguely she realised that her cunt was pulsing, expanding and contracting in time with his strokes. In the midst of the pain, she was close to climax.

Gregory paused dramatically, just long enough for her to miss the kiss of the whip. Then, with expert skill, he flicked the leather thongs between her legs. The knots caught her clitoris, distended and protruding between her aching lips. It was enough.

The orgasm broke over her, hot and strange, her raw

skin crackling with electric twinges, her sex, it seemed, turning inside out. The room turned red. Kate hung helpless in her bonds, writhing, twitching, undone.

When she returned to awareness, she found that Gregory was unfastening her wrists from the walls. He massaged her shoulders and upper arms, urging the blood to flow. She let her arms drop to her sides and stood there before him, silent. What could she say? Her body spoke for her.

Gregory stood back a bit, looking her over. 'Once again, Kate, you surpass my expectations. Now, indeed, you look as my slave should look, well-whipped, and well-satisfied.'

'Come here,' he said softly, 'and let me show you.' He led her over to the mirror.

Kate was shocked by the image that greeted her. The same full breasts and full hips, the nipples still erect, but now the white skin was marked with red. Each lash of the leather had left a rosy track on her flesh, that still burned slightly. She could see now that Marshall had planned his strokes for visual effect as well as for the sensation. There was a symmetry, a pattern to the marks, that was both disturbing and pleasing.

It was hard to believe this was her own body, her own flesh. She traced one of the welts on her breast with a hesitant finger. The skin answered with a muted sting. Something was familiar here, she thought. Then she remembered the roses, red veins on creamy white.

Gregory stood behind her, watching her reaction. 'You should see your ass, Kate. Lovely red tracks across your sweet skin. The marks will be gone by tomorrow. But I know that you will not forget the pattern.'

He put his hands on her buttocks, brushing his fingertips over the reddened skin. Kate sighed and leant against him, exulting that he was touching her at last. The heat that came from him made her sweat. His eyes met hers in the mirror as he continued to stroke her nether cheeks.

Then his touch changed. While one hand continued

to caress those twin globes of flesh, the other found its way into the crack between them. Once again, Kate knew mingled shame and pleasure as his long fingers began to probe her rear.

Marshall was less tentative than Somtow had been. Or perhaps her anal passage was a little less tight now, from Somtow's attentions. Gregory pushed one finger deeply into her, then two. Kate couldn't help the moan that escaped her.

'Ah yes, Kate. I thought you'd like that.' He grinned at her in the mirror, a wicked look on his face. 'Bend over,' he ordered. 'Rest your elbows on the dressing table.' Kate could see the nervousness and excitement in her own face as she complied.

Gregory pushed a third finger into her arse. She winced as the circle of muscle was stretched to a new limit. Then suddenly the man behind her removed his hand. Kate flushed, realising that she desperately wanted him to continue.

He stepped to one side of her so she could see him in the mirror. Slowly, he unbuckled his belt and unzipped his trousers. His cock rose from between his leather-clad thighs, longer and thicker even than she remembered.

'No!' she began, understanding his intent. 'I never . . . I can't . . .'

'Oh yes, you can, Kate,' he said. 'Spread your legs.'

He reached between her thighs, plunging his hand into her wet cunt. Pleasure surged through her. Then, as she watched, he ran his hand over his penis, across the glistening knob at the end, lubricating himself with her juices.

He positioned himself behind her again. 'You can, Kate. And you will, for me.' She felt the tip of his cock against the curled knot of muscle, then pressure as he began to push his way into her.

'Let go, Kate. Let go.' He pushed harder. Kate felt panic as sharp pain tore her virgin flesh. She looked at him in the mirror. His eyes were closed. She felt the intensity of his concentration, and his passion. His hands were like steel clamps on her buttocks, holding her open.

She suddenly understood that she would do anything for this man, this master who knew her so well, better than she knew herself. She put her head down between her hands and tried to relax the stubborn muscles keeping him out. Enter me, she thought, take me, use me as you will.

Sensing the change in her flesh or her thoughts, he thrust hard. Agony and ecstasy flooded her as his member stretched her wide and he filled her most private cavity with his hot, hard flesh.

He hung there for a moment, pinning her with his cock. Kate couldn't believe the sensations exploding inside her: all the dirty pleasure of being full, down there, and the desire to let it all out; the tremors in her clitoris, another climax gathering; the pain at the gateway, where her delicate tissues were stretched near to tearing; the sting where his hands clutched her leather-kissed skin.

There was a long moment of stasis; the feelings grew till they were almost unbearable. Then Gregory pulled out, letting her feel the guilty delight of being emptied. Then he thrust in again, deeper, deeper than Kate would have believed possible. In and out, Gregory ploughed her arse. The rougher his thrusts, the more abandoned Kate became. He worked his cock around inside her bumhole, grinding his hips, fierce, raw, finally letting go his own control. Kate clung to the dressing table, moaning, as he reamed her, buggered her, sodomised her like the sluttish slave that she was.

Dimly, Kate heard a low, guttural cry and realised that it came from Marshall. New fire exploded in her. She opened her eyes and saw Gregory in the mirror, his head thrown back, his hair tangled on his sweaty shoulders, his mouth open in animal yell as he pumped himself into her rear passage. She was shocked and amazed at the raw power that flowed from him, usually in check, now set free. He pulled his cock from her arse, leaving her empty, gaping. Moisture trickled from her stretched hole and dribbled down the backs of her thighs.

Kate felt dirty, violated, sore, and blissfully satisfied. Her master helped her stand up, then swept her up in his strong arms and laid her gently on the bed. The cool, quilted silk was soothing against her raw skin.

Gregory looked at her, silent, for a long time. Kate held his gaze bravely, proud that she had endured his trials and come out the other side. Finally, he bent and kissed her tenderly on the lips. There was amazement, even awe, in his voice as he murmured, 'You really do trust me, don't you?'

Kate was too exhausted to answer. In any case, there was no need; Gregory knew her, body and mind, saw her clearly through the masks of respectability and independence. The things he showed her about herself, she was not sure she was ready to see. She had to believe that he would not push her further than she was ready to go – or perhaps a bit beyond.

Chapter Six
Lost in the City

Kate called DigiThai on Friday morning, pleading illness. She was not dissembling. Every muscle ached, and though the red embroidery on her skin had faded, sitting down woke painful memories in her still-tender flesh. Meanwhile, she felt as if she was stretched open and gaping. Her body reminded her continuously how she had been used – a dirty little toy in Marshall's hands, a helpless, willing pawn in his games of humiliation and power.

Away from the cold blue light of his gaze, Kate found herself confused, questioning, ashamed. She had been willing, that was the difficult thing to face, willing and even eager to be beaten, marked, used in the most obscene and degrading manner. She had enjoyed it all. In fact, even in the throes of her guilt and self-disgust, she felt the stirrings of perverse arousal.

She saw again the pattern of the whip's traces on her breasts and felt the muscled leather of Gregory's thighs against her buttocks. Almost unconsciously she lifted her hand to her throat. The slave collar was gone; Gregory had laughingly told her that he would keep it safe for her 'until the next time she wanted it'. But Kate could swear she still felt the warm clasp of leather around her neck. Her cunt throbbed; she wanted desperately to put her hands inside her robe and caress herself. What was happening to her? Who was she becoming? She barely recognised in herself the practical, rational, self-disciplined and self-reliant woman she had been in Boston.

It was Bangkok, this paradoxical city of beauty, decadence and indulgence, where every pleasure of the flesh had its price. It was making her crazy. She had to get away, somewhere sane, away from Marshall and Somtow and all the other fascinating and frightening temptations that Thailand offered.

Just then Ae entered; Kate felt a pang of raw, unnamed emotion at the liquid grace with which the Thai moved through the room. Just another example, Kate thought fiercely. Lovely and corrupt.

The young maid smiled, surprised to see that her mistress was still at home. 'Hello, madame. I did not expect you to be here. Are you unwell?'

Kate made up her mind suddenly. 'No, Ae, I am fine. But I am going away for a few days. I have some business in Singapore.'

In fact, Kate had never been to Singapore, but she knew that it had a reputation for cleanliness, order, and predictability. The Switzerland of Asia, a friend had once called it, half-laughing and half-admiring. She needed to get away, somewhere where she could be alone to sort out her thoughts and feelings. A clean, modern city without traffic jams or pollution, street vendors or go-go bars, seemed ideal. Kate threw a few clothes in a bag and grabbed her passport. Within forty-five minutes she was sitting in the lounge at Don Muang Airport, ticket in hand.

She looked around her nervously, afraid that someone would recognise her. Once, she thought that she caught sight of Chaiwat, Edward Harrison's lascivious chauffeur, but she convinced herself that this was only her imagination. Still, she breathed a sigh of relief when the plane was finally airborne and winging towards Singapore.

As she gazed out at the mountains of cloud piled around the aircraft, Kate resolutely pushed away the images and recollections crowding her thoughts. Later, she promised herself, later she would consider the situation, the implications, and the alternatives. For now, she wanted the peace of an empty mind.

Immigration formalities in Singapore took only a few minutes. There were no long lines or inexplicable delays; the human traffic flowed smoothly and efficiently. Kate found this enormously comforting. Before long, she had checked into a tourist class hotel near one of the major commercial districts and was strolling down a wide boulevard.

Glittering shopping plazas lined the street, for block after block. There were many pedestrians, mostly Chinese, well dressed and polite. They did not make eye contact, respecting her privacy. Kate recalled, in contrast, the good-natured curiosity of the Thais when she walked the Bangkok streets, the calls of the hawkers and the frank stares of the Thai men. She felt an odd mixture of relief and loneliness.

The store windows offered elegant clothing, sparkling jewellery, electronic gadgets, and oriental handicrafts. Kate did not feel like buying anything. She wandered, in a kind of daze, through the crowds, which flowed around her without touching her.

Later, she took the subway to the famed botanical gardens on the outskirts of the city. As she queued at the entrance to the train, waiting for the doors to slide silently open, she noticed that there was no rubbish on the spotless tile floors, no ragged figures stretched out on the benches, no loud radios. A recorded feminine voice warned travellers in three languages to be careful of the gap between the platform and the train and to stay clear of the closing doors.

The gardens were lovely, refreshingly cool and uncrowded. Kate walked aimlessly up and down the paths, under the moss-hung limbs of old, twisted trees. Bright birds flashed like jewels in the green thickets and then were gone.

The scene was peaceful, idyllic, but Kate felt anything but peace. She sat down on a bench and finally allowed the thoughts and memories to flood over her.

The gardens reminded her of the shady grove in Ayuthaya where she and Somtow had coupled under the watchful eye of the guardian Buddha. Kate closed her eyes. She could taste the salty sweat, smell the moist fragrance of her own sex. She felt again the delightful fullness of Somtow's cock inside her, the ache to impale herself more deeply. Her nipples hardened and her clit swelled. Little twinges, echoing the pain from the previous night, rippled down from her breasts to the hot folds between her legs.

The scene changed and now Gregory knelt before her, working her cunt with his slick fingers, calculating just how much arousal she needed to balance the bite of the clamps. He played her like a fish on his hook. She had taken every bait, she realised, fallen into every trap. He had said that she chose to answer his call, but was this really her choice? Who would consciously choose pain and humiliation?

Kate heard voices and opened her eyes. A young couple strolled past her, holding hands and laughing softly together. Just before they rounded the bend and left her sight, the young man leant over and shyly kissed his companion on the lips.

How sweet, thought Kate, with a tinge of bitterness. How innocent and pure!

Then she heard Gregory laughing. She could clearly imagine his reaction, his words: 'Be honest, Kate! Is that what you want, innocence and purity? You would be bored. You would be hungry.'

She knew it was true. Even with David, she had felt something missing. She had craved the dangerous, the forbidden, the extreme. In Somtow she had found a lover who, it seemed, had no shame, who would do anything in the pursuit of sensual pleasure. And with Gregory she had gone further, allowing him to strip away her illusions and disguises, to show her the true darkness of her desires.

Dark. Dark. In fact, the light was fading in the quick tropical dusk. Kate sighed and headed towards the gate. So, it probably is me, at least partially, she thought. Gregory may evoke it, amplify it, twist it to his own ends, but the desire is mine. I love being helpless, giving him control. I love being used in new, shameful, deviant ways. Even the pain I love, because it comes from his hands, because it proves my submission to his will.

I can accept this about myself, she mused, and continue to explore this disturbing and exciting path. Or, I can reject it as unbalanced and unhealthy, and return to a normal sex life. Whatever that means.

Kate was suddenly certain that if she were to tell Gregory that she wished to end their association, he would not try to convince her otherwise. She imagined such a scene and saw regret in his eyes, and respect, but his persuasive powers were held in check. He had seduced her once, but he would not try to do so again.

Then she thought about his fevered hands, his devilish grin, the hard rod of flesh that he used as an instrument of punishment and fulfilment. Could she bear to relinquish these things, even if it was the healthy thing to do?

The clean, uncluttered streets seemed bleak as she walked from the subway kiosk back to her hotel – as bleak as the prospect of turning away from Gregory and her own submissive fantasies.

Alone with her thoughts, Kate enjoyed a fiery Szechuan dinner in the hotel restaurant. David would have appreciated this, she thought, full of longing for his comfortable presence. Recklessly, she ordered a bottle of Bordeaux and drank two-thirds of it with her scallops in garlic sauce. Then she weaved her way up to her room, definitely unsteady on her feet.

The room spun a little as she lay naked and exhausted

on the cool sheets. The room was basic, utilitarian, no plush carpets or silk curtains. Through the open window came the muted sounds of evening traffic. The ceiling fan washed her bare skin with an intermittent breeze, rhythmic and soothing like surf on a distant beach.

So, she thought, here I am, in a strange city, nearly a thousand miles from Bangkok and its temptations. But I can't run away from myself.

She ran her hands over her breasts, across her belly, lightly down her thighs, savouring the smooth curves of her own body. Gregory had said that she was born to be his slave. Some part of her resonated in agreement. Her sex stirred and tingled at the thought. She closed her eyes and listened to the whisper of the fan.

Is there anything that he could ask of me that I would not do? she wondered. As if in answer, images began to play against her closed eyelids. She saw herself bent over a chair, her rump exposed and vulnerable, while Gregory swung a flexible bamboo cane that whistled through the air and left long red welts on her skin. Then she was on her hands and knees and he was fitting a bridle and bit in her mouth; she felt the horsehair tail embedded in her arse, tickling the backs of her thighs, saw the riding crop leaning against the stool in front of her. Now a more subtle picture: kneeling behind Gregory as he held open the cheeks of his own buttocks, commanding that she service his anus with her lips and tongue. A shiver ran through her. Would she, could she do this? Here, by herself, the thought was disgusting and yet fascinating. Kate rolled over and stuck a pillow between her legs, as she used to do when she was a girl. She rocked back and forth, the indirect pressure on her clit building a different kind of arousal.

The pictures continued to unroll in her wine-loosened imagination, becoming more vivid and elaborate. Where was she getting these ideas? She had never thought about such things before. Had Gregory somehow planted these notions in her subconscious? She felt his presence, as if he stood beside the bed watching her.

She was kneeling again, but now it was Noi, the seductive *mamasan*, who stood before her, one booted foot elevated on a stool so that her sex was spread and visible. The Thai woman's pubic area was shaved smooth; Kate could see every detail of her labia, ripe-looking folds of flesh that glistened with moisture, and of her fat clitoris that peeked out between them. 'Eat her,' she heard Gregory say. 'Eat her well or, believe me, she will whip you so hard that you'll think my beatings were mere tickling.'

Kate moaned a little as she ground the pillow harder into her groin. Her nostrils were filled with the rising odours from her own sex. Or perhaps this was Noi's scent? She saw herself lapping at the other woman's cunt, exploring the secret tastes and textures while Gregory watched.

The scene shifted again. She was bound, hanging from an iron hook in the ceiling. Her legs were spread by a rigid bar fastened to her leather anklets. Gregory circled her, inspecting her, then returned carrying a lacquered wooden box. He opened it before her, to display an array of phalluses and dildos made of rubber, leather, even stainless steel. The smallest was longer and thicker than Gregory's own enormous cock.

'Your choice,' he said, his tone mocking and bright. 'What is your pleasure, my dear?' Leaning forward conspiratorially, he added, 'You must choose one for the front, of course, and one for the back . . .' Kate thrashed and writhed on the pillow as she imagined Gregory forcing the huge prongs into her orifices. Suddenly she craved penetration; she needed desperately to be filled. She rolled over on her back and thrust all four fingers into herself. But this still left her unsatisfied.

She opened her eyes and looked around the sparsely furnished room. Little help here, it seemed, and then she noticed the bedposts. The bed had a plain wooden headboard, ornamented with smooth posts topped with a knob, like chessmen. Drunk on wine and her carnal fantasies, she was on her knees in an instant, trying to unscrew one of the posts from the frame.

It seemed at first that the ornament must be glued, or of a single piece with the headboard, but then she felt movement. A few minutes' work and she held the detached post in her hand.

It was heavy, solid mahogany, and nearly a foot long. It tapered slightly near the end then bulged out into a globe about two inches in diameter. Kate ran her hands over its polished length. Her limbs trembled. Surely, she didn't dare . . .

Then she heard Gregory's voice in her mind, through the haze of alcohol and desire. 'You want to do it; you know you do. I want you to do it.'

She lay back on the bed, her knees bent and spread. Remembering Marshall as he prepared to bugger her, she wet the wooden rod all over with juices from her lust-drenched sex. Then she positioned it between her legs and pushed.

For a moment, nothing happened. Kate doubted that she could penetrate herself with something so large and rigid. Then, as she continued to push, she felt the flesh begin to stretch, and the post slid into her well-lubricated channel.

Oh, the feelings! Just as she craved, the makeshift dildo – solid, unyielding, tremendously exciting – filled her. She pushed it in as far as it would go, then rocked and twisted her pelvis, feeling the smooth head moving against her inner flesh. Then she pulled it almost completely out of her, so that just the knob remained within. With her other hand, she played with her clit, rubbing it against the hard ball resting at the entrance. She continued to massage herself as she thrust in and out, harder and faster, fucking herself with her bedpost.

Kate was yelling now, oblivious to the fact that her neighbours might hear, oblivious to everything except the climax building with each wooden stroke. Her eyes closed, she saw Gregory's face, smiling with approval.

'If I were there with you, of course,' she heard him say, 'that bedpost would be in your ass.' Just the words were enough, enough to send an orgasm screaming through her.

As the seizures of pleasure shook her, she dimly realised that she was calling Gregory's name.

Katherine woke late. Sunshine streamed in through the window and across the rumpled bed. It was warm, even with the fan. She felt clear-minded and refreshed, no trace of the alcohol-induced confusion that had fogged her thoughts the night before, and, fortunately, no hangover.

She rolled on to her stomach and arched her back in a delicious stretch. Her hand brushed something hard and slightly sticky. The bedpost! Smiling a little to herself, she took the thing to the bathroom, washed and dried it, and screwed it back into its place, an innocent part of the furnishings. Kate found she was not embarrassed or ashamed by her actions of the previous evening. Strangely, she felt light-hearted, relieved. The weight of self-doubt and guilt that had dogged her was lifted. There had been no conscious decision, no real resolution, but somehow her orgiastic fantasies had cleansed her of the need to resolve or control the situation.

I don't understand this, she thought, and I don't know where it will end. But for now, I'll simply trust my intuitions. And Gregory's.

It was already past seven o'clock in the evening when she arrived back at her house in Bangkok. Ae had left for the day. Kate found a note in the maid's simple block-printed English:

MR MARSHALL CALL 3 TIME. PLEASE CALL
HIM 243 0657

Kate felt a rush of pleasure. Gregory had never telephoned her before. Still, she was annoyed to realise that her heart was pounding and mouth dry with nervousness as she dialled the number and listened to the repeated rings.

She was almost ready to hang up when he answered. 'Hello. Marshall here.'

'Gregory, it's me. Kate.'

'Kate!' She heard warmth in his voice, and relief. 'Where have you been? I was concerned about you.'

'I had to get away, away by myself, and think. The time at the hotel was so – intense. And confusing. I needed to sort things out.'

'I understand,' said the voice on the other end of the line softly. 'I pushed you hard the other night. Maybe a bit too hard. It seems to come so naturally with you that I forget your inexperience.'

'No,' answered Kate, almost whispering. 'It was not too hard. I see a little more clearly now how it is between you and me. I see myself more clearly.'

'Ah, Kate! You have so much to learn! If you still want it of course.'

'I do want it. I want you.' She found herself blushing at her forwardness.

'And I want you, Kate, in ways you probably cannot begin to imagine.' Kate recalled her night of fantasy as he paused. 'Or maybe you can.

'Still,' he continued, 'I think I will give you some time to recover. And next time, perhaps, offer a lesson that is less physical.'

Kate felt a stab of disappointment.

'Don't worry,' he said, laughing, as if he had read her thoughts, 'you won't find it easy.'

'Next Saturday night?' he asked. 'Will you make yourself available?'

'Of course,' Kate answered, thinking that it would be a long week.

'I will send you instructions. I will expect you to obey.'

Kate was silent, wondering what new indignities he would contrive for her.

'Till then, Kate, be well.' His liquid voice was like a caress. 'Good night, my eager little slave.'

She had a busy week ahead of her, busy enough to distract her from thoughts of Gregory Marshall. Monday morning she repeated the projected 3D demonstration for Edward Harrison. He was, if possible, more enthusiastic than Roj had been.

'Marvellous, Katherine, simply astounding!' he raved. 'The illusion of depth, of solidity, is perfect.'

Katherine herself could still see flaws and discontinuities. However, she noted that the problems she had fixed the previous week had produced a discernible improvement.

'This will be a real coup for DigiThai,' he continued. 'I see all sorts of possibilities for new contracts. We will leave our competitors in the dust.'

'I still have a great deal more work to do on this,' she cautioned her boss. 'This is not ready for customer use, by Gregory Marshall or anyone else.'

'Marshall!' snorted Harrison. 'He's small potatoes compared to the people I have in mind. But of course, you are right, we must keep this under wraps for the moment.' He patted her shoulder paternally. 'Keep up the good work, my dear.'

Katherine resented his tone and his familiarity. She drew herself up to her full height and said stiffly, 'Thank you, Edward. I'll do my best.'

Wednesday evening saw a reception sponsored by the Minister of Science and Technology. His Excellency, the Minister, had invited representatives of all the major high-tech companies in Bangkok to eat, drink, network and politick. Harrison insisted on escorting her. Katherine would have preferred Somtow's company, but she had not heard from him since his departure for Hong Kong. She was not even sure that he had returned to Thailand.

It was Katherine's first formal occasion since her arrival. She opted for what she thought was simple elegance: a short cocktail dress of black satin with cap sleeves and a deeply scooped neckline. On her left shoulder she wore the intricate dragon brooch of red gold that David had bought for her last birthday. The jewellery matched her hair, which she had swept off her neck and into a pile of curls at the back of her head. When Harrison arrived to pick her up, she could tell by his expression he was impressed.

As she settled into the back seat with her employer, Chaiwat looked over his shoulder at her and grinned. 'Good evening, Miss O'Neill,' he said. His tone was respectful, but his insolent gaze made her uncomfortable.

Dusk was deepening into night as the Mercedes pulled up at the entrance to the luxurious Imperial Hotel. Harrison opened the door and helped her out of the car. 'You look stunning, Katherine,' he said appreciatively. 'DigiThai is fortunate to be represented by someone with your beauty as well as your intelligence.'

In the US, Katherine realised, such a comment would be viewed as sexist and inappropriate. Here in Thailand, though, the rules were different. She was silent as Harrison took her arm and led her into the ballroom.

The room was full of men and women of many nationalities, all gorgeously attired. Like a flock of tropical birds, thought Katherine, delighted with the scene. There were Indonesians and Malaysians in intricate, earth-toned batiks; Indian women wearing flowing, jewelled saris and men in embroidered tunics and satin turbans; Chinese women in fitted choengsams of red or gold brocade.

The Thais were, perhaps, the most splendid of all. Many of the women wore traditional costumes, sarong-like skirts and tight bodices in rainbow hues, silk embroidered with gold and silver thread or woven into shimmering multicolour patterns. The Thai men, meanwhile, wore spotless white military uniforms decked with brass buttons and bright ribbons or the typical high-collared tunics of striped cotton or silk.

'Can I get you a drink, Katherine?' asked Harrison. He gestured toward the bar near one wall. An elaborate ice sculpture of a swan towered above the heads of the barmen. Tables piled high with hors d'oeuvres were scattered through the room, decorated with fruit carvings and exotic flowers.

'Yes, thank you, Edward. White wine, please.' Katherine watched him wind his way through the crowd. She felt relieved to be out of his company.

'Katherine!' Somtow's familiar voice made her whirl around. 'I did not expect to see you here this evening!'

Her Thai prince stood behind her, his face alight with welcome. He took both her hands in his own and simply stood for a moment, gazing at her with something akin to adoration. Katherine was both embarrassed and pleased.

'I didn't realise that you had returned from Hong Kong, Somtow,' she said.

'Only this afternoon. A difficult but profitable trip. It took me all week, but I managed to negotiate two new contracts with Hong Kong advertising agencies.'

Katherine had assumed Somtow provided only financial backing to DigiThai. Suddenly she saw what an asset he might be, with his connections and his charm, in winning new business.

'Well, welcome home.' She squeezed hands enthusiastically. 'You were missed.'

'As were you,' he replied, with a twinkle in his eye. He lowered his voice slightly. 'When can I see you again, privately? Are you available this Saturday evening? I will be free.'

Gregory's mocking face rose in Katherine's mind. 'No, I'm afraid not. Would Sunday be a possibility?'

He shook his head. 'Regretfully not. I have promised my children that I will take them to the Elephant Festival in Chonburi on Sunday. I really cannot disappoint them.'

'Well . . .' Katherine began. Just then a woman approached them, stunning even in this crowd of the wealthy and beautiful. She took Somtow's arm and smiled at Katherine. 'Hello,' she said graciously.

Katherine was confused. Somtow looked momentarily discomfited, but quickly recovered his poise.

'Katherine, I would like to present Nongseurat, my wife. Nong, this is Katherine O'Neill, from DigiThai.'

The woman extended a graceful hand. 'I am delighted to meet you at last, Katherine. Somtow has told me so much about you.'

Katherine wished that she could drop through the floor. She could not bear to imagine what tales this dignified and elegant creature had heard about her.

Meanwhile, she felt like a drab little mouse next to Nongseurat. Somtow's wife was as lovely as he was handsome. Her gleaming black locks were piled high on her head in an intricate pattern, framing her flawless oval face. Black brows arched over almond eyes that sparkled with intelligence. Full, red lips brought a sensual touch to her otherwise cool and classic features. Her slender, curvaceous body was garbed in a tight, strapless gown of turquoise silk, shot with threads of gold. Around her neck was an exquisitely wrought necklace of sapphires, while matching gems dangled from her earlobes. Katherine glanced down at her plain black frock, felt the tiny red-gold studs in her ears. 'I – um – I'm pleased to meet you,' she said, ignoring Nong's outstretched hand and stumbling over even the simplest pleasantries. 'But I must go now. I hope that you will excuse me.'

She turned and fled, nearly tripping on her high heels as she raced for the door. Even as she ran, she saw in her mind's eye the puzzlement on Nong's face and the hurt and concern on Somtow's.

Katherine searched the hotel corridors until she found a door leading to the garden. She pulled it open and stepped from the air-conditioned interior into the warm, humid night.

The air was heavy and still. The heat of the day had not fled with the darkness. The garden was empty, the hotel patrons preferring the comfort of the salons and ballrooms inside. Katherine removed her shoes and wandered barefoot and aimless along the deserted paths.

Her feet ached. Her heart ached. Tears gathered in her eyes as she remembered the humiliating meeting with the gorgeous Mrs Rajchitraprasong.

Somtow had told her that his wife knew about his extracurricular activities and that Thai custom accepted and approved multiple sexual liaisons. His wit and sincerity, not to mention his consummate skill as a lover, had soothed Katherine's scruples when his wife was an abstraction. But to come face to face with her was too much to bear.

It didn't help that Nong had been so friendly and pleasant, so beautiful and charming. In some ways, this was worse. If Nongseurat had been cold, sarcastic, or accusing, Katherine might have felt some slight justification for her activities with Somtow. To see her act so graciously towards Katherine, and so affectionately towards her husband, made Katherine feel lower than dirt.

Katherine heard the unmistakable sound of falling water. She came into a clearing centred on an elaborate fountain. The sculpture dominating the fountain, she recognised, was a *kinnaree*, a woman-swan from Thai mythology. She remembered the tale, how a man spied on the *kinnaree* while she bathed, stole her feathers and refused to return them until the creature agreed to marry him.

The bronze figure had a bird's feet and tail, a woman's face and breasts. The main jet of the fountain rose from between the woman's hands, held together at chest height in the traditional *wai* gesture. Around the sculpture, six other jets rose and fell, pulsing in a complicated cycle.

Katherine sat down on the edge of the fountain and put her face in her hands. She began to sob, finally releasing the pressure in her chest. She just couldn't bear it, all the beauty and strangeness. She didn't belong here; she wasn't safe here, where she was prey to decadent, polygamous princes and seductive, irresistible sadists.

She sensed a brightening through her closed eyelids. Looking up, she saw the moon was rising, ripe and full. Katherine remembered the night of her arrival, the cold, mysterious moonlight washing the city. Had she really been here a month? How lost she had become in these few weeks!

A fresh storm of tears shook her. Her eyes burned. She knew that her mascara was smeared over her cheeks, that her dress was streaked with dust. Like the little tramp I am, she thought harshly.

'Katherine!' She looked up to see Somtow approaching.

'Leave me alone,' she said, looking down at the runs in her stockings. 'You don't need me. Go back to your beautiful wife.'

'I do need you, Katherine. You do not understand.' He seated himself beside her on the narrow edge of the basin and lifted her gaze to his.

'Nongseurat is beautiful, yes, cultured, refined, loving, a wonderful mother and a jewel of a wife. But she is not like us.' He laid special emphasis on the pronoun. 'To Nong, sex is at best a mildly pleasant activity, at worst a duty. She has no comprehension of the infinite variations, the wild impulses, the rich, tangled web of the erotic, which you and I know so well. Most of my ideas, my desires, I cannot even discuss with her. She would find them distasteful, or worse, silly.'

'Katherine, I have waited so long for someone like you. Someone who combines intelligence and loveliness with a sex drive that matches my own.'

Katherine tore her gaze away. 'I can't do this, Somtow. I can't be the other woman. Here in Thailand that might be considered acceptable or even honourable, but I am not Thai. Every time I touch you, I will be thinking about her.'

'But she wants you to, Katherine! She is delighted that I have found someone who fulfills my needs so completely. She says that I had never been such a loving and considerate husband before meeting you.'

Katherine shook her head, once again feeling that she was wading through quicksand. Were her scruples silly, inappropriate? She remembered Nong's kind smile. Perhaps Somtow was telling the truth.

Somtow leant close. She smelt the faint trace of sandalwood on his skin. He was breathing heavily. 'Katherine,' he murmured, moving to kiss her lips.

'No.' Katherine twisted away, still not sure that she was comfortable with this arrangement. As she moved, Somtow continued to approach her; his looming bulk threw her off balance. There was a blurry moment of confusion, then Katherine found herself tumbling backward into the fountain.

The water was cold, a shock to her skin. Her head went under and she came up sputtering, half-laughing and half-crying at her ludicrous position.

'Katherine, are you all right?'

'Of course,' she said, a little scornful. She looked down at herself. Her dress was probably ruined. Ah well, that seemed symbolically appropriate. She reached under her skirt and pulled off her knickers and stockings, which clung unpleasantly. She looked around, then threw them at the centrepiece of the fountain. They caught on the *kinnaree*'s tail and dangled there. Someone will wonder tomorrow, thought Katherine with just a hint of a smile.

The cool water washed pleasantly against her bare legs. After a moment, she grabbed the hem of her dress and pulled it over her head. She stood naked in the moonlight, framed by the jets of the fountain.

Somtow stood watching her in confusion and amazement.

'Come here,' she said, with a trace of impatience in her voice. 'What are you waiting for?'

The impetuous Thai began to climb into the basin.

'Take your clothes off, first,' she ordered, stifling her laughter. 'No reason why both of us should destroy our Sunday best.'

Somtow stripped off his jewelled tunic and white trousers faster than Katherine would have believed possible. In two breaths he was beside her, taking her in his arms.

'You see, Katherine,' he murmured, nibbling at her earlobe while his hands roamed over her body. 'We are two of a kind.'

Katherine didn't answer. She leant her head back, savouring the silky touch of his skin against hers. Mist from the fountain settled on them, till everything was wet, inside and out. Somtow rubbed his erection against her; she grabbed it, guided it into the hungry space between her legs. Then she clamped him between her thighs, her ankles locked behind his back, and began to ride his cock.

Her strong muscles flexed and strained as she ground herself against him. He supported her, one hand on each buttock, but allowed her to control the pace and intensity. 'Ah, Somtow,' she moaned, realising that she had never known a lover so devoted to her pleasure. His body was familiar now, but no less exciting. It was not merely his lithe frame and hairless flesh, his delicate touch and exotic scent. It was the desire that burned in him, like a lamp, illuminating him from within. She almost felt the light streaming out of her cunt as she moved on his rigid cock, stroking her way ever closer to climax.

The water rushing around them drowned any other sound. Katherine remembered, fleetingly, how exposed they were. Any hotel guest or employee, retreating into the garden, might happen upon their mingled flesh. She did not care.

Somtow was moaning too, as she gradually accelerated her thrusts. He grew larger and, if possible, harder inside her. Yes, thought Katherine, he is right, this is right. How could it not be?

Her partner began to move, in an awkward gait enforced by her legs clamped around his waist. What? she thought. Then she had no time to think any more. A burst of cool liquid flooded her cunt. Somtow had manoeuvred her over to one of the jets, which now spurted directly up into her sex.

She had an instant to admire his inventiveness, then the sensations took her – hot flesh, cold water, the alternating flashes and chills of orgasm singing through her. As the fountain pulsed against her, she felt an answering pulse within as Somtow's cock released its hot shower.

In the fountain, in the moonlight, clenched in her lover's arms, drenched with water and sweat, Katherine felt the world shift. Maybe this was where she belonged, she thought, this was the person she was meant to be. Maybe the Boston Katherine was a mistake, a diversion, a displacement. Perhaps she was not lost at all, but had finally found her real self.

Chapter Seven

Performance

Kate arrived at work early, eager to tackle the technical problems that she knew awaited her. Complex as they were, she knew they would be less of a challenge than the riddles of her personal life.

She checked her email immediately, half-expecting a commanding note from Gregory. She struggled against disappointment when she found only a reminder from Anchana regarding the weekly staff meeting.

Every ring of the phone raised her expectations. But there was no word from her unpredictable master. Well, it is only Thursday, thought Kate. Still, she burned with curiosity, wondering what plans he might be laying.

The staff meeting was routine. Kate found her attention straying to the previous evening. She recalled vividly her humiliation and despair, yet somehow the time with Somtow had washed all the hurt away. He had left her with a promise to call soon. Her cunt dampened and her nipples hardened merely at the thought of seeing him again. Then she wondered what Gregory would think, if he knew of her relationship with the Thai.

It's my business, not his, she thought. After all, who knows what other women he 'entertains' in that devilish hotel room? What would she do, though, if he demanded that she break off with Somtow?

Edward Harrison's voice interrupted her worried reverie. 'Katherine, could I speak with you for a few minutes?' The meeting was breaking up, the employees leaving the room in twos and threes. She heard Wang's boisterous laugh, telling Ruengroj some joke. In a moment she and Harrison were alone.

'Katherine, I'm quite concerned about the security of your work on the 3D project. If there were a leak, what is to prevent someone from hacking your PC and stealing your work right from under our noses?'

'I'm very careful, Edward. I back up my work every night and encrypt the archive. Even if someone broke into our network, found and downloaded the files, they couldn't use them without the password.'

'What if something were to happen to you, Katherine? I mean, what if you became ill? Or, heaven forbid, what if you were involved in an car accident? You know how reckless taxi drivers are! Does anyone else know the password?'

Katherine was irritated, sensing that he didn't trust her care and professionalism. 'If you like, I'll make sure that Malawee knows how to access the files, in case of an emergency. Will that make you more comfortable?'

'Definitely!' The burly man beamed at her. 'Your work is one of DigiThai's most valuable assets. We must protect it at all costs.'

When Kate returned to her desk, her first thought was to check her email. Then she realised something was odd. Her computer screen showed her work as it was when she was called to the meeting: various windows showing code, diagrams, video stills, documents. What should have been showing was her screen saver, a kaleidoscope of geometric patterns that she always triggered when she left her office. The screen saver served the dual functions of extending the life of her computer monitor, and protecting her work from prying eyes. Once started, the patterns could only be dismissed by someone who knew her password.

Could she have forgotten, this one time? She was

preoccupied, true, enmeshed in thoughts of her twisted relationships. But turning on the screen saver was practically a reflex, an automatic act that required no thought.

Was it possible that someone had stolen her password? She knew that there were software packages that surreptitiously recorded keystrokes. Or perhaps someone had simply watched her typing.

Edward's paranoia is rubbing off on me, Kate thought. Of course I forgot. Is it any wonder, with everything that I have on my mind? She sat back down to work, resolving to be more careful in the future.

Thursday and Friday were uneventful. There was no word from Gregory – no email, notes, or phone calls. Kate began to wonder if she had misunderstood him. Or perhaps he had sent her a message via some esoteric medium which she had not recognised. Contrary emotions stormed through her: frustration, longing, relief, annoyance. Damn him, she thought, he's doing it again, playing with my mind. Patience. He was trying to teach her patience, knowing full well what a difficult lesson it was for someone like her.

By Saturday morning, Kate was sure that he had forgotten. Sitting out on her patio, lulled by the birdsong and sound of falling water, she was philosophical. Perhaps it was for the best. A week had passed since the shameful and delicious scene at the Montien, but she was still not sure that she could look him in the eye.

She began to wonder if Somtow was still available that evening. How could she get a message to him without having to speak to his wife?

Kate jumped as the telephone rang inside. She caught it on the second ring, breathing heavily, a little dizzy from standing up so quickly.

'Good morning, Kate.'

It was, of course, Gregory.

'I hope that you have had a relaxing and productive week.'

'Ah – yes.' Kate found herself tongue-tied.

'And you are fully recovered?'

'Yes, I think so.'

'Good. Then I can give you your next assignment.' He spoke so softly she could barely hear his words over the sound of her own heart pounding in her ears.

'Tonight, I want you to perform at The Grotto.'

'Perform?' Kate felt a little thrill of nervousness.

'Yes, I want you to dance, up on the stage with the other girls. I want to watch you, along with all the other horny men, as you flaunt your body and your sex.'

'But –' Objections clamoured in Kate's mind. She would be so obvious, a westerner among the Thais. If anyone from DigiThai heard about it, she would be ruined professionally. What if one of the customers tried to buy her a drink, or take her out of the bar? Underneath all these excuses, though, Kate acknowledged the hum of excitement. She wanted to do this, despite the risks and the embarrassment.

'Noi will arrange an appropriate disguise. No one will recognise you, Kate. You can be the anonymous, outrageous slut you have always dreamt of being.'

Kate was silent. What could she say? Knowledge or intuition, she couldn't tell, but once again Gregory Marshall saw her true desires.

'Be there around seven. I will meet you and introduce you to the girls. Then I'll leave you in Noi's capable hands and just blend into the audience. But you will know I am there, watching.'

Of course she would. Didn't she feel his gaze even now, when he was half a city away?

'I'll be there,' she said simply.

'I will look forward to it,' he replied, laughter lurking in every word. 'Till tonight, my Kate.'

Till tonight. Kate wondered how she was going to live through the daylight hours.

She was early. She wandered through the district for a while, watching the vendors setting up their tables and the girls arriving for work. She had dressed like a tourist, T-shirt, sandals and shorts. No make-up. No one gave her a second glance. That was fine. She was about to become someone else.

By ten to seven she could delay no longer. The neon sign lit up just as she pulled open the heavy door of The Grotto and began to climb the stairs.

The bar was mostly empty. Rock and roll played in the background, but the stage was bare. The video wall was blank. The light was still tinged with red, but much brighter than on her last visit. A pale, balding, heavy-set man nursed a beer in the corner, the only customer.

She stood just inside the entrance, at a loss. The customer looked up from his drink and gave her a bleary-looking smile.

'Welcome, Kate!' She started at Gregory's voice in her ear. He had come up behind her, silent as a cat. 'Welcome to my world.' His hands were on her shoulders, and then, naturally, on her breasts, gauging the stiffness of her nipples. The customer watched, his beer halfway to his mouth. Marshall turned Kate around to face him, then bent to kiss her fiercely.

Kate's whole self leapt up in response – body, mind, soul. Heart. Yes. She drank his kiss as if it were the most potent of wines, wrapping her arms around his neck. After a moment, he broke the embrace. 'My, my, you are feeling passionate tonight! All the better. The customers will definitely appreciate that.'

He pulled himself to his full height and smiled down at her, only half mocking. 'Come along, now. You must get ready.'

He led her through a curtained doorway, down a dim hall, to another door. Surprisingly, he knocked.

'It's me,' he called out. 'The boss.'

Noi opened the door. 'Ah, hello, boss.' Kate heard the hint of ridicule in Noi's voice, and wondered at it. 'Hello, Kate,' the Thai woman added, taking in her deliberately casual outfit. 'Come in. Come in.'

Kate entered the room, with Marshall close behind. It

was crowded with beautiful young Thai women, in various stages of undress, chattering and laughing as they readied themselves for the night.

'Hello, boss Ji!' they called when they realised he had entered.

'Hello, girls,' he answered, with surprising gentleness. 'This is Kate. A friend of mine. She will be joining you tonight.'

A chorus of greeting answered him. Kate recognised several faces, including the lovely *katoey* she had met on her previous visit.

'Hello, madame,' Lek took both her hands and squeezed them affectionately. 'Hello. It is so good to see you again!'

'It is good to see you too, Lek. How are you?'

'Oh, very well, madame.'

Gregory turned to Noi. 'Help Kate get ready. I promised her that no one would recognise her tonight.

'Kate, put yourself in Noi's hands. She is an expert.' He bent down to whisper in her ear. 'Remember, I will be watching.' She felt a hard pinch on her bottom. 'Break a leg,' he said in a jocular tone, and then was gone.

Noi took Kate by the hand. 'Sit here,' she ordered, 'and take off your shirt.' Kate stripped off the T-shirt. She was bare-breasted beneath, but the women around her didn't give her a second glance. She sat at the dressing table that Noi indicated, looking at herself in the mirror.

She was flushed. Her green eyes seemed darker than usual and sparkled with suppressed excitement. The few freckles on her pert nose seemed especially prominent. She looked pretty, alert, and very Irish.

Meanwhile, her nipples were red and rigid, perched high on her full breasts. Touch me, they almost screamed, pinch me, suck me.

As if reading her thoughts, Noi caught Kate's left nipple between her thumb and forefinger, and gave a little twist. Kate gasped. 'You will be very popular,' observed the *mamasan* dryly. Kate couldn't keep from blushing.

Noi began to apply make-up. Kate watched, fascinated, as her ruddy skin became pale, her freckles disappeared, her eyebrows darkened and arched, her eyes became shallow and almond-shaped. In a short time, she was looking at an Asian beauty – perhaps half-Thai, half-American – with moist, full lips and curly red hair.

'My hair . . .' protested Kate. Noi reached behind her and produced a wig of straight, black locks. She gathered Kate's own ringlets into a tight ponytail, then fitted the wig.

The transformation was complete. A black fringe cut straight across her forehead; black tresses decorated her shoulders. She looked nineteen instead of twenty-eight. And most assuredly Thai.

The other girls gathered around. 'Oh, madame, you look so beautiful.' Kate couldn't help but smile, surrounded as she was by gorgeous female faces and forms.

'Here is your costume,' said Noi. 'Gregory selected it especially for you.'

Kate grew a little paler. Was she really expected to wear this, in public? She looked at Noi in silent entreaty, but the *mamasan* just grinned. 'Get dressed,' she said. 'The dancing will start in just a few minutes.'

A corset of black vinyl, laced up the front, which cinched her waist and left her breasts bare. The briefest of G-strings, a tiny vinyl triangle that barely hid her bush plus a thong that settled deep in the crevice between her buttocks. Thigh-high vinyl boots with four-inch heels. And, finally, the leather collar she had last worn while Gregory's cock ploughed her rear hole.

Fully attired, Kate checked herself in the mirror once more. A stranger stared back, a sultry Asian temptress. The body was more voluptuous than that of a typical Thai, full breasts and thighs that belied the woman's youthful face. Her red-painted lips were half-open, luscious and inviting. Her skin shone already with light sheen of sweat. Kate raised her arms above her head and swivelled her hips as she had seen the other dancers do. The figure in the mirror moved gracefully, languidly, every motion beckoning the viewer to watch, touch, taste, possess her.

'Here is your number, Kate.' Noi handed her a plastic chip with a pin on the back. Kate had noticed all the girls wearing them; apparently they served as a simple accounting mechanism, for tallying the tips the girls received whenever a customer bought them a drink. Kate smiled wryly, noting that Gregory had assigned her the number 69.

'The dancers for each set are written up here.' The *mamasan* pointed to a small blackboard with columns of numbers. 'Five or six girls dance at once, rotating positions with each song.' Noi casually put her arm around Kate's shoulders. 'As you can see, you are in the first set. We don't want you to stand around getting nervous!'

Many of the bar girls had already left the dressing room. Kate hesitated, taking one last look at herself. 'Come on, let's go!' said Noi, giving her a sharp little slap on the buttock. 'Get out there now!'

Teetering slightly on the spike heels, Kate traversed the corridor and pushed the curtain aside. The bar was transformed. The lights glowed dimly red; the video wall flashed and pulsed with bright images. Customers filled the tables that lined the room. Four dancers were already on the stage, moving with the music that pounded through the air. Kate saw, with some slight relief, that one of them was Lek.

She took a deep breath and began to mount the stairs to the platform. Her legs felt like rubber. Lek looked over at her and smiled kindly. Kate took hold of one of the poles that stretched from the stage to the ceiling and began to dance.

Hard rock surged around her. She could feel the beat through the floor, insistent, propelling her into move-

126

ment. The Rolling Stones, she thought. 'Under My Thumb.' How appropriate. She shook her hips in time, jerking her pelvis in lewd, explicit simulation of the sexual act. A roving spotlight picked her out; she felt the heat on her bare breasts. She gave a defiant little shimmy with her shoulders, setting her lush flesh vibrating.

A memory flashed through her: her breasts shivering with the force of Gregory's whip-strokes. She could almost feel the sting. The spotlight moved on.

Kate looked over the audience – exclusively men: fit young sailors, long-haired hippies, businessmen in their suits and ties, rowdy-looking trucker types. Some were engaged in conversation or flirtation with bar girls crowded around them or sitting on their laps. Quite a few, however, had their eyes glued to the stage, drinking in the sight of near-naked bodies only a few feet away.

There was no sign of Gregory. Kate could feel his presence, though. She sank down on her haunches, still grinding her hips provocatively, and cupped her hands under her breasts, as if offering them to the crowd. She saw a viewer, a middle-aged, harried-looking man, lick his lips.

The thong of her G-string stretched taut across her anus, teasing that sensitive area. The vinyl was hot and tight against her clit. Kate brought her hands down to her thighs, then moved her palms slowly from the knees towards her groin, swivelling her hips with the music all the while. Now her fingers lay lightly against the skin of her inner thighs while her thumbs pressed against the little black triangle between her legs. Lust flooded her. The string between her cheeks became slick as it slid back and forth in her dampening crack.

She was so tempted to push her thumbs under the minimal garment, to dig into her curls towards the centre of her pleasure. The man watched her avidly, leaning forward in his seat. His hands moved from his beer bottle out of sight under the table.

Kate smiled directly at him. She rose gracefully from her squatting position, then pivoted so that her back was to him, still looking over her shoulder. Then she bent over, running her hands down the back of her thighs until she grasped her ankles. She swayed back and forth seductively in this indecent position, presenting her bare arse for his inspection. Hair hung all around her face; looking between her legs, she could see her fan, his mouth half-open, panting.

She trailed her hands back up her legs, touching herself ever so lightly. Then she hooked her thumbs under the elastic encircling her hips. She began to move it down across her buttocks, in tiny increments, as if she were about to remove it. The man's gaze was glued on her slowly moving thumbs, hoping, praying, that she would continue.

The song ended. Kate sighed and pulled the G-string back up around her hips. The dancers shifted positions on the platform; now Kate was nearer the front. She was breathing heavily, from excitement as much as exertion. Her admirer was now only a few feet away. Kate caught his eye and held it as the next song began, a slow, moody ballad with a haunting melody.

The music took her, loosened her, flowed through her limbs. She raised her arms above her head, crossed them at the wrists as if she were bound, and moved in voluptuous waves, sinuous undulations that began in her sex and travelled up her spine. Eyes closed, she savoured the knowledge that the other eyes were ranging hungrily over her body.

Gregory was watching. She could feel the heat, imagine the wild light in those blue eyes. Now she danced only for him, breathless and desperate. Do you like what you see? she thought. Take me. Can't you see that I'm yours? Let me please you. I know that I can.

Too soon, the song ended, and the set. As she left the stage, Kate remembered her admirer. She gave him one last smile, wanting him to remember the vinyl-clad Thai vixen who had played with him.

Gregory was waiting on the other side of the curtain. 'Well, well,' he said, grabbing her wrists and pinning them behind her back. 'You are a naughty little girl, aren't you?' He leant over, catching her right nipple between his teeth. He was not gentle. As pain and heat spread from his mouth, Kate was determined not to cry out.

'Did you enjoy that?' he asked after a moment. Kate wasn't sure whether he meant the dancing or the bite. 'Of course you did.' He released her wrists and cupped her buttocks. His thumb slid under the thong and brushed over her tight rear hole. Unable to control her reaction, she writhed under his touch. 'I am afraid, Kate,' he said, still continuing his lewd caress, 'that this performance was too easy for you, too natural. I think I should set you a more challenging task.'

'It's almost time for the live sex show.' He smiled down at her. 'I'm sure that you remember watching this the last time you visited here.' Kate was swept with sudden panic. 'Tonight, I would like you to participate.'

Kate's heart pounded in her chest. Indeed she remembered, the tall, lithe young man with the enormous cock. Would Gregory enjoy seeing her impaled that way, by someone else?

'Unfortunately, tonight is Uthai's night off,' he commented, once again seeming to read her mind. 'But I feel confident that we can find a substitute.'

'Come, now,' he said brusquely, pulling her after him into the dressing room. 'Off with those fancy duds. No more hiding your glory.'

He began to unlace the corset, oblivious to the handful of girls in the room who watched curiously. Kate blushed, embarrassed that they should see her so pliant in their boss's hands. At the same time, every time his skin brushed hers, she felt that familiar surge of lust. Now he was pulling the G-string down around her ankles. 'Step out, and take off those boots. Leave the collar on, though. To remind you.'

Kate was naked now, save for the leather circlet

around her neck. In fact, her costume hadn't concealed much of what was now revealed, but she felt a thousand times more exposed.

Gregory handed her a silk kimono. 'Put this on, and wait behind the curtains until you hear the music. After that – you will know what to do.'

'I know that you won't disappoint me, Kate,' he added, and then he was gone again.

Standing in the dim hallway, Kate fought the urge to run. She fantasised about sex in public places, she acknowledged; she had enjoyed the risk of discovery in her recent, outrageous experiences with Somtow. This was different. How could she fuck a stranger, surrounded by strangers who were watching purely for their own entertainment? Being discovered in the midst of passion was one thing; deliberately exposing the most private of acts to public view was something else altogether.

She had no choice, she told herself. Gregory had required this of her, and she was bound to obey him. She knew she was lying to herself, though. Mixed with her trepidation was a secret, shameful excitement.

The first wails of the saxophone reached her from beyond the curtain. She recognised the tune. Kate pulled the kimono tight around her, swallowed hard, and stepped into the spotlight. In the bright light, Kate could see nothing. She moved towards the stage, feeling light-headed. It seemed as if she floated up the stairs.

Her partner awaited her.

It was the sweet little vamp who had been Uthai's companion in the previous performance. A woman! Gregory was diabolical.

The Thai woman caught her eye. Kate saw kindness in her face, and amusement. Slowly, she began to untie her robe; Kate did the same. The silken fabric slid from their bodies at the same moment. A low murmur rippled through the audience.

The woman held out her hands to Kate, beckoning, inviting. Kate glided across the stage, the music reaching her despite her fear. They clasped hands, standing face to face. We could be sisters, thought Kate. They were exactly matched in height; like her, the young woman was more generously endowed than was typical for a Thai

Still holding Kate's hands, her partner's arms encircled her; the Thai kissed her, open-mouthed. Kate felt a shock at the woman's soft lips and probing tongue. For a moment, she struggled against the invasion. However, her arms were pinned at the small of her back; though seemingly gentle, her partner was remarkably strong.

Perhaps Gregory has instructed her, thought Kate, as she surrendered to the strange and delicious sensations of the woman's kiss. There was a faint taste of peppermint. The woman drew back and smiled at her.

'Please,' Kate whispered, 'you'll have to help me, tell me what to do. This is all new for me.'

'*Mai khaojai,*' the Thai returned in a whisper. '*Pood pasa Angkrit mai dai kha.*'

Kate knew little Thai, but she understood the gist. Her lovely companion spoke no English. They could communicate only with their bodies.

The woman's hands were on Kate's breasts now, stroking and fondling. Her touch was unlike anything Kate had known, delicate yet focused, savouring both the smooth skin and the swelling flesh beneath. Kate's hands hung at her sides, awkward. Her partner's nipples, pert and upturned, seemed to wink at her. Come, don't be shy, they seemed to say, we long for your touch. Hesitant, Kate cupped the twin mounds in her palms, felt the silkiness under her fingers. It was so strange, like caressing herself, but with an extra spark. After a moment, she brushed her thumbs ever so lightly across the woman's nipples. Electricity ran up Kate's spine as the Thai stiffened and then relaxed, throwing her head back and thrusting her breasts forward.

The music changed, moved into a bridge, and the Thai woman regained control. She half-danced with Kate over to one of the poles, so that Kate was leaning back against it. Then she sank to one knee in front of her and used both hands to part the hair hiding Kate's sex.

Panic rose again in Kate's throat. With the spotlight in her eyes, she couldn't see the audience, but she heard their hot breathing. This passionate dance was too private for their gaze. Yes, she wanted this woman, but she would not, could not, allow herself to be so taken under their crude inspection.

Then thought was erased by sensation as her partner's tongue swept through her sex in one long, hard stroke that ended with a flick to her clit.

'Aah . . .' The Thai woman's tongue danced within her, a thousand places, a thousand pleasures. It thrust into her cunt, thickening and lengthening until Kate could almost believe it was a cock. Then it tickled and teased her lower lips so that she craved deeper penetration. The Thai woman put her mouth around Kate's clit and began to suck on it, pulling, nibbling, rasping her tongue up and down over that supremely sensitive flesh.

Kate raised one knee and pressed her bare foot against the steel pole, turning her thigh outward to give her partner better access. The girl responded by burying her face in Kate's cunt – lips, teeth and tongue all working to bring Kate to a frenzy.

The moist smell of sex rose around them; suddenly, Kate wanted the taste as well. She rested her hands on her partner's shoulders. Exquisitely responsive, the woman rose. Kate kissed her deeply, savouring the salty ocean taste of her own juices. Then, she knelt before the woman, closed her eyes, and tentatively poked her tongue into the fragrant folds between those shapely legs.

Dark, wet, secret, powerful; moss-hung caves and hidden rituals. The woman's scent and taste brought misty, half-formed images to Kate's mind. She tried to concentrate, noting the different textures: silky hair, slick flesh, taut muscle. Dimly she heard the music, and she let her tongue dance in time. Even in lust, she had half-worried about her inexperience, feared she could not satisfy a woman. But hands, lips, tongue, all seemed to know how to make this sweet girl writhe and moan.

The song was swelling to its climax; Kate licked harder and faster. Then, without warning, she was on her back, neatly flipped. The Thai woman straddled her face, still eager to be eaten, and Kate was happy to oblige. Meanwhile, her partner spread Kate's thighs and rolled Kate's aching clitoris between her lips. At the same time, she sank two, three, four fingers into Kate's hungry cunt. Kate responded, grabbing the woman's buttocks and then, hardly believing her audacity, stroking a finger across the knot of muscle between them. Upping the ante, the Thai pushed one long, slender finger into Kate's anus. Bucking and groaning, Kate did the same.

The song had ended. The only sounds now were moans and sighs as the two women ground their sexes into each other's faces and fucked each other's arseholes. The men watching were absolutely silent, hardly believing what they could see so clearly in the spotlight. Kate and her nameless partner were oblivious, climbing higher and higher towards final ecstasy.

In the split second before climax, Kate remembered: their hungry eyes, their sweaty flesh, their dreams and their judgements. Slut. Lesbo. Freak. It didn't matter. Nothing mattered. Screaming, she and her partner toppled over the edge together.

It was applause that brought Kate back to her senses: clapping, yelling, lewd whistling. The Thai woman rolled gracefully off Kate's face, rose to a standing position, and offered Kate a hand. This raised a new round of hoots and catcalls. Burning with shame, Kate pulled herself up beside her. They bowed together, holding hands. Kate looked sideways at her lovely partner for this carnal ballet. She smiled back, almost innocent. '*Khorp khun kha*,' she whispered. Thank you.

'*Khorp khun kha*,' Kate responded, shy and a little proud despite her shame.

A few minutes later Kate sat shaking on an empty bench at the back of the bar. She couldn't believe what she had done.

Her arms were crossed over her breasts. Through the thin robe, she could still feel her erect nipples. Her thighs were damp; on her lips she tasted the salt and musk of the Thai girl's cunt.

A new bevy of dancers gyrated on the stage. The audience seemed to have forgotten the recent spectacle. Where was Gregory? Kate scanned the faces in the rosy dimness.

She froze and shrank back into the shadows. There, directly across the room, she recognised the face of Edward Harrison. He seemed a bit tipsy. His gestures were expansive and exaggerated as he addressed himself to the two other men at his table.

They looked familiar also, thought Kate. How did she know them? One was clearly Arabic, thick dark hair and a bushy moustache beneath a noble but prominent nose. The other was short and nondescript with a fringe of sandy hair bordering a shiny bald spot and horn-rimmed glasses. Neither was particularly remarkable, but Kate knew that she had seen them before.

Then it hit her; both these men had been guests at the Ministry of Technology reception earlier in the week. This suggested, she thought, that they might be competitors to DigiThai. She was suddenly very curious to know the topic of conversation.

Just then Lek approached her. 'Madame,' she asked, concern in her voice, 'are you OK?'

'Yes, I'm fine, Lek. Just a bit tired.' The *katoey* didn't appear to have been the least embarrassed or disturbed by the sight of her ravishing another woman.

'Lek, would you do me a favour?'

'With pleasure, madame.'

'Do you see those three men over there? The heavy American, the Arab and the short, bald guy?'

Lek nodded.

'I would like you to go over there and be friendly to them. Flirt, get them to buy you a drink. And listen to what they are saying. I need to know what they're talking about.'

'Of course, madame,' Lek smiled delightedly. 'That will be easy.'

Kate watched the willowy creature move gracefully through the crowded bar, over to Harrison's table. She grinned to herself as she saw the enthusiasm with which the threesome welcomed the lovely transvestite. In just a few moments Lek was seated on Harrison's knee, while the Arabic man fondled her breasts through her semi-transparent blouse. Harrison was still talking non-stop, even as Lek rubbed her cheek against his chest.

Kate watched the silent tableau in grim amusement. Harrison tried to place his hand between Lek's legs, but she deflected this gesture with ease, burying her hand in his crotch instead. Finally, she rose and gathered their glasses, apparently going off to get them another round of drinks. Instead, she detoured over to Kate's corner.

'Did you hear what they were talking about?' Kate asked.

'Yes,' said Lek. 'But I did not understand it.'

'Tell me!'

'Well, they were talking about business. Lots of money – millions of baht. And then the American promised to bring them 'the three dee code'. What is that? Are these men secret agents, like James Bond? I did not understand.'

Kate frowned. 'Something like that, Lek. It sounds like something secret, and illegal, to me. Did they say anything else?'

'The man with little hair asked when the American could "deliver the goods". The American said, next Wednesday or Thursday. He said that he knew the magic word – at least I think that is what he said – and that he would call them as soon as he had used it.'

Lek shrugged. 'It really did not make much sense to me. Do you understand it, madame?'

Kate's lips pressed firmly together. 'I'm afraid that I do. Dirty work, Lek. Theft and deceit.' The gist was clear. Harrison was double-dealing. He was about to sell out DigiThai, handing over her work and who knows what other intellectual assets to competitors in return for a personal fortune. She must get to Somtow as soon as possible, to let him know his partner was planning to cheat him.

'Thank you, Lek! You have been tremendously helpful. Wait here a minute.' Kate rose and moved towards the curtained doorway, planning to get her purse from the dressing room. Lek deserved a generous tip for her assistance.

As Kate crossed into the light, though, Harrison noticed her. He stood up and waved, beckoning her to join them. Kate was terrified. He knows who I am, she thought. Then she realised the truth; he recognised her, but only as the abandoned Thai wench who had recently given him such a show. Her cheeks flamed.

She pretended to ignore him. He stood up, wavering a little, and pushed through the crowd, making his way towards her. Damn, thought Kate. She ducked behind the curtain, barged into the dressing room without knocking and grabbed her purse and sandals. As she emerged back into the hall, she heard his gruff voice on the other side of the curtains.

'Hey, you sexy little thing! Don't run away! You're beautiful. I won't hurt you. I just want to talk to you!'

Kate fled down the hall, praying there would be an exit. Rounding a corner, she came upon a door, propped half-open with a cinder block. She slipped through and found herself in an alley. The flickering of multicoloured neon reached down the alley from the street at the end. Music filtered from the surrounding bars, a dozen different beats. Kate paused only long enough to put on her shoes then headed towards the lights. There would be taxis cruising along Suriwong Road. She was fairly sure she had Somtow's card in her wallet.

All of a sudden, Kate froze. There was a car parked near the entrance to the alley, a white Mercedes that she recognised. She could clearly see Chaiwat in the driver's seat. He was smoking a cigarette, his elbow resting on the open window. She could not possibly exit the lane without him seeing her. Meanwhile, the other end of the alley dead-ended in a concrete wall.

Kate debated with herself. Did she trust her disguise enough to walk right past Chaiwat?

Her deliberations were interrupted by the sound of voices. Harrison and his companions! They had obviously found the same door she had used as an escape route. Desperate, Kate sank into the shadows beside a rubbish bin and tried not to breath.

'The little minx has given us the slip!' laughed her boss. 'Too bad. She was quite a little piece, don't you agree?' They were coming towards her.

The other men murmured their assent. The trio was now directly across from Kate's hiding place.

'Actually, she reminded me a bit of this American tart I hired last month. The idea was that she would distract Somtow, keep him busy, so he wouldn't notice that we were ripping him off.'

'Did your plan work?' asked the bald man.

'Like a charm! Somtow is totally obsessed with her. He hasn't been in the office or looked over the books in weeks!'

Kate realised that they were discussing her. Anger and humiliation fought within her. How dare he use her as bait! The arrogant fool! Here she was working her tail off to provide DigiThai with a technological break-through, and he viewed her as nothing more than an unwitting whore!

'Not only has she thoroughly seduced Somtow, she turned out to be smart as well. The projected 3D software is mostly her work.'

Mostly! thought Kate indignantly.

'But she wasn't smart enough to figure out my plans.' Harrison chuckled unpleasantly. 'By the time she does, I'll be on a plane to South America.'

Oh, yes? thought Kate. We'll see who is smarter, Mr Edward Harrison!

Her boss and his guests climbed into the Mercedes. Chaiwat started the engine and pulled slowly out of the alley. Kate released the breath she had been holding. She was fuming. Wait until Somtow heard about this.

She raced into the street and hailed the first cab that passed. Handing the driver Somtow's card, she remembered that she was still wearing the wig and make-up. How would she explain this to Somtow?

Never mind, thought Kate. I'll cross that bridge when I come to it.

Chapter Eight

Quartet

*T*he half moon, just rising over the roof of Somtow's house, provided some light. The building itself was dark. Kate hesitated before the door, acutely aware of her nakedness under the brief robe. Never mind, she thought, and resolutely rang the bell.

She expected to see Orapin's dignified figure answering the summons. However, there was no response at all, even after several attempts. Tentatively, Kate tried the knob. The heavy slab of teak swung open.

Peculiar, thought Kate, and slipped into the dim entryway, carefully shutting the door behind her.

Leaving her sandals with the other footwear clustered near the entrance, she started down the corridor. 'Somtow?' she called. Her voice sounded weak and uncertain. 'Are you here?'

The hallway was lit as before by sconces on the walls. There were shadows everywhere. Katherine moved cautiously. Her heart beat loudly in her ears.

The doors lining the corridor were all shut. The rooms behind them were dark. Then Kate noticed, near the end of the hall, one that was slightly ajar and showed a flicker of light through the frosted glass. 'Somtow?' she called again, barely louder than a whisper.

She paused on the threshold. Muffled sounds reached

her from the other side of the door – human voices, but no words. She took a deep breath and pulled open the door as silently as she could.

Then she grabbed the doorknob to steady herself. Surprise, shock, embarrassment and arousal swept over her in swift succession as she grasped the nature of the scene before her.

Oriental carpets two or three deep covered the floor, strewn with pillows and bolsters. A warm, golden light spilt from two candelabras on either side of a low sofa. Just in front of the sofa, half-turned so she saw only his profile, stood Somtow, completely naked. His pale skin glowed as the candle flames flickered and danced.

Kneeling before Somtow, sucking eagerly on his cock, was a naked woman. It took a moment for Kate to recognise her. Her black hair was tangled all around her face. Her long fingernails bit into Somtow's thighs as she pulled him towards her, devouring his rigid flesh. It was only when the woman released him for a moment to lick his balls that Kate realised that this horny lady was the composed and stately Orapin.

But that was the least of surprises. There was a third participant in this erotic tableau. Behind Somtow, his hands gripping Somtow's shoulders, his shaved head tilted back and his eyes closed, was Uthai. His night off, thought Kate with an inner grin, and he clearly is getting off.

As in The Grotto, Kate could see every detail of this performance. The younger Thai's hefty penis was buried deep in Somtow's arse. Kate's sex twitched and ached as she watched the thick shaft slide in and out of Somtow's well-stretched rear hole. Somtow moaned, and pushed his hips back, mutely requesting deeper penetration. Uthai was eager to oblige. Kate could see the muscles in his buttocks tense with the force of each thrust as he tried to stuff the whole amazing length of his cock into Somtow's back passage.

She should have known, thought Kate. A hedonist like Somtow would not limit himself just to women.

Her pulse raced as she remembered her own activities earlier in the evening. Who was she to comment? She had never allowed herself to feel attracted to women, but now, she saw, Orapin was as desirable as Somtow.

The tempo quickened. Uthai grabbed Somtow's hips and rammed in his cock, all the way to the root. Somtow cried out and held on to Orapin's shoulders for balance. Orapin grasped Somtow's hard rod with both hands, milking him to orgasm.

A hoarse growl gathered in Uthai's throat, mingling with Somtow's yells. His whole body jerked in long spasms as he spent inside Somtow. Orapin opened her mouth to catch the jets of Somtow's come. As Uthai collapsed exhausted against Somtow's back, Orapin tenderly licked every drop from her master's cock and balls.

All was quiet. Kate realised she was panting, and then that she was squatting on the threshold, her thighs spread and her hand buried in her crotch. She stood up hastily. Somtow looked up at the sound, his eyes slightly unfocused.

'What . . . Who are you?' he began, and then stopped in amazement. Kate pulled off her wig.

'Katherine?' Somtow said uncertainly.

'Good evening, Somtow,' she said, trying to sound nonchalant and unaffected by the orgiastic scene she had just witnessed. She couldn't tell him about Harrison, of course, until they were alone. 'My previous engagement for the evening ended unexpectedly early.' She glanced at his companions, Orapin still on her knees, Uthai sitting on the sofa. 'But I see you have other business tonight.'

Somtow took her by the hand and led her to the sofa. 'Nothing that could ever exclude you,' he said, kissing her delicately. He nodded to Orapin and then to Uthai. They rose silently and left through a door at the back of the room.

'Forgive me, Katherine, but when you told me that

you were not available, I thought I would console myself in some less precious but still pleasant flesh.'

'So I see.' Kate smiled. She took both his hands in hers. 'I don't know what amazes me more about you, Somtow: your exquisite politeness and consideration, or your insatiable and diverse appetites.'

'Well, I could say the same about you, Katherine.' He leant back, surveying her Asian make-up and half-open kimono. 'I do wonder about the nature of your previous engagement.'

'I'll tell you sometime, I promise.'

'Now that you are here, though, can I offer you some wine?' Kate nodded and he began to fill a glass. 'And some hospitality?' His eyes twinkled. 'Uthai is a very talented young man.'

'So I see,' Kate replied.

'I am sure that he would be happy to pleasure you.' Somtow's fingers began a lazy trip up the inside of her thigh. 'Front or rear, whichever you prefer.' His fingertips rested on her clit, teasing. He could obviously feel the dampness of her curls.

Kate felt the heat rising in her sex. She sipped her wine and gazed into Somtow's lively face.

'You would enjoy that, wouldn't you?' she said. 'Watching him fuck me?'

'Watching him give you pleasure,' he said softly. 'Oh yes, I would enjoy that very much.'

Kate felt crazy and reckless. Why not? The graceful, muscular Uthai definitely turned her on. She had craved his cock ever since she first saw him in The Grotto. Why not give in to that craving?

'Well, then,' she said, so low that he could hardly hear her. 'Let's do it.'

Somtow beamed and kissed her again. She didn't see him give any signal, but almost immediately Uthai reentered, obviously fresh from the shower. Orapin followed close behind.

'Uthai,' said Somtow formally, 'this is Katherine, a dear friend of mine.'

Uthai smiled shyly and bowed.

'Katherine, may I present Uthai.'

'My pleasure,' said Kate gently, trying to put the young man at ease.

'Uthai, Katherine would like –' Then, incongruously, Somtow leant over and whispered something in Uthai's ear. He nodded his close-shaven head as Somtow continued to whisper.

Somtow turned to Kate. 'Front or rear?' he asked.

Kate blushed furiously. 'Front, I think,' she said. Her rear hole still felt ghost sensations from her Sapphic partner's fingers. The thought of new probing there made her heart pound. Somehow though, she believed that orifice belonged to Gregory and his minions. Patience and discipline, she thought. I'll save my darkest and dirtiest self for him.

Somtow settled back comfortably on the couch. Orapin knelt next to him. They turned their eyes towards Uthai and Kate.

Uthai approached her, gliding across the floor until they stood face to face. His cock was engorged and ready. Kate vividly recalled the opening moves of his Grotto performance. She shrugged off the silk robe and held out her arms. He put his hands on her waist and lifted her as if she were light as a feather above his head. Her crotch was just even with his face.

Kate understood immediately. She spread her thighs and lifted her hips until she could rest her bare feet on his shoulders. Then she relaxed into his grasp, as he began licking her cunt and nibbling on her clit.

The effects were electric. Hot sparks moved from her sex-flesh up her spine. His tongue probed and tickled, building the tension, stoking the fires. Meanwhile, Kate savoured the sensation of being suspended in mid-air, maintained by his astounding strength. She was flying.

The more he worked on her with his mouth, the more she craved his cock. Still, she let him set the pace. He was the expert, after all. Just when she thought she could wait no longer, he lowered her slowly and settled her wet cunt on to his near-vertical erection.

He slid in easily, and yet he felt huge, the size of a Coke bottle – no, a wine bottle. The image made her burn. Her flesh was stretched taut, like the strings of some celestial instrument. His slightest movement set up exquisite vibrations.

Kate wrapped her legs tightly around him, but Uthai gently loosened her grip, signalling her to relax. He supported her, one hand under each thigh, and moved her up and down his pole. On the down stroke, he let her weight drive him deep into her until all ten inches of his cock filled her sex.

Uthai had complete control of her body. Kate didn't even need to hold on. She cupped and caressed her breasts, pinched and pulled on her nipples. Her cunt muscles contracted deliciously.

Kate ventured a glance at Uthai's face. He was serious, attentive, focused. She smiled at him as she reached between her legs and grasped the slick rod of tumescent flesh where it entered her. She could hardly get her fingers around it.

She squeezed as hard as she could. Uthai moaned and then broke into a shy grin. He doubled the speed of his thrusts, plunging in and out of her like the piston of some powerful engine.

Kate closed her eyes, concentrating on the volcano of pleasure erupting inside her. Rivers of sensation coursed through her body – hot, wet, all-engulfing.

Uthai slowed his strokes as she came, but did not stop. He continued to sweep his cock-flesh over her sensitised tissues, triggering delightful aftershocks.

Kate suddenly realised she had forgotten their audience. Uthai's physical prowess had completely distracted her. She stole a glance over at the sofa.

Somtow was watching intently, his sensual lips half-parted, his dark eyes bright with lust. However, he was not just watching.

He lay on his side on the couch. In front of him, her

back to his chest, lay Orapin. Her knees were drawn up. Kate could clearly see Somtow's shaft languidly sliding in and out of the Thai woman's sex.

Orapin had the ripe body of a mature woman. Her breasts swelled to large, dark nipples. Her cunt hair grew more thickly than the girls Kate had seen at the bar, though it was still sparser than Kate's own. Her ivory-toned skin looked silky-soft. Kate longed to stroke her fingers over that flesh, to trace the fullness of those hips and the roundness of that belly.

The Thai woman's eyes were closed. She was breathing heavily and gave a low moan as Somtow, noticing Kate's scrutiny, increased the pace and force of his thrusts. Obviously she was not simply a passive servant to her master's desire.

Uthai shifted his hands to Kate's buttocks, recapturing her attention. She clamped him with her legs as he squatted, his cock still inside her, and laid her on her back on the lushly carpeted floor. Still on his haunches, he resumed his thrusts. He kept hold of her arse, so that her hips were suspended a few inches above the floor. As he pushed deep into her, he twisted and rotated her pelvis, stimulating every corner and crevice of her inner depths.

After orgasm, the sensations in her cunt were subtly different, less urgent yet more acute. Kate felt wider, more open. Uthai still fitted snugly but no longer stretched her. He moved fluidly, with confidence and grace. As if he were dancing, thought Kate.

Little birdlike cries came from the direction of the couch. Kate could no longer see them, but she knew that Somtow had brought Orapin to climax. As if this were a signal, Uthai paused and, much to her disappointment, withdrew from her.

'Turn over, please,' he said, the first time he had spoken since their introduction.

Kate rolled over and on to her hands and knees. Uthai was now kneeling behind her. She gave a sigh of relief and pleasure as he sank his cock back into her aching cunt.

In this new, grounded position, Uthai was rougher and more forceful. His shaft was a battering ram, hammering at gates of her womb. An edge of pain tinged his strokes as he raked his cock across her raw, swollen tissues. She loved it.

Her eyes squeezed shut, she wriggled and pressed her arse against him. More, she begged silently. Harder. She remembered his face, fierce and passionate, as he buggered Somtow. Did he have that expression now?

Kate felt a disturbance of the air, a presence in front of her, and soft lips on hers. It was Orapin. The Thai woman smiled at her sweetly and brushed the damp curls from her forehead. Then she lay down on her back and pushed her body forward between Kate's arms. Within moments, Orapin's glistening sex was directly below her nose and Orapin's tongue was lapping at her clit.

The added stimulation was almost more than Kate could bear. The servant was as expert in her own way as Uthai. First she flicked and teased the rigid, sensitive flesh protruding from Kate's lips, barely touching it, till Kate screamed inside for more contact. Then she took Kate fully into her mouth, sucking and kneading with her tongue until the sensations became overwhelming.

The hot musk of Orapin's sex rose to Kate's nostrils, recalling the taste of Kate's nameless partner earlier that evening. Before Kate could react, Somtow joined them. He straddled Orapin and inserted his organ into her well-lubricated channel, inches from Kate's face. Then he bent to kiss Kate, long and hard.

She watched, fascinated, as his cock ploughed his servant's ripe cunt. She knew, so well now, what Orapin was feeling.

A great joy welled up in her. Uthai and Somtow thrust in the same accelerating rhythm. Orapin's tongue danced over her clit. The world smouldered with magnificent lust.

Kate bent her head and burrowed through Orapin's bush. Her tongue found the Thai woman's clit and played there, urging her on to climax. Then, a slight adjustment, and she was licking the juices off Somtow's cock, following it down into Orapin's folds.

Orapin gave a muffled cry as climax took her. Her hips writhed and jerked, wringing a moan from Somtow and bringing him over the edge. In her ecstasy, she clamped her teeth down on Kate's clit. Kate was too far gone to distinguish pain from pleasure; her sex convulsed with an orgasm so intense that it brought tears to her eyes. Dimly, through the veils of her own pleasure, she heard Uthai growl and felt the surging energy of his release.

Four exhausted, sweaty bodies sprawled on the rich carpet. As Kate regained her senses, she realised that she was inexplicably, deliriously happy. Joy bubbled inside her like champagne. Laughter threatened to overwhelm her.

Her head rested on Somtow's flat, firm stomach. He gently stroked her hair, running his fingers through the tangled ringlets. His other hand stroked Uthai's buttocks. The performer lay face down, his shaven skull in Orapin's lap. The maid sat leaning against the couch, a serene smile on her full lips.

No one spoke, but Kate could sense Somtow's gratitude and delight. Meanwhile, she scrutinised her own emotions. Why did she feel so buoyant, so joyous? It was only sex. Then she understood her own error, that the line between sex and love was so thin that it might easily dissolve in the warm flood of mutual pleasuring.

She felt love for Uthai, for Orapin, and most of all for the shameless and insatiable Somtow. Finally, too, she felt love for herself, so free and ready to savour whatever carnal treats her life might offer.

Then she had another realisation. She could not tell Somtow about Harrison and his plot, not now. He was open and unashamed about his sexual adventures, but it would be a terrible loss of face for him to learn that his preoccupation with her had jeopardised his company. Perhaps after the situation was resolved she could break the news to him gently. For now, though, she would have to look elsewhere for assistance.

She would have to ask Gregory for help. With his skills and connections, he would undoubtedly be able to devise a plan. Kate wondered, half in anticipation and half in fear, what he would demand in return.

Chapter Nine
Crime and Punishment

*K*ate's telephone was ringing when she walked in the door the next morning. She wasn't surprised to find that it was Gregory.

'Kate! What happened to you last night?' She warmed at his tone of concern. 'I came looking for you after your most remarkable performance. Lek told me you had left in a great hurry.

'I hope that you were not upset by what you did with Arun,' he continued. Kate silently noted the name. 'You seemed, at the time, to find it quite natural.'

'It had nothing to do with Arun,' she replied. 'I saw Edward Harrison in the bar, and he saw me. I had to get away before he recognised me.'

Gregory caught the edge in her voice. 'Was that all?'

'Well, no. With Lek's assistance, I learnt some very disturbing things about Mr Edward Harrison.

'Gregory, I need your help.' Kate tried not to sound like she was pleading. 'Harrison is about to commit a crime, and I need your help to stop him.'

A hint of his characteristic irony crept into Gregory's voice. 'This sounds intriguing. Tell me about it.'

'Not over the phone,' she replied. 'Meet me tomorrow afternoon in the Montien Hotel bar. Five o'clock. Then I'll give you all the details.'

'I'm looking forward to it,' Gregory said smoothly. 'See you then.'

She felt a little flare of anger as she hung up. Why wouldn't he take her seriously?

At DigiThai on Monday, Kate tried to act normal. Harrison was out of the office until noon, so that helped. When he did arrive, he seemed preoccupied. He greeted her with his usual effusiveness, then spent the afternoon behind a closed door.

Kate tried to stay alert, to notice anything out of the ordinary. On her way to the laser printer to pick up some output she passed Wang, engaged in heavy conversation with Malawee. The woman looked a bit perplexed. On her way past in the other direction Kate slowed and tried to eavesdrop.

'Come on, Malee,' said Wang, 'you can trust me. Mr Harrison wants to make sure that at least three of us know the password . . .'

Kate pondered what she had heard. Was Wang in on the plot, or simply Harrison's innocent dupe? She decided to take no chances and changed the password on her archived code before leaving to meet Marshall.

She walked into the bar promptly at five to find that Gregory had already arrived. He lounged at a round table in a dimly lit corner of the bar and surprised her by rising as she approached and taking her hand.

'Kate! You look lovely, as usual.' She was wearing a simple cotton blouse and straight skirt. 'Though not as lovely as the last time I saw you.' He grinned provocatively. He was dressed more formally than was his custom, in a suit of jet-black raw silk. There was a silver ring on every finger and, now, Kate noticed, a silver stud in his left earlobe.

Kate blushed. As usual, the heat of his touch inflamed her. She sat down, trying to mask her embarrassment.

'Good afternoon, Gregory,' she said. She ordered a gin and tonic from the tuxedo-clad waiter who appeared almost immediately. Marshall already had a beer sitting before him.

'Now then, Kate,' he said, settling back and smiling at her. 'Tell me your tale.'

Struggling to sound coherent and in control, Kate related the conversation that Lek had overheard. She also told Marshall about the success of her recent projected 3D demos and how she had hidden in the alley while Harrison and his cronies strolled by discussing the plot.

'Lek said that they talked about "millions of baht",' she concluded, her voice shaking despite herself. 'And Harrison promised to hand over the software sometime this week.'

Gregory rested his hand on his chin, thinking hard. 'I believe I know the identity of Harrison's partners. Sayed Hakim and Herbert Malachevsky, co-owners of TFX Limited. Definitely a second-rate company, but in the same general business as DigiThai. I wonder how they would manage to pull together that much money.'

He turned his attention back to Kate. 'Is there anything else, Kate?' he asked. 'You seem upset. I can understand you being angry that they would steal your work, but this seems more – personal.'

Damn his intuition, thought Kate. She couldn't tell him about her own role as decoy, not without revealing her relationship with Somtow. 'No, that's all,' she said.

'Kate –' Marshall speared her with his gaze '– you must be honest with me. Don't be afraid.'

His mixed tone of kindness and authority melted her resistance. Her anger and shame both rekindled as she told him what she had learnt in the alley.

Gregory chuckled. 'So Harrison hired you, Kate, to distract Somtow! I suspect that he got a bit more than he bargained for!'

'I can't stand the thought that he used me this way!' Kate exclaimed. 'And I hate to think that I brought trouble on Somtow.'

'Don't blame yourself, Kate.' His voice held a sudden gentleness. 'After all, who could resist you?'

Kate was silent for a moment, pondering his good-natured response to the news that she had another lover.

'I knew you were seeing Somtow,' he remarked, once more showing an uncanny awareness of her thoughts. 'I decided not to say anything; I was waiting for you to tell me.' Kate looked down at her lap. 'I know him reasonably well. He's a good sort. I thought you might need someone like him to counterbalance me. That perhaps you were not ready for a steady diet of domination.

'At some point,' he continued softly, 'you may decide to give him up, understanding that you need and want only me. Until then, you may continue your innocent little fling.'

Innocent! thought Kate. If only Gregory knew of the scene they had played on Saturday night!

'By the way, where were you Saturday night, after you left The Grotto?' Marshall shifted in his seat and leant towards her. 'I called you at home again and again, but there was no answer.'

Kate was mortified. 'I was at Somtow's house,' she said briefly.

'And . . .?' He lifted her chin and looked into her eyes. 'Tell me, Kate. All the juicy parts.'

So she found herself describing her encounter with Uthai, Orapin and Somtow, watching his expressions change as she added one graphic detail after another. She was trying to shock him, but he merely looked amused. Meanwhile, her sex grew wet and her nipples swelled as she relived the experience.

'Thank you, Kate,' said Gregory when she had concluded. 'That was well told.' He stroked her cheek affectionately. 'You never cease to amaze me.'

He sat back again. 'Now, let's make some plans. I'll bet that I can do a fairly decent impersonation of Harrison over the telephone . . .' He seemed to slump a bit, his gaze defocused, and he rubbed one hand over the other, one of Edward Harrison's distinctive mannerisms. 'Katherine, my dear, I appreciate all the effort that you have expended on behalf of DigiThai. Be assured that you will reap your reward.'

Kate was astonished. The voice, the inflections, the sentence structure, were all Harrison's.

'That's amazing!' she exclaimed. 'How did you do that?'

Gregory grinned. 'Observation, and practice. When I got out of college, I spent several years with a theatre troupe, travelling around Australia. We did everything from Strindberg to slapstick. I left when I thought I had learnt all that they could teach me.'

'I knew it,' Kate said. 'The first day we met, I thought you had dramatic training. You seemed so thoroughly adept at manipulating the emotions of your poor audience.'

'Well, now I'll put those skills at your service. I'll give Malachevksy a call, pretending to be Harrison, and set up the exchange. Meanwhile, you need to put together a package that will convince them it's the software Harrison promised them. We don't want them to discover, at least not for a while, that Harrison has fleeced them.

'Then, we will think up a suitable punishment for Edward Harrison, to compensate for your humiliation. Something that he will find painful – and personal.'

Kate shivered despite herself. She would not want Gregory Marshall as an enemy.

'Let me consider this for a while and work up something appropriate. I'll call you tomorrow or Wednesday to let you know how things are going. How does that sound?'

Kate felt intense relief. She had no doubt that she and Marshall could thwart, and punish, Harrison.

'Thank you, Gregory,' she said sincerely. 'I really appreciate your help.'

His eyebrows arched and a mischievous twinkle came to his eyes. 'Well, I am wondering what I should ask of you in return.'

Kate blushed again. By now, she should be used to

his manner, but he still managed to simultaneously thrill and embarrass her.

'We could go upstairs to Room twelve-sixty-three,' he continued, as if talking to himself. 'I rather thought that was what you had in mind when you suggested that we meet here at the Montien.'

Kate started to protest, then stopped short. Was there any truth at all in his statement? Why in fact had she chosen this place for their rendezvous?

'Unfortunately,' he said, his voice sincere but his eyes laughing, 'I have an appointment later this evening. So I couldn't give you the time and attention that you deserve.'

Kate squirmed in her seat. Disappointment washed over her. An image briefly flashed through her mind: her own naked body bent double over a chair, while Gregory stood behind her wielding a heavy leather strap. The picture was so vivid and unexpected that she sucked in her breath. Her cunt muscles contracted. She searched Gregory's face. Was he responsible for her wayward mind?

The black-haired giant kept his expression bland and pleasant, offering no clues and no admissions. 'I do feel that you owe me something for my help, though – beyond the normal obedience that you owe me as your master.' A flame kindled suddenly in his dark eyes. 'Under the table. Now.'

'What –' Kate began to object, but his probing gaze silenced her. She glanced around nervously, to see if anyone was watching. The bar had filled up, but the patrons all seemed to be engrossed with their own companions. Besides, the table Gregory had chosen was in a shadowy, out-of-the-way corner. Without further hesitation, she slipped under the table and rested there on her knees, awaiting further instructions.

Perhaps he wants me to suck him, she thought, her heart beating faster. Perhaps tonight she would taste his come. She itched to go ahead and unzip his trousers, but she knew better. She knelt, hands in her lap, and waited.

'Slip off your undergarments,' she heard him say, a little muffled by the table between them. 'If you're wearing any, that is,' he added, in a tone she knew was calculated to embarrass her. With some difficulty due to the cramped space, she complied.

'Now, lay yourself across my lap, with your skirt up around your waist.'

No! she thought. Not here, in this public place! Yet even as her mind protested, her body obeyed. He leant back on the upholstered bench, away from the table. She pulled up her skirt, then wriggled up into the space he had made, trying to cause as little disturbance as possible. In a moment, her abdomen and hips rested against the textured silk of his suit. With some satisfaction, she realised that she could feel the delicious hardness of his incipient erection pressing into her. Meanwhile, her bare bottom was available and exposed, just below the level of the table-top. Her head and shoulders rested, fairly comfortably, on the plush upholstery of the bench. She buried her face in the crook of her elbow, as if by shutting out the visual world no one would see her.

They remained still in this position for what seemed like eons. Kate was intensely aware of her naked flesh; she imagined it gleaming in the dim bar like some secondary moon. Ghostly fingers seemed to be caressing her buttocks, but she knew this was only the suspense acting on her mind. Then came Gregory's voice, soft and commanding.

'You ran off last night, Kate, before the last act. I had planned a final performance for you, with just me as the audience. Too bad. I understand why you ran, without my permission, but I still need to punish you. You understand that, don't you?'

Kate replied with a muffled assent.

'So I am going to spank you now, because you need to be punished. It won't hurt as much as the cat-o'-nine-tails. However, you don't really know who will be watching, do you? There could be a crowd gathered round admiring the reddening fullness of your lovely ass.'

Kate shook her head, still shutting out the light. Incredulous, she realised that her sex was damp and tingling. Merely by describing her humiliation, he could make her hot.

She'd been expecting further discourse from her beloved torturer, but instead she felt the sting of his palm on her skin. It hurt for a moment. Then the warmth spread across her flesh, creeping between her legs. A second slap followed on the other cheek, and then a dozen more until her whole arse burnt, tender and alive.

He stopped for a moment and then Kate heard the accented English of the waiter.

'Would you like another beer, sir?' With his left hand, Gregory spread her thighs and sank three fingers into her drenched cunt. With his right, it seemed, he drained the last of his beer mug and handed it to the waiter.

'Yes, thank you.'

'And your lady companion?' Kate wanted to sink into the ground. She had no idea whether she was visible to the Thai across the table from Gregory. 'Will she be returning?'

Gregory worked her with his fingers. He pressed his thumb against the tight muscles of her anus, seeking access. Her heart beating wildly, Kate relaxed and let the thick digit enter her.

'She went off to the powder room. Please bring her another gin and tonic.'

'Of course, sir,' said the waiter. Kate could only hope he was gone. Meanwhile, she writhed in Gregory's lap as he clenched his hand, bringing thumb and fingers together. He rubbed his thumb against his fingers through the thin wall of flesh that separated her rear passage from her forward one. The pleasure was so acute Kate thought she would faint.

Her orgasm began deep, deep inside her, welling up irresistibly. Part of her fought against it, unwilling to be so easily manipulated and controlled. But there was no help for it. Gregory's hand blazed within her, urging her on, teasing, commanding. She stuffed her wrist in her mouth to stop her screams as the climax raged through her like a forest fire. Just as she was coming, Gregory roughly removed his hand from her sex and rained a new set of blows on her raw buttocks. This only fanned the flames.

'Your drinks, sir.' Kate lay panting in Gregory's lap, his hard cock pushing rhythmically into the space between her open thighs. He'll ruin his lovely suit, she thought, deliriously happy despite the pain and embarrassment. However, he seemed to be in complete control of himself.

'Thank you. Could you bring our check, please?' Then he leant over and whispered into Kate's ear. 'Sit up. Pull yourself together.'

Kate did her best to obey. Her skirt clung to her sticky thighs. Her nipples ached, and she was still breathing heavily.

Gregory took her chin in his hand, his left hand, and leant over to kiss her. As his hot tongue probed her mouth, she smelt her own mingled scents on his fingers, the salty musk of her cunt and the sweet, dark, scary fragrance of her bumhole. It was enough, almost, to make her come again.

'My little Kate, it's so difficult for me to be stern with you.' Gregory sighed. 'I suspect that you need a firmer hand than mine.'

No, thought Kate to herself, your hand is exactly what I need. Your hand, your whip, your cock. She snuggled against him. He didn't resist or chastise her. Rather, he seemed lost in thought.

Kate was a little worried. Gregory appeared uncertain, at a loss, for the first time in their acquaintance. She didn't know what to say, and so she sipped her drink and said nothing, acutely aware of his silence.

After what seemed like a long while, he gave a little laugh. 'I have just the thing!' he said. 'Just the right sort of punishment for Edward Harrison who clearly does not have sufficient respect for you or for women in general. And just the right sort of scene for you.'

Kate's eyes grew wide as he recounted his plan. It was bizarre, crazy, perhaps a little dangerous. It played like a scene from some pulp detective story, full of intrigue and drama. But it might work.

Meanwhile, Kate could tell even from his brief description, it would be more extreme and perverse than anything she had experienced under his tutelage so far. She had to admit to herself that she was looking forward to it.

Kate arrived at DigiThai before seven o'clock the next morning. She needed some private time, free from interruption or surveillance by her co-workers.

The first thing she did was rename the archive holding the projected 3D work, and move it to an out-of-the-way area on her temporary disk. Then she began to systematically construct a decoy archive. She grabbed whatever files she could find – computer games, word-processor software, jokes emailed to her by friends back in the US – and renamed each one to match one of the files in the original 3D archive. To avoid suspicion, she made sure to include some source code, tutorials that had come with her compiler. She loaded all the renamed garbage files into a new archive called PROJ 3D and added the real documentation file she had produced which contained details on the files included and their contents. Finally she encrypted it all, using the password she had shared with Malawee.

By eight o'clock she was writing the decoy archive to a CD-Rom. The process was nearly complete when Edward Harrison interrupted her.

'Good morning, Katherine! You're certainly here early. And you're hard at work already!'

'Good morning, Edward,' Kate replied, her calm voice

hardly betraying the anxious pounding of her heart. 'I was just finishing up fixes for the final bugs in this first version of the 3D software.' She smiled sweetly. 'I thought we might want to invite Mr Marshall in later this week for an initial demo.'

Her suggestion produced the desired effect. Harrison was visibly flustered as he replied. 'Oh, no, I think that's premature. You told me yourself, Katherine, that work was far from complete, that you needed to deal with multiple viewpoints and a host of other details.'

'Still, Edward, since Mr Marshall has commissioned the work, we should keep him apprised of its progress.'

Harrison squirmed. 'Well, perhaps next week. This week is impossible; I already have too many commitments.'

I'm sure you do, thought Kate as he left her office. Such as your commitment to sell out DigiThai. She put the decoy CD in her briefcase and waited to hear from Gregory.

Just before she left for lunch, her phone rang. Anchana was at the other end of the line. 'I have a call for you,' she said. 'Someone named Gary Murdock. He sounds British.'

Kate didn't find the name familiar. 'Go ahead and transfer me,' she said, curious.

'Ms O'Neill?' The voice was suave, cultured, higher in pitch than she had expected.

'Yes, this is Katherine O'Neill. How can I help you, Mr Murdock?'

'Well, you could get down on your hands and knees, and stick your hot, juicy cunt in my face.'

The crudeness was totally inconsistent with the tone and delivery.

Then light dawned. 'Gregory!' Kate couldn't help but laugh a little. 'You are impossible!'

'At your service, madame,' he said, reverting to his normal voice. He paused, then continued. 'As I know that you are at mine.'

Kate tried to ignore the thrill that ran through her.

'I have spoken to Malachevsky, in the persona of Edward Harrison. The transfer is arranged for tomorrow morning. Do you have the fake material?'

'I finished it this morning,' she said, glad she had been so diligent.

'Great. Can you drop it off at The Grotto tonight on your way home? I won't be there, unfortunately, but you can give it to Noi.'

'Whatever you say,' she answered demurely.

'Indeed. Well, we'll see about that.'

'Now, tomorrow you should skip work as we discussed. Leave home early in the morning, and spend the day somewhere you will not be recognised. Don't talk to anyone, especially not your maid. Then meet me at seven in the evening in front of the Montien.'

'I'll be there,' said Kate.

'Come prepared to be kidnapped,' Gregory added. She could imagine the glint in his eye. Then he hung up.

Kate reviewed the plan in her mind. She would disappear; Harrison would wonder where she was, would worry that something had gone wrong. Then, late in the day, Gregory would telephone Harrison, masquerading as some anonymous thug. Katherine had been kidnapped, Gregory would tell Harrison, and furthermore the plot to defraud DigiThai had been discovered. To save Katherine, and himself, Harrison would obey Marshall's instructions. Gregory would lure the American to some out-of-the-way spot. Then he and Noi would use their skills to humiliate and punish her boss – while Kate watched with satisfaction.

Kate wondered just what Gregory and Noi would do to Harrison. She was still turning over ideas in her mind when she reached The Grotto. Noi was waiting in the doorway, a strange smile on her lips.

'Kate,' she said softly. 'It is good to see you again.'

Kate blushed as she remembered the last time Noi had seen her, with her face buried in another woman's sex.

'Good evening, Noi,' she said, struggling for composure. 'Here's the material for the swap.' She handed Noi a sealed manila envelope that held the CD.

'Would you care to come inside?' asked Noi, her smile widening. 'I am sure that the girls would love to say hello.'

'No, thank you, I have to be going.' Kate was surprised at her own discomfiture. Then she realised that it was more from anticipation of the next time they would meet than from recollection of the last time.

The next day had the vague, portentous quality of a dream. She left her house early in tourist garb, sunglasses and a floppy hat. She spent the morning in the National Museum, admiring the grace of the Buddha statues and the gilded complexity of the paintings. Resolutely, she shut out the vivid, obscene images that assailed her imagination. At lunch, in an open-air restaurant overlooking the Chao Phya River, she ordered a beer to calm her nerves. The alcohol intensified her feelings of unreality.

The afternoon flowed on, bright and endless. Kate tried to go shopping but instead found herself just sitting in the cafe in the middle of some busy shopping centre, sipping her ice tea and staring at the passers-by, while one perverse scene after another unrolled in her mind.

Finally it was twilight. She stood under the awning at the entrance of the Montien Hotel, relaxed and still. She didn't know what to expect, but somehow she was prepared.

A black sedan with tinted windows pulled up to the kerb. Gregory pushed open the back door.

'Get in,' he said. Kate obeyed. He kissed her lightly, almost playfully, then produced a black silk scarf from one of his pockets.

'Close your eyes,' he said, almost in a whisper. She felt the cool fabric on her eyelids and a small tug as the knot was tied.

161

'Why a blindfold?' she asked, though in fact she really didn't care. All she wanted was to be where she was, with him, in his power.

'I don't want you to know all my secrets just yet,' said Gregory. The back of his hand brushed her cheek and then was gone, leaving a stroke of heat in its wake. 'Besides, it adds verisimilitude.'

'Let's go,' he said to the invisible driver, perhaps Noi. Then he didn't speak again.

Encased in darkness, Kate could feel the warm bulk of Gregory's body seated close beside her. Please touch me, she begged silently, please. Of course he didn't, as ever teaching her to be pliant and patient. Strangely, though, Kate had the idea that he was disciplining himself, that he yearned to reach for her but would not allow himself to do so.

The ride seemed to last a long time. Heat radiated from Gregory's flesh, so close to her and yet so distant. She remembered her back-seat encounter with Somtow, on the way to Ayuthaya, but she didn't dare try any such manoeuvre with Marshall. She knew he would only mock her and tell her she must learn how to wait.

Once she felt him shift and thought for a moment that he might be about to encircle her with his arm. Then he settled back into his seat a little further away. Again Kate sensed an inner struggle within the heart and mind of her master.

Finally the car slid to a stop. Without removing the scarf from her eyes, Marshall helped her out of the car. She smelt salt and rotting seaweed, and heard the distant boom of a foghorn. They must be somewhere on the Gulf of Thailand, she thought, near the mouth of the river.

Gregory held her elbow, steadying her as he led her forward. She heard the crunch of gravel under the heels of her sandals, then the muted click of wood which gave a little under her weight. A bridge or causeway, thought Kate, wondering where they were headed and feeling, for the first time, a tiny prick of fear.

Squeaky hinges as a door swung open. 'Step up,' her guide said curtly. She followed his instructions, then felt a more solid floor beneath her. 'Stop,' said Gregory, then circled around her and removed the blindfold.

They were in a rough wooden shack, apparently on stilts over the water; Kate could hear the lap of the waves against the pilings beneath them. Two paraffin lanterns provided a yellow light that left the corners in shadow. Iron hooks and rings were scattered over the unfinished walls and embedded in the heavy beams that supported the corrugated tin roof. The shutters on the single window were fastened back. A salty breeze drifted in through the opening and Kate could see the lights of the squid boats and tuna trawlers twinkling in the misty distance.

'Strip down to your underwear,' said Gregory, his voice unexpectedly harsh. 'We don't have much time.'

Kate obeyed silently, handing her clothing to Noi who had followed them into the room. The *mamasan* looked stunning in spike-heeled boots with silver zippers running from ankle to thigh and a brief black dress with matching zip down the front. Noi smiled enigmatically as she took Kate's skirt and T-shirt, but said nothing.

'Sit there,' said Gregory, indicating one of several straight-backed wooden chairs in the room. The only other furnishings were a utilitarian-looking wooden table and a battered steamer trunk in a corner. Noi rummaged inside it. She emerged holding several lengths of rope, which she brought to Gregory, her heels clicking on the linoleum-covered floor.

Dressed only in her simple cotton bra and panties, Kate seated herself demurely in the chair. Gregory pulled her hands behind her, a bit roughly, and tied them at the wrists, weaving the rope through the rungs of the chair so that she was thoroughly attached. Then he bound her ankles together, looping the rope around the chair legs in the process. Although he did not seriously hurt her, he was not gentle. The twinge of fear grew stronger. 'Why are you tying me up?' she asked, hesitant to speak without permission.

Gregory Marshall leered at her. 'Well, you are a kidnap victim, after all.' He leant closer. 'Why? Don't you like it?'

Kate looked down and said nothing. It was true. Immobilised by the bonds, she felt helpless and aroused. Still, his strange mood and manner made her uneasy.

With my legs tied so tightly together, she thought, he can hardly access my sex.

As if to answer her thought, Gregory came up behind her. In one swift motion, his left hand swooped into her bra, captured her breast and twisted the nipple until she gasped. The other snaked between her pressed-together thighs and into her panties. His fingernail raked roughly across her clit. 'Keep quiet, Kate, or I will have to gag you. You are my prisoner now. Remember that.' He lingered a moment longer, wiggling his finger in the tight confines between her legs until she was wet and breathless. From across the room, Noi watched, that same strange smile on her lips.

A knock on the door made them all jump.

'Harrison!' said Marshall. 'Be still now, Kate.'

'Come in,' he called, deepening his voice and adding a hint of some foreign accent.

Hinges squeaked as Edward Harrison opened the door and hesitantly entered the room. Kate's half-naked, bound figure was the first sight to meet his eyes.

'Katherine!' he said, rushing towards her. His concern seemed genuine. 'Are you all right?'

'She is fine, Harrison,' said Gregory, stepping out of the shadows.

'Marshall?' Harrison appeared confused. 'What are you doing here?'

Gregory strode over to stand in front of Kate's boss. Though Harrison was a big, burly man, her master was taller still, and his air of authority and menace made Edward Harrison seem to shrink.

'Sit down, Harrison, and I will tell you a story.'

Edward seated himself uncomfortably in one of the other chairs. He rubbed one hand nervously over the other and darted pleading looks at Kate as Marshall continued speaking. Kate kept her face impassive.

'Once upon a time, there was a crook who masqueraded as a businessman. He gained the confidence of a Thai aristocrat and convinced the Thai to invest in a new company in order to capitalise on advancing technology. The Thai sank a significant fortune into the company, a fortune that the crook coveted. The Thai was something of a playboy, but nevertheless developed a real interest in the business. So the crook was unable to pursue his long-term goal of embezzling the company assets.'

Kate looked at Gregory. Was this true? Was Harrison stealing from DigiThai's coffers as well as selling its intellectual property? Gregory was watching Harrison's face, and, when Kate followed his gaze, the guilty nervousness she saw in Harrison's expression confirmed the tale.

'The crook conceived of what he thought was a brilliant plan. Knowing his Thai partner's weakness for the pleasures of the flesh, he hired a beautiful, sexy and intelligent young woman – ostensibly to work for their company, but actually to distract his partner's attention from business matters.'

Harrison glanced over at Kate. She met his gaze and held it until he dropped his eyes in shame.

'The plan worked perfectly. The Thai was smitten by the new employee and stopped his periodic examinations of the company books.'

'The woman turned out to be even smarter than expected. She developed an innovative new product which the crook realised he could sell to the competition and make even more money.'

'However, she was a little too smart. She found out about the plan to sell her work, as well as her unwitting role as a decoy, and she was furious. So she came to me.'

Gregory chuckled ominously. 'That was her mistake, of course.'

Kate searched his face anxiously, finding his tone disturbing. However, his attention was focused on his other captive.

'I impersonated you, arranged the exchange of the goods, and got hold of the money that you had hoped for.' Marshall nodded to Noi, who brought over an attaché case that had been hidden by the trunk. He opened the case to reveal neat stacks of crisp green bills.

Unconsciously, Edward Harrison leant forward, his greedy eyes caressing the money before him. He actually licked his lips.

'Yes, it is a lot of money,' said Gregory. 'Seven hundred and fifty thousand dollars. I have big plans for this cash.' Kate felt a surge of anger. Did Marshall really intend to keep these ill-gotten gains?

'Meanwhile, Hakim and Malachevsky have not figured out yet that you double-crossed them. But they will soon.'

'Wait a minute –' began Harrison, rising from the chair.

'Sit down,' growled Gregory. 'I'm not finished yet.' Harrison obeyed. 'Lock the door, please, Noi.' Noi glided across the room, put a padlock through a hasp, and clicked it shut. 'I don't want Mr Harrison trying to leave before we're through.'

'In addition to your partners in crime, I would expect that the Thai police would be interested in hearing this story. Not to mention Somtow Rajchitraprasong, whom I am sure you know has some powerful friends.'

'However, I will be satisfied with a private settlement of this matter.' Harrison relaxed slightly. 'First of all, I want a fifty-thousand-dollar ransom for Ms O'Neill here. Or else, you don't know what I will do to her, do you, Mr Harrison?'

Harrison looked seriously worried. Meanwhile, Kate seethed. Was Gregory really this mercenary?

'Second, you must submit yourself to the attentions of my partner, Noi, who will teach you to have more respect for women.'

Harrison fidgeted in his chair as Noi approached. In one gesture, she unzipped her dress and flung it off her shoulders. Underneath, she wore a costume out of some fetishist's dream.

A black leather corset cinched her waist and elevated her naked breasts. Matching silver rings pierced her chocolate nipples. Two silver chains ran between her legs from the front of the corset to the back. Otherwise, her sex was arrogantly bare, shaved smooth so each crevice and fold was clearly visible.

Noi's muscular legs were encased to mid-thigh by the supple leather of her boots. On one hip, Kate could see a vivid tattoo: a red heart speared by an arrow, engulfed in multicoloured flames. Kate shivered at the formidable vision, overwhelmed by a mixture of lust and fear. Gregory folded his arms across his chest and gazed at Noi fondly. 'Noi is my half-sister, and my pupil in the arts of discipline. However, you will find that she is far more severe than her teacher.'

His sister! Kate felt deep relief at the knowledge that fearsome Noi was not her competitor for Gregory's affections.

Standing in front of Harrison with her hands on her hips, Noi spoke for the first time. Her lilting Thai-accented voice was full of steely authority. 'Strip, Mr Harrison. Now.'

Harrison began blubbing in protest, but Noi interrupted quietly. 'Now, Edward – I assume that I may call you Edward, since we are going to get quite intimate – I am sure that you do not want Gregory to call the police. Do you?'

Harrison shook his head miserably.

'Then take off that expensive suit and let's get down to business.'

Harrison slowly began to comply. He removed his necktie and handed it to Noi, unbuttoned his shirt, pulled his undershirt over his head. He hesitated as he began unzipping his fly. A stern glance from Noi forced him to continue.

Before long he was standing in the middle of the room completely naked except for his socks.

'Leave them on,' said Noi, circling his pale, somewhat pudgy figure and looking him up and down. 'I have always found that naked men look particularly ridiculous with their socks on.'

Edward Harrison was certainly more prepossessing dressed than nude. Kate surveyed him critically, enjoying his obvious discomfiture. For a middle-aged man he wasn't in terrible shape, just a little bulge here, a little sag there. His skin was pale and soft-looking, though, and he looked amazingly vulnerable. His skin will mark nicely in response to the whip, thought Kate, and then was shocked at herself.

'Down on your hands and knees,' said Noi. Awkwardly, Harrison obeyed. Noi strode around him. 'Now, what should I do with you, Edward?' she said. She paused behind him and put one booted foot on his raised buttocks. 'Perhaps you'd like my boot heel up your ass,' she said sweetly, running the stiletto lightly up and down the crack between his cheeks.

'No, no . . .' choked Harrison, clearly terrified.

'No? Well, let me think of something else.' She paused for a moment, her heel still teasingly close to Harrison's arsehole. 'I know just the thing for you,' she said. 'Don't move,' she added as she crossed the room to the trunk.

She returned with her arms full of paraphernalia, which she set on the table. 'You are going to be my little pony, Edward. I am sure that you will like that.'

From the pile, she fished out a mass of leather straps. She fitted them over Harrison's head. Kate could see that it was intended to simulate a bridle, complete with a soft bit that fitted between Harrison's teeth.

Kate's sex burnt as she remembered her fantasies in the Singapore hotel room. She knew what came next.

Noi was holding a long tassel of blondish hair. 'You will be my little palomino,' she told Harrison. She showed him the tail and the bulging rubber plug to which is was attached. Edward moaned, perhaps in protest, but with the bit in his mouth he was unintelligible.

Noi crouched down in front of him, her knees on either side of his head. She squirted some lubricant into her palm and spread it over the hard rubber, holding the obscene object only inches from his face. 'If I had thought of it earlier, before I bridled you,' she said with a hint of laughter, 'I could have had you suck on it to moisten it.' She stood up and circled behind him. 'Ah, well.'

With expert skill she held his cheeks apart with one hand while pressing the base of the tail against his hole with the other. 'Open wide, Edward.' Some muffled sounds came from Harrison's mouth. 'I said, open,' she repeated sharply. She gave a forceful twist and the plug disappeared inside Harrison. The tail reached nearly to the ground. Playfully, Noi lifted it and brushed the prickly horsehair against the back of Harrison's thighs. He squirmed. 'Nice pony,' she said. 'Be calm now, pony.'

She returned to face him and picked up another object from the table: a riding crop. Harrison's eyes grew wide with alarm. Noi tested its flexibility; the fibreglass whizzed through the air, almost invisible.

'Now, pony, show me how fast you can trot,' said Noi. She brought the crop down on Harrison's rear with a resounding *thwack*. Her victim moved awkwardly on his hands and knees, the blond tail dangling between his pale legs.

The sound, and the sight of the red welt rising on Harrison's skin, made Kate feel very odd. On the one hand she felt deep satisfaction at seeing Harrison punished. At the same time there was pity, and desire. She imagined herself in Harrison's place, the sting of the crop and the swell of the plug stretching her arse; she was overwhelmed with fearful excitement as she watched Noi stride back and forth, cutting at Harrison's tender flesh as he crawled around trying to escape her strokes.

Kate looked over at Gregory, wondering if he sensed her reaction. He was lounging against the wall in his tight black jeans and cotton singlet, his muscular arms still crossed, watching his disciple work. His face was in shadow. As if he felt her gaze, though, he turned to her. She could not decipher his expression; it seemed full of warring emotions. She saw lust, anger, affection, irony, something like desperation. She smiled, a little weakly, trying to lighten his darkness. As if he realised that he was exposing himself, his face became a mask, calm, confident, slightly mocking. He turned his attention back to Noi and her victim.

Harrison's rump was now criss-crossed with red stripes. He knelt in the middle of the room, panting as Noi ran her hands over his hair. 'Steady now,' she crooned. 'Good pony.' She straddled him, settling her bare cunt just above his buttocks. 'I'm going to ride you now,' she said, drawing up her knees and poking his thighs lightly with her heels as if they were spurs. 'Ho, pony! Let's go!' Harrison began crawling with his rider. His face showed utter misery; in fact he looked quite ridiculous. His leather-clad jockey urged him on with crop and heels. 'Faster, Edward, faster! I know you can do better than this!' With difficulty, Kate suppressed her laughter. This was serious, she reminded herself. Harrison more than deserved his punishment.

Finally, Noi allowed him to stop. She was panting a bit herself as she swung her legs off him. 'My, Edward, you have made me so hot!' she exclaimed as she removed the bridle. Sure enough, Kate could see a damp spot on Harrison's skin where Noi's sex had rested. She grabbed the tail by the base and pulled it out of Harrison's body. 'Not only that – I need to pee!'

Kate looked around. There was a door in one corner that might lead to a bathroom. Then she understood that this was not Noi's intent.

'Turn over on your back, Edward,' said Noi. Slowly, as if in pain, Harrison complied. He lay on the linoleum, gazing up miserably at his tormentor. 'Now, close your eyes, and open your mouth.'

Kate held her breath. She couldn't believe what she was seeing. She was horrified and yet her nipples hardened inside her bra, her sex ached.

Noi stood like a colossus over Edward Harrison's prone body, one leg on each side of his head. Then she squatted, her shaved sex just above his face. Her hands went to her nipples; she pulled slightly at the rings embedded in her flesh as she released a gushing stream of urine into Harrison's mouth.

Harrison sputtered as the hot liquid continued to come. 'Swallow it, Edward,' said Noi sweetly. 'Swallow it all.'

Though no one was watching her, Kate wanted to sink into the floor with shame. Because watching Noi bathing Harrison in her pee turned her on. Gregory, she thought, what have you done to me? What have I become? She squeezed her eyes shut. I can't watch any more of this, she thought. She heard Gregory's voice, close to her ear. 'What do you think, Kate?' He laughed softly. 'Isn't Noi doing a fine job?' He brushed his hands across her swollen nipples, so lightly that he hardly touched her. 'Just wait, though. She has lots more in store for our friend Edward.'

Kate opened her eyes and turned to look at her master, but he was gone, back leaning nonchalantly against the wall. Had she imagined his voice?

Noi finally finished pissing. She stood, picked up a towel, squatted again and wiped the remaining moisture from Harrison's face. 'Mmm, that felt good,' she said. Then she noticed, at the same time as Kate, that Edward Harrison, lying helpless and humiliated on the floor, had an enormous hard-on.

'Well!' Noi said, a note of irritation creeping into her voice. 'It seems that you enjoyed that, too. That is definitely not the idea here, Edward. I'm afraid I'm going to have to punish you more severely.'

'On your feet,' she said harshly. Glaring at her, he obeyed.

'Lean over the table,' she commanded. 'Butt in the air. Let your hands dangle on either side. Spread your legs.' As Harrison adopted the position she described, she looked over at Gregory. 'I need rope. Could you please untie our Kate?'

Without comment, Gregory removed the bonds from Kate's wrists. As he knelt in front of her, untying her ankles, Kate had the overwhelming desire to touch him. Timidly, she reached down and stroked his dark, shiny hair. He looked up sharply, and she jerked her hand away as if scalded. His face was unreadable, but he didn't seem angry. Silently, he completed his work and handed the ropes over to Noi.

In no time, it seemed, she had tied Harrison's ankles to the table legs. 'Now, I need something for your hands,' she said to Harrison. 'Oh, I know exactly the thing.' She retrieved Harrison's necktie from the pile of clothing he had shed. 'No!' exclaimed Harrison, 'that's a Dior! You'll ruin it!'

'That should be the least of your worries, Edward,' purred Noi as she used the silk tie to fasten his wrists together under the table.

'Can you move around, Edward?' she asked. 'Try it.' All he could do was shift his rear a bit from left to right. Otherwise he was immobilised. 'Are any of the ropes too tight? Are they cutting off your circulation?'

'No,' replied Harrison sullenly.

'Good. I am glad that you are comfortable.' Noi picked up Harrison's discarded trousers and extracted the Gucci belt from the belt loops. She showed it to Harrison. He said nothing.

'Now I am going to teach you a real lesson, Edward. This belt is going to hurt a lot more than the crop. I am going to beat you with it until you sincerely apologise to Kate for your arrogance, dishonesty, and disrespect.'

'I apologise!' said Harrison eagerly. 'I am truly sorry, Katherine.'

'I do not believe you, Edward, and I suspect that Kate does not believe you either. You are just trying to save your skin.'

Noi raised her arm. The belt whistled through the air and landed with a snap on Harrison's already reddened left buttock. He gave a surprised whelp. 'I will know when you have had enough pain, when you are truly sorry. I will hear it in your voice.' The leather seared his other cheek.

'I'm sorry! I apologise!' Harrison wailed.

'I don't think so,' said Noi, with another stroke.

Kate's eyes followed the Thai dominatrix with fascination. Noi danced gracefully around the man's rear, delivering her blows with power and precision. Her victim squirmed and twisted, trying in vain to avoid her reach. Harrison had stopped talking. Now the only sounds were his cries and groans, the singing of the leather slicing through the air, and the slap as it found its mark.

Kate found she was leaning forward in her chair, eager not to miss any detail. Suddenly Gregory spoke up.

'Noi, perhaps Kate would like the chance to punish Mr Harrison personally.'

'Oh, Ji, that is an excellent idea. Kate, would you care to take a few whacks at our guest here?'

Kate wavered, indecisive. Surely she could not do such a thing. Looking at her boss's raw, plump bottom, though, she was extremely tempted.

Harrison mumbled feebly. 'No, Katherine, please! I have always had the highest respect for you . . .'

Kate recalled his arrogant bragging in the alley, his characterisation of her as an 'American tart' and 'quite a little piece'. 'Definitely,' she said, walking over to stand next to Noi behind Harrison's back. 'His ass looks really sore, doesn't it?'

Noi smiled delightedly. 'Oh, we are going to make it a lot sorer!'

She handed Kate the riding crop. 'Try this; it is a bit easier to control. Use your whole arm to build momentum, then add a flick of your wrist on contact so the tip digs into the skin.'

Kate was breathing heavily. The braided leather of the crop handle felt comfortable and strangely familiar in her palm. She marked with her eyes an area that seemed less red than the rest of Harrison's arse. She raised her arm above her head, then brought the crop down hard, right on target.

Harrison cried out. As her instrument of discipline met the flesh of her victim, Kate felt pride and elation. 'Very good,' said Noi. 'Try swinging through a larger arc, with a little less force.' Kate followed instructions. The leather loop at the end of the crop gave a satisfying snap as it landed on the back of Harrison's thigh.

'Excellent, Kate!' Noi glanced over at Gregory, who was smiling broadly. 'I think you have a real talent for this.'

After Kate's third stroke Noi said, 'Let's both work on him. That should bring him around fairly quickly. You concentrate on his butt; I will work on his thighs, which, as you can see, have barely been touched.'

Kate and Noi began beating Harrison simultaneously, Kate with the riding crop and Noi with the belt. They quickly fell into a pattern of alternation, so that each had time to prepare and deliver a careful stroke and yet Harrison never had a moment's respite.

Kate realised she was in a state of heightened awareness. She breathed deeply and steadily; her body flowed smoothly from one position to the next, as if she were dancing. Her mind was clear. She noted each change in the colour of Harrison's flesh, each moan, each change in his breath. She was gloriously aware of her own strength and power. She felt the same power emanating from the woman beside her.

There was excitement, incredible arousal, but it was controlled, harnessed, focused on her victim. She realised suddenly that she no longer felt angry with Harrison, that she felt only pity and amusement at his plight.

He began moaning and crying in a new voice. 'Please, forgive me, Katherine. I'm sorry, so sorry. Please accept my apology. Please, please, stop. I can't take any more.'

Noi paused and Kate did likewise. 'What do you think?' the Thai asked. 'Is he sincere? Should we stop?'

Kate stood next to the table, looking into Harrison's tear-stained face. She knew that her own face was flushed, and that her undergarments clung to her body, damp with her sweat. She didn't care. She was full of power.

Harrison looked at her, true contrition in his face. 'Please, Katherine,' he said.

'I think he really means it,' said Kate finally. 'I think he'll think twice in the future before underestimating a woman.

'Should I untie him?' she asked Noi, who was over at the trunk again.

'Not quite yet,' said Noi. 'He has one more lesson. I want to teach him what it feels like to be fucked.'

As Noi returned to the table, Kate caught her breath. The Thai had a large, realistic phallus strapped to her groin. With her swelling breasts, muscular physique and the magnificent, erect cock, Noi looked like a fantastic hermaphrodite.

Kate sank back into her chair, feeling a bit weak. She found the sight unbelievably erotic.

Noi walked around to where Harrison could see her. She thrust the rubber phallus into his face. 'Suck it,' she said, her voice a bit husky. 'Get it nice and wet. The wetter you make it, the less it will hurt.'

Harrison seemed to have given up all resistance. Meekly, he took the simulated cock into his mouth and liberally anointed it with his saliva. Kate watched intently as the bizarre scene continued to unfold.

Noi returned to her former position behind Harrison. She grabbed his strap-reddened cheeks and held them open as she positioned her dildo against his anus. 'Relax, Edward,' she said briefly; then, with a jerk of her hips, she entered him.

A loud groan came from Harrison's lips. Kate could see that half of Noi's phallus was buried in his arse. The Thai pulled back so that only the tip remained within the tight circle of muscle, then pushed again, penetrating more deeply.

Harrison did not move or struggle. He simply lay there, moaning, as Noi ploughed his hole, slow then fast, straight in and then from an angle, the muscles in her buttocks tensing beautifully with each thrust.

Kate slipped her hand inside her soaking crotch. She couldn't help herself. She could see that Noi was getting excited, too. Perhaps the dildo was double-ended, the Thai having a matching rod buried deep in her cunt. The thought thrilled her. Noi's eyes were closed and she was panting. Straining, every muscle taut, she pushed every inch of her cock into Harrison's aching hole and ground her pelvis against him.

Noi gave a little cry as her frame went limp in the spasms of orgasm. Kate was only moments away from her own climax when she felt a hand on her shoulder. 'Stop,' said Gregory. 'Not yet. Not quite yet.' He gently took her wrist and pulled her hand away from her pulsing sex. Then he raised it to his lips and kissed her fragrant, sticky fingers.

'Ah, my Kate,' he murmured, nuzzling her hand. In the midst of sexual frustration, she felt a different kind of relief. His cold, harsh manner was gone. Had it all been nothing more than an act for Harrison's benefit?

Noi had recovered and was now bustling around, untying Edward Harrison's arms and legs and helping him to sit up. 'Are you all right?' she asked him. He nodded mutely. 'Good. Then get dressed and get out of here. We are finished with you.' Slowly, stiffly, he began to don his clothes. He looked around for his tie.

Noi was wearing it around her neck. 'I think I will keep this,' she said with a little laugh. 'To remember you, Edward.'

Now Gregory spoke up. 'If I were you, Harrison, I'd get out of the country. It won't be long before Hakim and Malachevsky come looking for you. Didn't I hear something about South America?'

Harrison gave a tired nod. 'I already have the tickets. I'll move up my departure plans and leave tomorrow night.'

He paused. 'What about the ransom, the fifty thousand dollars for Katherine's release?'

'As you can see, Edward, Kate is here of her own free will.' Kate blushed at the implication, then shook her shame away. What did she care what Edward Harrison thought of her? Given what she knew, what she had seen tonight, she could damage his reputation far more than he could injure hers. 'Besides, with seven hundred and fifty thousand dollars in hand, I hardly need fifty thousand more.' Gregory pulled himself to his full height. 'Now get out,' he said, a hint of menace in his voice. 'I never want to see your face again.'

Noi unlocked the padlock and Harrison scurried out the door, slamming it behind him.

In the wake of his departure, the three of them stood there, looking at each other. For a moment, Kate had the urge to laugh. Then she sensed the tension, the electricity flowing among them. The dynamics had shifted. Her power had subsided, sinking back into the hidden recesses of her soul from whence it had emerged. She was, once again, Gregory's slave.

Gregory gave her a smile that was at once both sweet and mocking. 'Now it is your turn, Kate. I, for one, have not forgotten that you are my prisoner.'

He laughed a little. 'Get out of those wet clothes,' he said, 'and get up on the table.'

Kate unfastened her bra and peeled off her sodden

knickers. She stood next to the table, unsure of what was expected.

'Chest on the table,' said Gregory, 'and ass in the air. More or less the same position as your hapless former boss.'

Her heart pounding, Kate complied.

'Should I tie her, Ji?' asked Noi.

'Oh, I don't think that will be necessary,' said Gregory. 'Kate knows how to be still and obey.'

Noi came close to the table, checking and adjusting Kate's position. She folded Kate's T-shirt and put it like a pillow under Kate's cheek. The Thai was tall enough that her sex was just even with the table edge. Kate could not take her eyes off the smooth folds and dark crevices. She caught a whiff of Noi's scent and, before she realised it, stuck her tongue out, reaching for that fragrant valley.

'Aha!' said Noi. 'So you want to taste me, do you, Kate?' Mortified, Kate closed her mouth. Noi leant close and kissed Kate's lips. 'Some other time, Kate, I will make you eat me until I come. Tonight, though, we have other plans for you.'

Now Gregory came into view. 'Which would you prefer, Kate? The strap or the crop?' Kate realised that Noi had kept Harrison's belt as well as his necktie.

Kate considered the question seriously. She longed to feel and understand the sensations she had inflicted on Harrison with the riding crop. On the other hand, Noi had said that the belt was more painful. She wondered if she could endure it.

A part of her mind followed this internal debate, horrified and amazed that she could be engaged in such an argument. She pushed that part of her away.

'The strap,' she said finally.

'You're sure?' asked Gregory with respect and concern in his voice. 'You know that Noi will not spare you.'

She nodded, feeling she had made the right choice. 'I know,' she said.

The first cut made her wonder, though. The hard edge of the leather left a burning trail on her flesh which became more painful over time instead of subsiding. She whimpered in spite of herself. Noi did not pause, but delivered sharp, rhythmic blows that felt like knives carving into her. She felt her skin tearing open, though she knew from watching Noi with Harrison that her strokes would not draw blood. Kate gripped the edges of the table and gritted her teeth. Gregory sat in a chair opposite her, observing her face and Noi's artistry.

Through half-closed eyelids, Kate watched her master watching her. His steel-blue eyes flitted from her face to her leather-torn flesh. His sensual lips were parted; she could see his excitement. His powerful hands rested on his thighs and, as she watched, began to move up and down in rhythm with Noi's strokes. He was so beautiful, so wild, seething with energy barely held in check.

The pain had begun to blur; she relaxed and concentrated on the sensations as the leather kissed her again and again. Her sex tingled and twitched, hungering for penetration, but she did not strain or rub herself against the table. She was perfectly still, perfectly open, a willing sacrifice to her master's pleasure.

'Enough,' she heard him say sharply. 'I think we're losing her.' The blows stopped, and suddenly the pain rushed in like a tidal wave. She felt dizzy, and a little scared.

'I'm all right,' she reassured him, her voice shaky. 'I'm fine.'

'You deserve a reward,' said Gregory, smoothing her hair away from her eyes. 'Noi, come over here so Kate can see you.'

The Thai came into view. She had removed the corset; she was now gloriously nude, aside from her boots. As Kate watched in fascination, Noi snapped a leather harness around her waist, anchoring it with straps around her thighs. Then she attached another dildo.

Unlike the realistic phallus she had used to bugger Harrison, this one did not mimic a cock. It was bright

179

purple and circled with concentric ridges. It bulged, much wider at the end than at the base. And it was obviously much larger than the seemingly enormous one Noi had used on Harrison. Kate judged that at its narrowest, the dildo was four inches in diameter, an inch or two thicker at the end.

'I'll bet your hot little cunt is really hungry after tonight's activities,' laughed Gregory. 'But I think Noi can satisfy even you.'

The *mamasan* positioned herself behind Kate in exactly the same position she had used on Harrison. Kate gasped in pain as the Thai dug her fingernails into her lacerated bottom, and then in pleasure as Noi slid the hard rubber dildo into her eager cunt.

Despite the size of the toy, it went in easily. Gregory was right, of course; her whole being ached to be fucked. And Noi was ready to oblige.

The rubber felt foreign; solid and unyielding, no respite, no escape. Noi hammered into her, then pulled out slowly so that Kate could feel each of the ridges as it caught and then released the edges of her hole. The huge dildo stretched her deliciously, but she wanted more. She pushed her hips back towards the woman fucking her, begging for deeper penetration, harder strokes.

As if in answer, Noi removed herself entirely. 'No,' cried Kate, 'please don't stop!' The next instant, she was full again, but this time with living, burning flesh.

Gregory! It was not possible, of course, but he felt longer, thicker, harder than the outrageous dildo. She could feel his cock pulse, shift, probe – alive and aware – seeking the heart of her pleasure.

As before, she felt his heat, his inner fever igniting her. Blazing, searing, hot desert winds blowing through her inner canyons, tropical sun scorching her. Pain and yet not pain. She saw herself naked on an altar, consumed by the flames of sacrifice.

'I'll fuck you for ever, Kate,' she heard Gregory say, his breathing laboured. 'I'll fuck every hole, every inch of your body, in every crazy, profane, perverse way you can imagine. You are mine, my slut, my slave, my goddess of sin.'

She felt him swelling, ballooning, about to explode. She let herself float, be pulled along with him.

'Fuck you, Kate, fuck you!' he yelled, his cock bursting within her. 'I love you.'

Chapter Ten
Chinatown

*K*ate awoke after the scene at the fishing shack with the disquieting feeling that the world had changed. The red traces of Noi's strapping were still clearly visible, tattooing her buttocks. She swallowed hard as she looked over her shoulder, studying them in the mirror. This was the first time her encounters with Gregory had left lasting marks. She guessed it would not be the last.

The sight of the livid stripes criss-crossing her flesh scared and fascinated her. Gingerly, she touched one of the welts with her finger. It stung, though the pain was a faint echo of the original stroke. Details from the previous night ran in her mind: the intoxicating flow of power, rushing through her arm to the crop as she punished Harrison; Noi, glorious and severe with her pierced nipples and strap-on; rapture and release as Gregory's cock seared her sex. She ached there now, remembering, wanting him.

She recalled his harshness and his moodiness. It was atypical. Normally he remained serenely in control, confident and a bit condescending as he observed and manipulated those around him. Last night he had been different, torn, unsettled. She had caught flashes of some darkness in him, some confusion or indecision. She did not understand.

He had driven her home, stonily silent for the entire trip. Kate wondered if he was angry. Had she displeased him somehow? His brutal passion in the shack suggested otherwise. He had kissed her tenderly when he left her at the threshold then disappeared without a word, leaving her perplexed and disturbed.

She could only wait, be patient and see what happened next. She found this passive stance strangely comforting.

Kate dressed for work, selecting a loose skirt and eschewing underwear. Even so, the slightest brush of fabric on her skin reminded her of her hidden badges of submission. Each twinge brought a little smile to her face and increased the dampness in her crotch. Have I really come to this, that I take such pleasure in my fall? She knew it was an idle question.

At DigiThai the next morning, everyone seemed to know that Harrison had disappeared. His office was emptied of personal belongings. Kate assumed the role of temporary manager. She reassured the staff and encouraged them to get on with their work. Then she asked Anchana to make an appointment for her to see Somtow, realising she could not put off her confession any longer.

She sat in her office, staring blankly at the screen and trying to collect her thoughts. Anchana rang to tell her that Somtow would come by at two o'clock. She had hardly hung up when the telephone rang again. It was David.

'Kate! I'm glad that I caught you in!'

'Hello, David. It's good to hear your voice.' It was. His warm tone and familiar inflections immediately soothed her jangled nerves.

'How are things?' he asked.

'Oh, David, you wouldn't believe it if I told you!' Then she did tell him, an edited version of the tale that included Harrison's double-dealing, unmasking and flight, but omitted her Grotto performances and the very personal punishment meted out to her former boss.

'So now what?' David asked when she was through. 'Will you be staying in Thailand? Or are you coming home?'

'At the moment, I am the acting general manager of DigiThai. I certainly can't leave until they find someone to replace me.' In fact, Kate realised in surprise, the thought of leaving Bangkok had not even crossed her mind.

'So you'll be there for the next week or two.'

'It looks like it.'

'That's great. Because I'm coming to visit, next week.'

Kate felt a surge of panic. David, here? What would she do about Somtow, about Gregory?

'Are you sure you can get the time off, David? It's such a long trip; you shouldn't plan to come for less than two weeks.'

'It's already done. I picked up the tickets this morning. I arrive in Bangkok around midnight next Wednesday.'

Kate said nothing, full of discomfort. She cared deeply for David; he was her faithful friend and long-time lover. Somehow, though, she couldn't imagine him here, couldn't fit him, mentally, into the crazy patchwork of her current life.

Across the miles, David sensed her hesitation.

'I really miss you, Kate,' he said softly. 'But I understand that things might be different between us. I just want the chance to see you, a chance for us both to see where we stand.'

His generous spirit melted her. 'Of course, David. I miss you, too. I'm so confused by everything that's happened here that I really don't know what I want or need.' Or who, she added to herself. She was beginning to understand that the time for choice was coming.

'Wonderful. I'll send you my detailed itinerary by email. Can you meet me at the airport?'

'I'll be there,' she replied, noting that he didn't ask if he could stay with her.

'I made a hotel reservation,' he said quietly. 'I wasn't

sure that you'd be comfortable with the idea of having me as your house guest.'

Bless his sensitivity. 'Thank you, David. You are truly a remarkable person.'

'So are you, Kate.'

There was an awkward pause.

'I'll see you next Wednesday, then,' said Kate finally.

'Next Wednesday. I can hardly wait.'

Somtow arrived promptly at two. Kate met with him in the conference room. Somehow she felt that she needed to keep a table between them. She made sure that the door was closed.

'Katherine, you are looking lovelier than ever,' the Thai began.

Kate felt the tracks on her buttocks burning. 'Please, Somtow. There are serious things that we need to discuss.'

'I was definitely serious,' he said earnestly, but his eyes were twinkling. 'However, I suppose that you called me here to talk about Edward Harrison.'

Kate nodded. 'I have some very disturbing things to tell you,' she said, trying to figure out how to get started.

'I already know,' said Somtow simply.

'Know what?' she asked, startled.

'Everything.' He smiled kindly and reached across the table for her hand. 'Gregory Marshall called me this morning and told me the entire story.'

'Everything?' Kate asked, wondering exactly how much Gregory would have shared.

'About Harrison's embezzlement and industrial espionage. About how he hired you to distract me. About how you discovered the plot and how you and Marshall foiled it.'

Kate searched his face, trying to grasp whether he really knew the details.

'I know that you and Marshall have a relationship. I have known that for some time. He's a strange character, with some tastes that even I do not share, but basically he is a decent person.' The handsome Thai smiled wryly. 'I understand, Katherine, that I could never hope to keep you completely for myself.'

Kate shook her head. 'Somtow, I can't go on like this. It's too confusing, too draining. David, my lover from Boston, called this morning. He's coming to Bangkok next week. What am I going to do, with three men in one city? I've got to simplify my life before I go insane.' She sighed. 'The trouble is, I want you all. Each of you is unique and exciting in his own way. How can I choose between you?'

Somtow saw she was in significant distress. 'From my perspective, you do not need to choose. I see no reason why you should not take as many lovers as you wish.' A mischievous gleam lit his face. 'However, if you really do believe that you must make a decision, I have a suggestion.'

Kate brightened. 'Anything would help.'

'Why not have a contest, a showdown of sorts? Invite all three of us to make love to you at once. Seeing us, feeling us, knowing us, side by side, may help you see your own desires more clearly. When you compare us directly, perhaps your path will be obvious.'

'Are you serious, Somtow?' Kate didn't know whether to laugh. What a typical suggestion to come from her debauched prince!

'Definitely. Maybe you will discover which one of us is right for you, which one of us pleases you the most. Maybe you will change your mind and decide you still want us all. Either way, it will be an adventure that you will remember all your life.'

It was a crazy, reckless idea. Still, as Kate mentally reviewed the last six weeks, the wild things that she had done, the wild person she had become, the proposal had a certain symmetry that attracted her. What more appropriate way to conclude this period of sexual excess and unbridled lust than by staging the most extreme, orgiastic episode of all?

'I'm willing to do it,' she said finally. 'And you're obviously willing. Even eager,' she added slyly. 'But what about Gregory, and David? Will they agree?'

'If they want you,' said Somtow, 'they will. And I cannot imagine that they would not want you as desperately as I do.'

Somehow he was behind her. His arms went around her waist. He buried his face in her hair, left soft kisses on her neck. 'Leave all the arrangements to me, Katherine,' he said. 'I will reserve a suite at the Oriental Hotel where we can all relax in comfortable luxury. I will also speak to Gregory, and to David if you like. It will soothe their masculine egos to think of this as a competition between us men, rather than as a show for your sole benefit where you will choose your favourite performer.'

Somtow was as good as his word. Gregory called her Friday afternoon to confirm his intention to participate in the gathering.

'I wouldn't miss it,' he told her, the usual edge of mockery in his voice. 'The chance to watch you being fucked by other men, to see you writhe and hear you moan! A most delightful show, I expect!'

He paused. 'I have no doubt about your ultimate choice, my sweet. I have known that you were mine from the very start. However, if it amuses you to play this scene, I will let you have your fun.'

Kate felt a stab of annoyance at his conceit that almost cancelled out her excitement.

'Don't be so sure, Gregory,' she said smoothly. 'You have never met David, and you hardly know Somtow.'

'But I know you, Kate.' His voice was low, barely audible. 'I know you better than you know yourself.' He was silent for a moment, then continued briskly. 'In any case, I called for another reason as well. I want to offer you a job.'

'A job? I have a job.'

'Well, I thought this might stimulate your creative

juices, as they say.' He gave a little laugh. 'I've decided to use some of the money from the TFX deal to start a new club.'

'You're planning on keeping that money?' Kate found his greed depressing.

'Certainly. I earned it, didn't I?'

Kate didn't trust herself to respond rationally.

'Anyway, what I have in mind is something more modern than The Grotto, and more – specialised. A cyberclub that better reflects my particular interests and talents.'

'An S and M cyberclub? You can't be serious!'

'Oh, I most definitely am. Bangkok is already considered the sex capital of the world. There is a significant minority of visitors, not to mention residents, whose inclinations are less – shall we say – traditional than my customers at The Grotto. I will offer immersive fantasy as well as live performances; the watchword will be "interactive".'

'I'm considering calling it Club O. Or perhaps, Justine's. What do you think?'

'Where do you see me fitting into this new venture?' Kate asked a bit stiffly. Was he envisioning her as one of the performers? Was this all an elaborate plan to subject her to ever-increasing humiliation and punishment?

'I would like you to design the environment – be my technical and creative resource. Your projected 3D work would fit right in, but that would be just the start. I'm sure that you can come up with lots of ideas, given your recent experience and training.'

'And of course you will always be welcome on my stage at Club O . . .'

Kate sighed. He was so infuriating, and so appealing. 'I'll think about it,' she said. She certainly couldn't put such an engagement on her CV. Still, she found the possibilities interesting, from both a professional and a personal perspective.

'Let me know when I see you at the showdown,' he

said. 'Until then, I'll stay out of your hair. By next Saturday, I want to be sure that you're missing me.

'Oh by the way,' he added in an offhand tone, 'I gave about two-thirds of the TFX money to the royal charities for slum children. I figured that I needed some good karma to balance out the evil intentions I have for the remainder.'

He hung up before she could voice her astonishment.

Friday afternoon brought her a second offer of employment. Somtow called to ask if she would take the position of Managing Director for DigiThai on a permanent basis. 'I do not know if I will be staying in Thailand, Somtow,' she answered. 'Depending on how things turn out at the "showdown", I might decide to return to Boston with David.'

'That would be a great loss,' said her prince. 'I think you belong here, Katherine, in this sensual, experimental, changeable city. However, I do not need a decision now. I just want you to know that I value your intelligence, skill, and dedication, as much as your more tangible assets.'

Kate leant against a pillar in the arrivals area of the international terminal waiting for David. She scanned the double doors nervously. The monitors indicated his plane had landed, but she knew from experience how long it could take to clear immigration and customs.

Her feelings about seeing David were incredibly mixed. She recalled their closeness, the easy comfort of their relationship, with a kind of amazement. Life had been so simple then. She reviewed all the good times they had shared; movies and the concerts; gourmet meals and lazy evenings in front of the television; deep conversations and strong, sweet lovemaking. Somehow she couldn't make it real. They felt like someone else's memories.

I have changed. I am not the woman who loved David, not the woman he loved. He will see that. The thought filled her with a poignant sense of loss.

Then she remembered David's boldness in the Boston airport, and their long-distance dalliance a few weeks before. Perhaps David had changed also. Maybe this time in Thailand would encourage him to explore and develop the kinkier, more adventurous self that she had glimpsed in those encounters. Certainly, Bangkok has had that effect on me, she thought wryly.

The doors to the secured area swung open and a stream of passengers began to emerge. Kate moved over to the railing, pushing her way through the cheerful, noisy crowd so she could see better.

When David finally trudged out, she didn't recognise him for a moment; he wasn't her usually energetic, well-groomed lover. He was pale and drawn, with dark circles under his eyes. His brown curls were dishevelled and stuck up from his head. One tail of his wrinkled shirt dangled outside his trousers, while the other was tucked in. He wearily dragged a suitcase behind him, as if he barely had the energy to put one foot in front of the other.

Did I look that bad when I arrived, Kate wondered, her heart filling with affection and concern. 'David!' she called out. 'Over here!'

He looked up and scanned the crowd. His face brightened as he located her. 'Kate! You have no idea how glad I am to see you!'

His pace quickened and in a few moments he was at her side. Kate held out her arms. 'Welcome to Bangkok, David.'

She felt his arms encircle her as he returned her hug: strong, warm, comfortable, familiar. They hung there motionless for what seemed like a long time, neither wanting to end the embrace. Finally David loosened his grip and kissed her with closed lips. 'Thank you for coming to meet me.' He stood back a bit and eyed her hungrily. 'You look wonderful, Kate. Life in the tropics agrees with you.'

'To be honest, David, you look like hell!' She smoothed his curls with gentle fingers. 'Believe me, though, I understand exactly how you feel! Let's get you to your hotel, and to bed.'

Kate took David's suitcase pull in one hand and his hand in the other, and led him towards the ranks of waiting taxis. 'Which hotel are you booked in?' she asked.

'The Montien,' he said, not noticing the odd look that flitted across her face. 'It's on Suriwong Road, near the business district, or so I was told.'

'Yes,' said Kate quietly. 'I know it well.' She turned to the driver and used her rudimentary Thai to bargain for the fare. Soon they were on the highway into the city, the neon signs and tenements shooting past.

David leant back and closed his eyes. 'God, I'm exhausted,' he said. 'I knew you were far away, but I don't think I really understood how far.'

Kate took his hand. 'I know you must feel pretty limp and bleary-eyed at the moment. It takes a couple of days to get over it. It helps to think in terms of the current time zone. Don't keep reminding yourself what time it is in Boston. Instead, try and adapt yourself to the schedule here as quickly as you can. Force yourself to go to bed when it's night-time here. Don't allow yourself to nap during the day, even if you think you can't keep your eyes open. And so on.'

'I certainly could use a bed right now!'

'Go ahead and doze. I'll wake you when we arrive.'

David settled back into the seat. In five minutes he was snoring softly. Kate took the opportunity to look him over more thoroughly. Rumpled and worn as he was, he was still attractive. In sleep, his boyish features were peaceful and relaxed. Red-brown curls framed his smooth, tanned forehead. The hint of a smile curved his full lips. His russet eyelashes were as thick as a girl's, but the blunt-fingered hands that lay in his lap and the wiry muscles exposed by his short-sleeved shirt testified to his delightful masculinity.

Kate remembered those hands on her bare flesh and gave a delicious little shiver. She allowed her gaze to travel to his crotch. In fact there seemed to be some swelling there. Perhaps he was in the midst of some lascivious dream. She longed to touch him, to stroke him to full hardness, but she restrained herself. He needed his sleep. They were in a public place. Most of all, given her own uncertainties about him, she felt it wasn't right to encourage him.

So she spent the ride in fantasy. She imagined unzipping his fly and waking him with her mouth. He would be rigid almost immediately, she knew. She would slide her tongue up and down his smooth shaft, then swallow him suddenly, burying her nose in the hairy tangle at the root. He would cry out, would nearly come, and she'd pull back, barely teasing him with her lips until he regained control. Then she would engulf him again.

She knew him so well. He would want to lay her down on the seat with legs spread wide. More than anything, he liked to be in her pussy. This time, though, she would take command. She would climb into his lap, her back to his chest, and ever so slowly take him into her. She felt the juices flowing there now as she pictured it. Then she would ride him, hard, the way she liked it. If he seemed too close to coming, she would stop for a moment. She could imagine their laboured breathing, smell the sweat and the sex as they sat poised in one of these moments. Then she would begin again, slamming herself down on his cock, twisting and grinding her way to orgasm.

David stirred in his slumber and murmured something unintelligible. His partial erection had become more prominent. Suddenly, Kate felt ashamed at her own selfishness. What about his pleasure? She had an inkling, though, that he would enjoy being taken that way, being used by her for her own satisfaction. It was, after all, a type of pleasure that she understood.

The cab pulled up at the hotel. Kate shook David's shoulder gently. 'We're here, David. Wake up.'

He opened his eyes, yawned and stretched. 'Mmm,

that felt good. I had some interesting dreams, too.' He grinned at Kate.

'About me?' she asked demurely.

'What do you think?' he said, his grin broadening. He glanced down between his legs. The bulge in his pants provided an obvious answer.

'You'll have to tell me,' said Kate with an answering smile. 'But not tonight. You need sleep more than you need me.'

'You think so?' he asked, his eyes serious though his tone was humorous.

'Come on, David!' Kate grabbed his suitcase and carried it in to the reception desk. She didn't want to pursue the conversation.

Though it was past midnight, the lobby was bustling. Loud laughter came from the bar. Kate could feel the pounding beat from the disco downstairs through the soles of her shoes. She remembered her first visit here, her trembling and hesitation as she opened the door of Room 1263. She felt a sharp pang of desire at the thought that Gregory might be up there at this very moment. This was swiftly followed by a stab of envy as she wondered who might be his companion.

'Do you want to come upstairs with me?' David's voice broke into her reverie. There was a hint of sadness in his eyes. 'You know I'd like you to.'

'Not tonight, David,' said Kate gently. 'You are very tired. And I'm – confused.'

'I understand, Kate. It's true, I'm beat.' He pressed the button to summon the lift.

'Why don't we get together for lunch tomorrow,' she said. 'Come meet me at DigiThai around noon and I'll take you to one of my favourite little places.' He nodded as she handed him her business card.

The elevator door slid soundlessly open. 'Until tomorrow, then,' said David, kissing her lightly.

'Tomorrow. Sleep well, David.' The door closed and he was gone.

Kate stood motionless in front of the lift, fighting

temptation. More than anything, she wanted to go up to 1263, to see for herself if it was occupied. Of course, she knew Gregory would not appreciate the intrusion. He would punish her severely for it. She didn't mind; it would be worth it.

Then again, perhaps the desire she felt pulling her towards the twelfth floor was actually his summons. Maybe it was a test of her sensitivity, of her obedience to his will. How could she not answer his call?

She shook her head, trying to clear her thoughts, and the spell faded. It was late. She was tired and over-wrought, tense from her encounter with David. She was allowing her imagination to overwhelm her good sense. Sleep was what she needed, as much as David did. Still, she felt a strange reluctance as she turned to find the taxi and make her way home.

David arrived promptly at noon. His sports shirt was freshly pressed and his hair was combed, but he still looked tired.

Kate wore a beige linen suit with a skirt that reached her knees. She had an appointment with some new customers in the afternoon, the proprietors of one of the oldest textile companies in Thailand.

'You look so businesslike!' said David, admiring her. 'Though a bit conservative.'

Kate laughed. 'This is my Managing Director uniform. My software engineer uniform is much more casual.'

She took his hand. 'Come on. Let's go eat.' She held open the door of the office suite for him, then summoned the lift.

The doors opened, and Somtow stepped out of the lift. 'Katherine!' he said, taking her hand briefly, then relinquishing it. 'I was just coming to see you. I was hoping to persuade you to join me for lunch. There are a couple of company issues that we need to discuss.'

Kate smiled despite herself at Somtow's attempts to present their relationship as purely business. 'I'm sorry,

Somtow, but I already have a lunch engagement. This is David Berman, an old friend from Boston.'

'David, this is Somtow Rajchitraprasong, founding partner of DigiThai Limited.'

David smiled and held out his hand. 'A pleasure, sir.'

Somtow answered with a smile of his own. 'Please call me Somtow. It is the custom here in Thailand to call people by their first names. The pleasure is mine, David.'

The two men stood for a moment with their hands linked, studying each other. Kate felt distinctly awkward. 'I was going to take David to Suda's restaurant, for a taste of authentic Thai food.'

'An excellent idea,' said Somtow. 'Would you mind if I joined you?'

Kate's discomfort grew. 'Well, David just arrived last night, and we really haven't had any time to talk. Perhaps some other time . . .'

'It's OK; I'd be delighted to have Somtow come along,' David broke in as her excuses faded off. 'You two can even talk business. Everything here is new and interesting to me!'

The three of them strolled the two blocks to the restaurant, an informal open-air place with plastic tables and vinyl chairs on a quiet side street. It was busy, full of Thais eating, talking and drinking Mekong, the local whiskey. When the proprietress saw Somtow, however, she hurried over to seat them and serve them herself.

'*Sawatdi kha*!' she exclaimed, with a respectful *wai*. 'Welcome!' Kate realised that everyone knew who Somtow was.

'Shall I order for all of us?' he asked Kate and David. 'The Thai menu includes many dishes that do not appear on the English version.'

'Sounds great,' said David.

'Can I assume that you, like Katherine, enjoy spicy food?' There was just a hint of mischief in Somtow's voice.

'Definitely! Back in Boston, Kate and I have to work

195

hard to convince the waiters in the Thai restaurants that we really did want the food hot, as hot as they would make it at home.'

'We should have no problem satisfying that request here,' said Somtow with a smile. He launched into a long discussion with the owner in animated Thai, gesturing and pointing to the menu.

David turned to Kate with a grin. 'This is fantastic! A lifetime's dream fulfilled!'

Kate was still feeling uncomfortable in the simultaneous presence of her two lovers. On the other hand, they both seemed perfectly at ease. She was sure that Somtow knew who David was. Meanwhile, though Somtow's behaviour had been perfectly proper and above reproach, she suspected that David might guess Somtow's true role in her life.

Somtow completed the apparently complicated process of ordering and turned his attention back to the two Americans. 'Would you like to try a Singha beer, David? Or perhaps some Thai whiskey? I know that you have a meeting this afternoon, Katherine, so I will not try to tempt you. But you are on vacation, are you not, David?'

'I suppose you could call it that,' said David quietly. 'Mainly, I'm here to see Kate.'

Kate blushed at the naked emotion in his voice.

'However, I do want to experience what Thailand has to offer,' he continued. 'We've had Singha in Thai restaurants at home. So let's order some whiskey.'

'David, it's execrable stuff! They sell it for fifty cents a bottle.'

'Katherine,' chided Somtow. 'Have you tried it yourself?'

She shook her head, embarrassed at her outburst. She was on edge, she knew, and making a fool of herself.

'Then why not allow David to make his own evaluation?' Somtow signalled the owner and soon she brought a bottle of brown liquid labelled in Thai, a bucket of ice and tongs, and two glasses. Somtow loaded each glass with a few cubes, then poured an inch or two of the dark liquid. He handed David one of the glasses and lifted the other himself.

'To Katherine,' he said, with a twinkle in his eye.

'I'll drink to that,' said David. 'And to new experiences.'

Kate had a sense of *déjà vu*. She recalled her first evening with Somtow, in the garden.

David took a sip and began to cough. 'Whew! That is strong!' He tried another, smaller nip. 'But you know, it doesn't taste bad at all.' His third drink was larger.

'May I try it?' asked Kate, feeling left out in spite of herself.

'Of course.' David passed the glass to her and she sipped it cautiously. It burnt her tongue and throat, but did have a pleasant, slightly sweet flavour – more like brandy than whiskey.

Somtow was watching her with a smile on his lips. 'You see, Kate. You should perhaps not make judgements without personal experience.'

Kate felt certain there was a deeper meaning to his comments. Was he making a reference to the planned showdown?

The food began to arrive, first one dish and then another, until the table was covered with fragrant savoury platters. Most of them Kate didn't recognise, but every one she tried was delicious. David appeared to be enjoying himself immensely. He ate with a hearty appetite while carrying on a lively conversation with their Thai companion.

Somtow was even more charming than usual. He regaled them with tales of Thailand: history, myth, folk tales, jokes. Before long, Kate relaxed. Clearly, Somtow and David got on well, despite the fact that they were rivals for her affection.

The table was littered with empty plates. Kate sighed in satisfaction. Then she looked at her watch and was alarmed at how late it was. She pushed back her chair. 'I apologise, but I have got to leave. I have an appointment on the other side of the city in less than half an hour.'

'Forgive me, David, for abandoning you. Somtow, could you please make sure that David gets back to his hotel?'

'Of course,' said Somtow, rising as she began to leave the table. 'On the other hand, I am free this afternoon. If you do not have other plans, David, perhaps you would like me to show you around the city?'

David had been looking slightly sleepy, but he perked up at Somtow's suggestion. 'I'd love it,' he said enthusiastically. 'I need something to distract me so I don't fall asleep. This jet lag is murder.'

'Then it is settled. Katherine, do not worry about David. I will take good care of him and give him some introduction to our Thai ways.'

I'm sure you will, thought Kate ironically. The same way, perhaps, that you introduced me? Then she realised how petty the thought was. Am I jealous? she wondered. Silly me. Somtow was gazing at her with something like adoration. Meanwhile David was watching Somtow.

'Have a good time, David.' She leant over and kissed his cheek. 'I'll give you a call at the hotel tonight. Maybe we can get together for dinner.'

'Goodbye for now, Somtow. I'll speak to you soon, and we can schedule some time to go over those business matters you mentioned.' She grinned wickedly at her prince, then turned to find a taxi.

Her meeting ran late and the traffic was even worse than usual. She didn't get back home until after seven. Kicking off her shoes, she settled down on the sofa and dialled the Montien.

The phone in David's room rang and rang, but there was no answer. He must be asleep, thought Kate. I'll bet Somtow ran him ragged, dragging him to every palace and temple in Bangkok. Deep down, though, she had other suspicions.

She was tired herself, and still full from lunch. She decided to take a shower, make herself a light snack and go to bed early.

Sometime around nine, her phone rang. She expected it to be David, but it was Somtow.

'I hope I am not disturbing you, Katherine,' he began. The contrition in his voice made her smile.

'Of course not. Is everything all right?'

'Well, yes. David and I just spent more time together than we had planned. I hope that you were not worried. I just dropped him at his hotel – he was exhausted.'

'I'm sure that you and he had a very active afternoon,' said Kate, allowing just a little irony into her voice. Somtow seemed not to notice.

'I spoke to him about the contest, Katherine.'

'And? What was his reaction?'

'First he laughed – a little sadly. Then he said that of course he would participate. I think that he would do anything for you, Katherine. He loves you dearly.'

'I know,' she said with a sigh. 'That doesn't make me feel any better about all this.'

'It is not your fault that you are irresistible.'

'Oh, stop it, Somtow!' Kate was chuckling in spite of herself. Then Somtow spoke again, in a much more serious tone.

'I need to see you, Katherine, before the contest.'

'That's not fair, Somtow. We agreed that I should not get involved with any of you until we all meet on Saturday evening.'

'Please, there is something that I want to give you. Have dinner with me tomorrow night.'

'Definitely not! I've noticed that you are especially dangerous at night!'

'Lunch then. Tomorrow. Please, Katherine.'

Kate hesitated. It was he who was irresistible, she thought.

'Have you been to Chinatown yet?' he asked in a lighter tone, sensing that she was hooked.

'No . . .' she began.

'There is a restaurant on Charoen Krung Road that has been in continuous operation for more than one hundred years. I know that you would love it. Tell me that you will meet me there.'

'All right, Somtow. But only for lunch. I do not want you planning to have me for dessert!'

'Of course, Katherine.' But, she realised, he didn't promise.

He gave her the address, then bid her good night. As she hung up the phone, she marvelled at his influence on her. He never commanded – he only requested. Yet she could no more refuse his requests than she could disobey Gregory's orders.

Kate took the bus to Charoen Krung Road. It was not far from DigiThai, no more than two or three miles, but it was a slow trip. The vehicle oozed through the heavy traffic. Pedestrians, *tuk tuks* and daredevil motorcyclists weaved their way through the snarl of cars and trucks.

Kate didn't mind the pace. The bus was air-conditioned. She sat next to a window where she could watch the passing sights.

The Chinese area of Bangkok was one of the oldest parts of the city. Tucked into a bend of the Chao Phya, it was a warren of narrow streets flanked by crumbling three-storey shop houses. Charoen Krung, the main thoroughfare, was barely wide enough for two cars to pass. The traffic crept sluggishly along its length, but the pavements bustled with commerce.

The street was lined on both sides with jewellery stores, their bright red signs emblazoned with gold lettering in English, Thai and Chinese characters. Some were glassed in, protected from the heat and the dust of the road, but many had open fronts stretching a quarter of a block or more. Inside, the walls too were crimson. Kate saw long counters and display cases with glittering contents. Customers sat on stools at the counters, bending over the cases or haggling with the proprietors.

In front of the gold shops vendors hawked everything

from fresh vegetables to movie posters. As Kate got off the bus, she took a deep breath. The air smelt different here. She caught spicy hints of anise and ginger mixed in with the normal exhaust fumes. She passed a traditional medicine shop, its murky interior lined with wooden drawers holding mysterious roots and herbs. A pale ginseng root floated in a glass bottle, its hairy extremities vaguely suggesting a human figure. The wizened, bespectacled shop owner behind the counter looked up as she paused. Flustered, she hurried on.

At the address Somtow had given her, she found a narrow door framed in Chinese script. There was no English sign. The door was open and led, she saw, to a steep, carpeted stairway. The building smelt of age, but there were also some rich food odours that she couldn't identify.

At the top of the stairs, she found a small ante-chamber made even smaller by the huge porcelain jars standing on either side of a curtained arch. She was met by an elderly Chinese man in a rusty black suit.

'Miss O'Neill?' he asked, his accent making it difficult for Kate to understand him. She nodded. 'Please come with me.'

He held the curtains aside for her. They entered a cavernous room, two storeys high. Fans turned lazily above them, hanging from the embossed tin ceiling. Round tables were scattered around the room, but only one or two of them were occupied. None of the diners was Somtow.

'This way,' said her guide, gesturing toward the back of the room. Here, Kate saw, there were wood-panelled walls that reached halfway to the ceiling. As they came closer, she realised that these were enclosed booths made of teak or mahogany, arranged around a central corridor. Floor-length curtains of heavy brocade covered the entrances, ensuring the privacy of the occupants. Halfway down the corridor, Kate and her guide stopped, and the Chinese man knocked on the door post.

Somtow's voice was muffled by the curtains. 'Come in,' he said, sweeping the curtains aside. 'Come in, Katherine.'

The interior of the booth was furnished with cushioned brocade benches and a table covered in white linen. It was surprisingly spacious. There was no sense of being confined. The top was open; immediately above their heads, Kate saw one of the fans twirling slowly.

Somtow closed the curtains and took her hands. 'Thank you for coming. Please, make yourself comfortable.' She seated herself on the bench. He smiled at her delightedly. 'Well? What do you think?'

Kate looked around her. 'Interesting,' she said. 'I've certainly never seen anything like it.'

'The Chinese conduct all important business over food,' explained Somtow. 'And sometimes, discretion is important. The Three Moons restaurant has seen five generations of negotiations, deals, intrigues and coups. Not too mention illicit meetings and lovers' rendezvous.'

Kate just smiled at his enthusiasm.

'In addition,' he continued, pouring them some tea, 'the food is exceptional. I took the liberty of ordering Peking Duck for us. They need twelve hours advance notice.'

Kate laughed. 'You are unbelievable! It seems that all you think about is food and sex!'

'Not so,' Somtow protested in mock seriousness. 'I will admit those are among my primary occupations, but I am also interested in business. You have not told me yet whether you will take the position I offered you.'

'After Saturday, I will let you know. After Saturday, everything may change.'

'I know,' said Somtow softly. 'Still, I am looking forward to it.' He reached across the table and stroked her cheek gently. Something inside her melted. Her eyes grew wet, and so did her sex.

'Are you hungry?' he asked after a moment. Kate nodded. He pressed a button on the wall that looked like an old-fashioned doorbell. In less than sixty seconds, there was a knock outside.

'Come in.' The elderly gentleman and a much younger man entered with two trays. The steam rising from them made Kate's mouth water. With remarkable speed, they set the food on the table and left the cubicle, closing the curtains behind them.

The food was wonderful, but they ate mostly in silence. Kate was surprised at Somtow's uncharacteristic reserve. She felt a strange tension growing between them. She picked up a morsel of duck with her chopsticks and placed it thoughtfully in her mouth. Was it because of David, she wondered? Or the coming moment of truth? She watched Somtow as he used his chopsticks to pull the juicy flesh from the bone then brought it to his lips. She was seized with the desire to kiss those lips, to run her hands over his smooth, firm limbs. She felt the pull of his body like magnetism.

Of course, she reminded herself, she had been celibate for more than a week now, in preparation. She had to laugh at herself. A week without sex these days seemed like a year.

Finally, she leant back on the cushions. 'I can't eat another bite,' she said. 'That was magnificent, though. Thank you.'

'I love to please you, Katherine,' he answered. 'As I am sure you know by now. As I told you, I have something for you. If you are finished, I will have them clear the dishes.'

He rang for the waiter and the dirty plates disappeared as quickly as they had arrived. The young man also brought them a fresh pot of tea.

When the curtains were closed again, Somtow reached into his pocket. He brought out a blue velvet box. 'I hope that you will accept this, Katherine, as a token of my love and respect for you. As something to remember me by, perhaps.'

Kate wanted to refuse the box, but the look in his eyes

stopped her. Silently, she took it from him and opened it.

It was a sapphire necklace, an oval pendant on a delicate gold chain. It was unbelievably beautiful.

Kate was overwhelmed. 'Somtow, I can't take this. This should be for your wife, not for me.'

'Nong has her own sapphires, Katherine. And she has the honour and misfortune of being my legal wife. I want you to have something tangible, something precious, something to convince you that you are more to me than just a playmate and a diversion.'

He was so sincere. Kate felt tears prick her eyes again. Without further comment she carefully fastened the chain around her neck. The stone sparkled in the hollow of her throat.

'Thank you, Somtow,' she said softly. 'I am deeply touched.'

Her prince watched her, a smile playing at the corners of his mouth. 'You look lovely,' he said. 'Of course, you would look lovelier still if you removed your blouse.'

'Somtow! You promised!'

'Promised what?' he said with mock innocence.

'That you would stick to the rules and wouldn't try to seduce me!'

Somtow grinned. 'I am sure that I never promised that!' He leant forward across the table. 'I would never make a promise that I could not keep. In any case, I have a feeling that you really want to take off your top.'

It was true, of course. The attraction that Kate had felt towards him during lunch was a hundred times stronger now. She glanced over at the curtains. They were tightly closed. 'The management would never enter a booth unannounced,' said Somtow. 'It would violate all the traditions.'

Without a word, she pulled her silk shell over her head. Then she unhooked her brassiere in the front and let it slide off her shoulders. She sat up straight, enjoying the hungry way he eyed her bared breasts.

'Ah, Katherine,' he sighed. 'I see that I was right.' He

picked up his chopsticks, reached across the table and deftly caught her left nipple between them. 'Quite stiff,' he commented approvingly. He applied a bit more pressure and the button of flesh swelled further. Her cunt muscles tensed and her clit tingled.

He switched to the other nipple, rolling it back and forth between the lacquered wood sticks. Kate gave a little moan and thrust her chest forward.

'You are incorrigible, Somtow,' she said when she had caught her breath. 'In any case, I'll bet that you're quite stiff yourself.'

'You would win that wager,' he chuckled. He stood up and Kate saw that he had already unzipped his trousers and released his erection, that he had been stroking himself with his left hand even as he used the chopsticks with his right.

'You know,' she said with a smile, 'I am still a bit hungry after all.' She grabbed one of the cushions from the bench and threw it on the floor in front of him. Then she knelt and began feasting on his smooth, cool flesh.

The slender Thai rested his hands on her shoulders and pressed his pelvis against her mouth. Kate worked his cock like a vacuum cleaner, sucking him as if to extract every drop of his come. She relished his slightly salty taste and the now-familiar whiff of sandalwood that came from him. He moaned, and she paused to admonish him. 'Shh!' she whispered. 'I don't want the management to come rushing in thinking that I'm doing you harm.'

'I cannot help myself, Katherine,' Somtow gasped.

'Maybe I need to gag you,' she said playfully, and then was a little shocked by her own words. Was her association with Gregory polluting her mind to such an extent?

She returned her attention to his cock, licking up and down its length before swallowing it again. The skin was petal-soft. She could feel the pulse of blood raging beneath.

As Somtow came closer to climax, Kate felt her own

heart beginning to pound. Her clit throbbed in the same rhythm as his cock, and she could feel her lower lips swelling, opening, aching for attention. She was determined, though, not to allow him access to her sex. Technically, at least, she wanted to adhere to the rules she had established. She wanted the contest on Saturday to be fair and unbiased. She sucked harder and lightly raked her teeth over his rigid flesh. Come on, Somtow, she thought. Come in my mouth, my sweet prince.

He hovered on the edge. Kate could feel his muscles tensing. But instead of letting go, he gently pushed against her shoulders, pulling out of her mouth. 'Turn around, please, Katherine. I want to share my pleasure with you.'

'No, Somtow. We all agreed, no sex until the showdown.'

'Oh?' He raised one eyebrow. 'And what do you call this that we have been doing for the last fifteen minutes?

'In any case, the notion that you should have no sexual contact with any of us was your idea. In my opinion, it is unnecessary, and unrealistic. You cannot segregate your feelings and desires that way. This lunch is part of the contest, Katherine.'

She realised he was right. Her body spoke for her even when her mind tried to remain uncommitted and in control.

'Please, Katherine,' Somtow almost whispered. 'Turn around.'

She did as he requested, resting her elbows on the table. He raised her skirt around her waist. However, he did't pull down her panties as she expected. Instead, he simply pushed the fabric covering her sex aside and entered her.

His shaft met no resistance. She was, she knew, wet and ready. He moved slowly, probing then withdrawing, somewhat constrained by the enclosing garment. The feeling was interesting, new, exciting.

Her buttocks and her bush were completely covered, yet there was this hard cock filling her. There was a kind of secret thrill to it, as if she could be fucked in the middle of a crowd and no one would know. As Somtow thrust harder, the force pulled on the fabric, tightening it deliciously against her clit. She reached down and stroked herself through the silk. The indirect stimulation sent sparks through her. She rubbed harder, but still kept the fabric between her fingers and her flesh.

Kate bit her lip to keep back her moans. 'Yes, Somtow,' she whispered hoarsely. 'Yes, my dear . . .'

As if her voice drove him to a frenzy, he began to pound his cock into her, burying the full length of it in her writhing body. Kate felt the spring of climax coiling inside her. 'Yes . . .'

There was a tearing sound. Strong as it was, the silk gave way before the force of his fucking. Somtow grabbed the torn scrap and pulled it off. She felt a breeze from the ceiling fan caress her bare cheeks as Somtow impaled her completely. The spring released itself. Exquisite vibrations shook her. Her cunt pulsed and shivered. And despite her best intentions, a loud cry of pleasure echoed in the high-ceilinged chamber.

For a long moment, the only sound was Kate's laboured breathing. She leant her head on her hands, still savouring the after-pulses of her orgasm. Somtow moved inside her, and Kate discovered with surprise that he was still hard. He had not come with her. She looked over her shoulder at his handsome, smiling face.

He stroked her arse gently. 'Katherine, my dear, you should never deny yourself.' He twisted his hips a little, so that his cock shifted slightly, bringing more vibrations.

'But what about you, Somtow? What about your pleasure?'

He paused for a moment. Then he rested a finger delicately on the tight knot of her anus. 'I would like to enter you here, Katherine. I want to explore your darker channel. May I?'

Kate was rocked by conflicting desires. On the one hand, his light touch raised memories of the intense pleasures awaiting her via that portal. His smooth, slender cock would feel glorious there, she guessed, dancing slippery and nimble in and out of her. Some part of her, though, still felt that dark door belonged to Gregory. He had taken her virginity there. It was probably absurd, but like virgins everywhere she attached special significance to this, felt that she owed him some special loyalty. Though Gregory had never asked for a promise, she realised she had made one, in her heart of hearts.

Still, how could she refuse sweet Somtow, so generous and devoted to her pleasure? But she could not bring herself to agree.

'No, Somtow. I hate to deny you anything, and I am deeply grateful for your asking. I will do just about anything that you request, but please, not that.'

Somtow looked surprised for a moment, then he seemed to understand. Did he, in fact, guess that her reservations revolved around Marshall? He leant over and planted a kiss on each of her buttocks.

'Of course, Katherine.

'In that case, would you be willing to take me, there?'

At these words a shock ran through Kate, followed by a surge of lust. She understood what he meant. Did she dare fulfill his request?

She turned to him, her heart pounding in her ears. 'How, Somtow? I don't know what to do'

He smiled gently. 'Use your intuition, Katherine. I trust you, and your sensual imagination.'

She nodded, still uncertain. Somtow unbuckled his belt and lowered his pants down to his ankles. He was hugely erect. He turned toward the table and bent over, his legs spread as wide as the trousers would allow. Another man in that position might have looked ridiculous. Somtow moved with simple grace, though, and his muscular, perfectly proportioned body changed what would have been a posture of humiliation into a gesture of lovely submission. He was offering himself to her, for his pleasure and hers.

Kate ran both palms over his swelling arse globes. The skin was smooth and soft as her own. The touch sent a thrill through her, tightening her nipples.

He was nearly hairless, but there was a touch of downy black around his scrotum. She reached between his thighs to cup his balls in one hand. They were tense, contracted by his arousal. She stroked her thumb over the wrinkled skin and Somtow moaned. She reached further forward and grasped his cock at the root. It was like iron, and pointed nearly vertical.

Still holding his shaft, she used her other hand to separate his cheeks. Here, there was no hair. The brown rosette lay naked, waiting for her. She blew upon it and saw the muscles tense in response to the moving air. She felt simultaneously drawn and repelled.

She remembered her fantasy in Singapore; Gregory ordering her to anal service. This felt very different. She was in control. She had the power to penetrate and to pleasure Somtow. Relinquishing her hold on Somtow's cock, she held his buttocks open and bent to touch her tongue to the tight curl of muscle.

The flesh was ridged and firm. The taste was strange, musty, but not unpleasant. She ran her tongue up and down the groove between his cheeks, then circled the entrance. Somtow made little noises of pleasure. She saw the muscles relax a little, inviting her. She lapped with the tip of her tongue against the tiny orifice that appeared. Then she pushed her tongue in as deeply as she could.

Somtow sighed and pressed his hips back, urging her further in. She twirled her tongue inside the opening. Her own anus twitched as she imagined the sensations she was providing. She felt powerful, daring, dirty.

She removed her tongue. It was not long enough. Instead, she licked her fingers until they were soaked with her saliva. Then she inserted two fingers, pushing them gently but firmly inside him.

It was hot, and damp. She could feel him clench down on her fingers. He rocked back and forth, sliding over her. She hooked her index finger and pulled back a bit, feeling the resistance at the entrance. Then she added a third finger. He twisted his hips. He was murmuring something in Thai.

She had small hands. Remembering him, skewered by Uthai's huge cock, she knew that her fingers were not enough to satisfy him. She wished for Noi's dildo. Heat flashed through her as she imagined herself with a strap-on, ploughing this open and willing arse before her.

Futile imaginings, though. She cast her mind about. What could she use to penetrate him as she knew he wanted?

Her eye fell on Somtow's chopsticks, lying on the table. Too thin, she thought. But the smooth lacquer might still feel interesting. She pulled out her fingers. A strong dark smell filled the cubicle. Somtow gave a little whimper of protest.

'Hush,' she said. 'I'll be right back.'

She grabbed the chopsticks and licked them well. Then she pushed one into him, a few inches only. She knew she had to be careful not to pierce the delicate membranes inside. She began to slide it in and out, as rapidly as she could. Somtow held very still, but the soft sounds that came from him told her he was enjoying it.

She held the stick motionless, just inside him. Then she carefully slid the second chopstick in next to the first. Rather than pushing them in, she pulled them apart slightly, stretching the muscles at the entrance.

'Oh, Katherine!' Somtow was barely intelligible. 'Oh, yes.' She pulled them further apart.

He wanted to be filled, stretched. How well she understood his feelings! But she lacked the anatomical capabilities to do what he desired, and she had few artificial possibilities available.

Still holding the lacquered sticks apart, she thought of the contents of her purse. She recalled her hairbrush. Perhaps that would do.

'I will be back in just a moment, my dear. Don't move.' She left the chopsticks protruding from him and went to get the brush. When she returned, she was struck by the perversity of the scene. Sensing her gaze, he tightened his sphincter and the sticks moved slightly. Kate gave a low laugh.

'I know, you want more. Well, I have something else for you here. Don't look, now,' she said with mock severity as he began to turn around.

The hairbrush was pale blue, made of hard plastic. It was the handle that interested her, a cylinder about six inches long and an inch in diameter that tapered near the end. Not in the same league as Uthai's cock, but, in her inexperience she might do damage with anything larger.

She looked again at Somtow's upraised posterior and the sticks rising from his anus. Incredible, she thought, stroking his pale cheek. She had a fleeting impulse to spank that white flesh, to see the red imprint of her palm. She suppressed this urge, almost before she was conscious of it. Her sex responded, though. New moisture flooded her.

Lubrication, Kate thought with an inner smile. Still gazing at her lover's body before her, she crouched down and slipped the brush handle into her cunt. With her other hand, she pressed her clit against the hardness. It was nearly enough to make her come again.

Not yet, she told herself sternly as she removed the makeshift dildo, now covered with her juices; she returned her attention to Somtow. 'You'll like this,' she said to him softly. Slowly, she pulled out first one chopstick and then the other. His rear opening was larger now. She blew on it again and watched the muscles contract.

'Relax,' she said, 'and open wide.' She positioned the tip of the plastic rod against him and pushed gently.

There was resistance for a moment, and then Kate could actually see his muscles release and open to her. She continued to apply a gentle, steady pressure. Little by little, the blue plastic disappeared into his hole, until finally all six inches were inside him.

211

'Do you like that?' she asked, incredibly turned on herself. The bristles of the brush stood up from his hole like some strange tail. Somtow only moaned.

'I'll assume that means yes,' she said softly. She took hold of the brush end and slowly pulled until only the tip remained inside him. Then, just as slowly, she pushed it back in. Gradually, she picked up the pace of her strokes, always careful not to press too suddenly or too hard. She spoke to him softly as she worked, building her own arousal and his.

'Somtow, you have no idea how hot you look, with my hairbrush in your butt. My princely lecher, you'd do anything for pleasure, wouldn't you?' She twisted the handle inside him. 'I know you'd like even more, something bigger and harder still, and, you know, Somtow, I'd love to give that to you. Someday I'd like to harness myself to a dildo and bugger you the way you really want it.'

Her pussy was gaping, moisture dripping down her thighs. Leaving the brush all the way inside him, she reached around his waist and grasped his cock. She circled it with her fingers. Somtow moaned but otherwise held still. She walked forward until her sex was even with his buttocks, then pushed her pelvis forward. As she raked her bulging clit back and forth over the stiff bristles, she squeezed Somtow's cock with all her strength.

He exploded in her hand, a long wail escaping his throat. His come flowed hot over her fingers. In the midst of his spasms, he thrust his hips backward, pushing the brush end deeper between her swollen lips. The sharp prick of the bristles on that tender flesh was what she needed, finally, to strip away the last shreds of her control. Kate yelled and ground herself against the painful barbs as her mind filled with the impossible image of the prickly brush-head disappearing into her vagina.

* * *

All was quiet save for the swish of the fan. Somtow still lay slumped on the table. Kate had collapsed on to the cushion on the floor. The Thai stirred, looked over his shoulder at his companion, and smiled in blissful satisfaction. He reached behind him and grasped the brush, pulling it out slowly. He closed his eyes, concentrating on the sensations as he did so.

He refastened his pants, noting with some chagrin that the tablecloth was damp with come. Then he knelt by Kate's side and kissed her until he roused her.

'Katherine, my sweet. How are you feeling?'

Kate sat up and looked around them. Her blouse and bra lay on the bench where she had discarded them. The tattered remains of her knickers and one damp chopstick sat under the table. In the throes of their passion, they had tipped over the teapot. The infamous hairbrush lay on the table in a puddle of tea.

Her breasts were sweaty and her hands sticky with Somtow's come. Her skirt was wrinkled and bunched up around her waist. There were little scratches on the insides of her thighs from the stiff brush.

She reached up and touched the sapphire at her throat, then gazed up at the sensitive, concerned face of her lover.

'Wonderful,' she said. 'I feel wonderful.'

Chapter Eleven

Showdown

Kate took the remainder of the afternoon off. In the state she was in, she could hardly return to the office. Even after she had straightened herself up as best she could, the taxi driver gave her a curious look. She could feel the residual dampness between her thighs as her bare bottom brushed the lining of her skirt.

Somtow had bid her farewell in such respectful tones that she was embarrassed. Even given his high opinion of her, personally and sexually, she guessed that she had surprised him that afternoon. She had surprised herself. She recalled the delicious feeling of being in control, the thrill of seeing Somtow's pliant, submissive body arrayed for her use. Was this what Gregory felt, she wondered, when he looked at her? She flashed back to the fishing shack, remembered being drunk on her own power as she scourged Edward Harrison. Perhaps she and Marshall were more alike than she had thought.

She had not heard from Gregory since the previous week, when he had called to share his cyberclub scheme. Unlike Somtow, he was sticking to the rules of the game. She smiled to herself, knowing that he was doing so only to frustrate her, to pique her desire for his attentions. She did want him. Her encounter with Somtow had awakened ideas that she wanted to explore with him. She could wait, though; she had learnt that lesson. Tomorrow night it would be her turn to make him wait.

The telephone was ringing when she let herself into the house. Slipping off her shoes, she ran to grab it. She sank wearily on to the sofa as she recognised David's voice. No guilt, she told herself. No regrets.

'Kate, I'm glad I reached you.'

'I just got home. I needed some time by myself – to prepare.'

Kate could almost see him nod. 'I understand. Look, I am really sorry that I conked out on you last night.'

'No problem.'

'No, really, I apologise. I really wanted to have dinner with you. But I was bushed. Somtow took me all over: the Grand Palace and Temple of the Emerald Buddha, the National Museum, Wat Arun, the textile market, and, finally, a sail through the canals on a rice barge. It was fantastic, but I couldn't put one foot in front of the other by the time we'd finished.'

Kate was silent, remembering her own barge trip with Khunying Somtow.

'I can see why you like it here, Kate. It's fascinating.'

'Yes,' she said, wondering if he would pick up on the irony in her voice. 'You never know what to expect.'

'And Somtow really is charming,' he continued quietly. 'I can understand why you would be attracted to him.' There was a brief but awkward pause.

'Anyway, I feel much more energetic today. How about dinner tonight?'

Kate felt torn. She craved the familiar comfort of his casual presence, the lack of pressure or tension. On the other hand, she did feel the need to be alone, to sort out her thoughts and calm her anxieties before the coming contest.

'I don't think so, David. As I said, I need some space tonight, to sort things out.'

'You know you can trust me, Kate. I won't try to

215

come on to or to influence you. Let's just have dinner, as old friends.'

Kate was tempted. She knew he was telling the truth.

'I don't think it would be a good idea, David. I'll see you tomorrow.'

He tried to keep the disappointment out of his voice. 'Whatever you say, Kate. I'll look forward to seeing you tomorrow night.'

Dusk was falling. Kate let herself into the garden and wandered barefoot in the grass, breathing deeply. She sat down on the bench under the miniature temple, close to the spot where she had observed Ae and Chaiwat's tryst that first night. Since then, she had learnt that this was called a spirit house. The Thais believed that when a new building was constructed, it was critical to provide a dwelling for the spirits of the land who were being displaced. Incense was smouldering now on the platform holding her spirit house. Ae had placed little bowls of rice and fruit as offerings.

She remembered finding Ae in tears a few days after Harrison's punishment and flight. The girl had sat on this very bench, her head in her hands, long black locks tangled around her face. Chaiwat was gone, the maid informed her when Kate inquired as to her trouble. He had disappeared without a trace, without even saying goodbye. His landlord had told Ae that Chaiwat left in the middle of the night, owing two weeks rent. The landlord had even wanted Ae to pay.

A new storm of tears shook the woman's slender body. Chaiwat had promised to marry her, Ae had told her. He came round nearly every night, after Kate was asleep, to make love to her, and to ask her questions about her mistress. 'He was always very curious about you,' added the maid, sounding a little jealous.

The bastard! Kate was not surprised that Chaiwat had dropped out of sight. By now, Harrison's would-be business associates would have discovered the double-dealing, and they surely knew his driver. Clearly, Chaiwat has used Ae to keep tabs on Kate's private life. No wonder Harrison had known so much about her relationship with Somtow.

Kate comforted Ae as best she could. Chaiwat was a crook, she told the girl. He and his master had been plotting to steal millions of *baht* from their company, her company, Khunying Somtow's company. (The girl perked up at this news. As Kate had surmised, Ae knew who Somtow was.) The planned crimes had been discovered, and Harrison had fled the country. Chaiwat had probably gone with him.

Ae sobbed on Kate's shoulder. Kate had awkwardly patted her head, trying to resist the urge to caress her more intimately. Eventually, Ae had calmed herself. Kate even brought a smile to her face by promising to give her a raise in her salary in gratitude for her faithful service.

Kate sighed. She closed her eyes and sat quietly, listening to the soft music of the fountain. Peace. She needed to centre herself, to find the truth in herself that would guide her in tomorrow's choice.

The doorbell chimed, waking her from her reverie. Ae had left for the day. Kate got up wearily, re-entered the house and padded over to the front door. She was too tired to speculate on who it might be.

It was Noi. The long-limbed beauty was dressed more casually than Kate had seen her before, in a simple black shift and sandals. Silver earrings dangled to her brown, bare shoulders.

'Good evening, Kate,' she said quietly. 'I know that you were not expecting me. May I come in?'

Kate felt clumsy and stupid, as she often did in this imposing woman's presence. She felt Noi's appraising gaze taking in every detail of her dishevelled appearance: her unbrushed locks, her wrinkled skirt, the bra strap peeking out from the neckline of her blouse. Noi must know, Kate thought, that she was bare underneath, that the tattered remnants of her underwear were stuffed at the bottom of her purse.

Kate blushed. 'Of course, Noi. Please do.' She stood

aside and the dominatrix slipped off her sandals and strolled into the living room. Noi took a seat on the couch. Kate remained standing, somehow unable to move without permission.

'Sit down, Kate. Don't be nervous. I am here as a messenger from Gregory, not on my own accord.'

She paused thoughtfully, her eyes still bearing down on Kate. Kate tried to meet her gaze, and failed.

'Gregory is very fond of you, you know. Perhaps too fond. If you were my slave,' she paused to lick her lips, 'I would be considerably more strict.' She settled back a little into the cushions. 'Still, I can understand why he wants you, little Kate. Even I find you hard to resist.'

Kate was silent. Her heart pounded in her chest and her nipples ached. What did Noi want, she wondered. She didn't dare allow herself to imagine.

Noi reached into the black bag hanging from her shoulder. Kate half-expected her to pull out a whip or a set of nipple clamps. Instead, she retrieved a flat box covered with red velvet, which she handed to Kate.

'In case you do not choose him, tomorrow, Gregory wants you to have this. To remember him by.'

Kate opened the box. Inside, cradled in more velvet, lay her leather slave collar. She touched one of the studs with her fingertip and understood the underlying message. Gregory was acknowledging that the choice was hers to make. It would be up to her to decide whether to cross the line and commit herself totally to him. If she decided otherwise, though, he would say goodbye. He was no longer willing to share her.

'Thank you, Noi. Please tell Gregory thank you from me. And tell him that I understand. I look forward to seeing him tomorrow.'

Noi smiled, almost kindly. 'I am sure that he is full of anticipation as well.' Then she grew serious. 'Do not disappoint him, Kate. I would never forgive you if you hurt him.'

Noi turned and was gone, leaving Kate bewildered.

How could she hurt Gregory? He was the master manipulator, the prince of pain. She was just his slave. Yet, despite his arrogance, she saw now that he was not sure of her. If he were, he would never have sent Noi to her with the collar.

She fastened it around her neck and went to look in the mirror. The black leather made her flesh look pale, tender and vulnerable. She gave a little shiver. Then she noticed the sparkle of Somtow's sapphire, hanging just below the collar in the hollow of her throat. She felt a pang, understanding that tomorrow she would choose one or the other of these ornaments.

Kate leant against the balcony railing, watching twilight enfold the Chao Phya. Twinkling lights marked the long-tail boats zipping up and down the river and the barges proceeding at their more leisurely pace. The towers of Wat Arun, the Temple of the Dawn, stood tall on the opposite bank, silhouetted against the still-golden sky. A cool, moist river breeze caressed her bare arms and she breathed deeply, inhaling the now familiar fragrances of tropical flowers, frying garlic and car exhaust.

The suite was spacious, lavish, gorgeously appointed with rare textiles and antiques. Plush oriental carpets soothed her feet. Low couches of carved teak, brocade-upholstered, invited her to recline. On a low table in the centre of the room, someone had provided a porcelain vase of orchids, an assortment of succulent-looking fruit, several bottles of wine, crystal goblets and a corkscrew. Kate sipped her chilled Pinot Grigio as she contemplated the twists that had brought her to this point in her life.

She had always viewed herself as sober, responsible, practical – someone who considered the alternatives and weighed the consequences before making any decision. Yet she had come to Bangkok, half a world from home, essentially on a whim, veering wildly off the course she had plotted for her life. She had allowed herself to be seduced, used, abused, fingered, fondled and fucked.

She had plunged willingly into a sea of debauchery and depravity.

She did not regret it, any of it. As dusk settled over the City of Angels, she knew finally that the controlled, pragmatic, sensible self she recalled was just a mask. She had found her true self here in the embraces and the bonds of those who had possessed her.

And now, the final act in this passion play was about to start. Kate refilled her glass and drank deep, trying to relax.

There was a soft knock at the door. 'Come in,' she said without rising from the couch. Somtow had the key, and he had promised that they would all arrive together to avoid any awkwardness. The door swung open soundlessly, and her three lovers filed in.

David came first, a spring in his step and a twinkle in his eye – a remarkable contrast to the weary, dishevelled young man she had met at the airport only a few days before. He wore blue jeans and a shirt of multicoloured batik that set off his rich brown hair and tanned skin. Before she could stop him, he knelt beside her and took her in his arms, his tongue probing her mouth, his hands wandering over her breasts. 'David!' she said, laughing despite herself as she pushed him away. 'That's not fair! We're supposed to draw lots.'

'I can't help myself,' he said, grinning. 'After all, it has been ages since I've seen you!'

Somtow entered next, elegant in a teal silk shirt and linen trousers. He too knelt beside her, opposite David. He took her hand and kissed it gracefully. Then, just as she was admiring his gallantry, he took her middle finger into his mouth and began to suck it. He ran his tongue in the sensitive groove between her fingers. The warm, wet touch sent electric sparks through her.

'Somtow, you have no excuse,' she said. 'Play by the rules!'

Finally, Gregory entered and stood towering over them all. Kate was interested to see that he had dressed all in white, vaguely nautical, a softly flowing shirt open at the neck and tight pants of white cotton. With his jet hair pulled back from his broad forehead and a silver hoop gleaming in his earlobe, he reminded Kate of some eighteenth-century pirate. His expression fitted the role: his eyes blazing and his sensual lips pressed together. He looked fierce, desperate, dangerous.

His voice was as melodious and controlled as ever. 'Good evening, my little Kate,' he said. He held out his hand to her, and she could not help rising to take it. Heat travelled from his fevered skin, up her arm, through her nipples, down to her sex. He didn't make any further advances. For a long moment they simply stood together, as the flames flickered through her body.

Somtow spoke, finally, breaking the spell. 'So, here we are, Katherine, at your service. Yours to command.' Gregory dropped her hand and looked at her sharply. 'How can we please you, mistress?' he said, with an edge of mockery she suspected that only she could hear.

'Have some wine, all of you,' she said. 'Relax and get comfortable.' As they followed her instructions, she continued. 'Thank you for coming. I'm grateful that you are all willing to indulge me.'

'Our pleasure,' said David with a gentle smile. 'And yours too, we hope.'

An awkward silence fell over the group. They sipped their wine.

'So, gentlemen, let's get started.' Kate felt the alcohol coursing through her veins, making her bold. 'Strip, please.' She heard a hint of authority in her voice that she liked. Her guests began to obey. She sank back into the cushions to watch them.

Gregory worked quickly, pulling his shirt over his head without unbuttoning it. The conflagration tattooed on his flesh came alive as he unzipped his fly and peeled off his trousers. He wore nothing underneath. His cock was already half-erect. Finished long before the other two men, he stood with his legs slightly apart, his hands clasped at the small of his back, as his shaft continued to harden. She smiled at him, but he merely stared at her with unnerving intensity.

Somtow undressed as if he were dancing. In fact, Kate felt sure that he was being deliberately seductive, entertaining her with an amateur striptease. He lingered over each shirt button, then stretched languidly as the silk slid over his skin and on to the floor. Using both hands, he slowly pulled down his zip. He stepped gracefully out of his trousers and folded them neatly. Finally he coquettishly turned half-away, as he removed his undershorts, revealing his gorgeously smooth buttocks and quivering cock.

David's style was simple and unselfconscious. His broad smile never left his face as he shrugged off his shirt and pulled off his jeans and boxers. Kate ran her eyes over his bronzed, compact body, remembering the delightful feel of the curly hair on his chest and around his cock. Like the others, David was already showing his excitement.

Kate suddenly became aware of her own arousal. She was wearing a halter-style dress of thin, floral-patterned silk. She felt dampness where the fabric bunched between her legs and circles of sensation where it brushed over her nipples.

Her throat was bare of adornment.

She stood proudly in front of the three naked men and unfastened the straps tied behind her neck. The dress drifted to her feet, revealing her to their hungry eyes. The curtain rises, she thought.

'Now,' she said, each of you has a chance to please me. You may do whatever you like – whatever you think that I would like. I want to feel, smell, touch, and taste each of you separately. I don't know whether it is best to be the first or be the last. However, let chance decide the order.' She took a pair of ebony dice from a celadon bowl on the table and handed them to Gregory. 'Whoever rolls highest, goes first.'

Without taking his eyes from her, the tattooed man shook the cubes in his palm and threw them on to the

222

table. Each die showed a single spot. 'Two,' said Gregory, almost growling. 'That represents the two of us, my Kate.'

Somtow rolled a three, David a six. 'I'm first!' the young man exclaimed in delight. He took a step towards her. She held up her hand.

'One moment.' She turned to Somtow and Marshall. 'Please sit, if you'd like, be patient, and wait your turn. You are free to watch, of course.' She smiled mischievously. 'I just hope you don't lose interest.'

Somtow relaxed on the sofa. 'I prefer to stand,' said Gregory softly. 'I'll have a better view.'

Kate was annoyed to realise that she blushed. She turned towards her visitor from Boston and reached out to him. 'David,' she said, 'come to me.'

He needed no further invitation, but was at her side at an instant. Taking her face in his hands, he kissed her deeply. His familiar taste brought back warm memories of shared pleasure and simple trust. Kate returned his kiss, trying to convey all the love and gratitude she felt towards him.

'Place your hands behind your head, Kate, and close your eyes,' said David softly. 'Just let me touch you.'

Kate followed his suggestions. She felt her breasts pushed forward as she crossed her arms at her neck. Memories flashed through her mind, unbidden: the last time she had assumed this position, the clamps and the pain. She pushed those images away. I must concentrate, she reminded herself, focus on the one I am with.

For a moment there was only the evening breeze stirring against her skin. Then she sensed the lightest of touches. Something like velvet brushed over the exquisitely sensitive area exposed by her upraised arms.

The touch sent electric currents down her spine to her sex. She adjusted her stance, slightly separating her thighs.

Barely in contact with her skin, symmetrical caresses travelled across her breasts and traced circles around her throbbing nipples. What was David using to arouse her in this way, Kate wondered? It wasn't his hands, she was sure, and it felt softer than any feather, though just as light.

The velvet left her for a brief instant, then she felt it again slowly tracing the line of her neck, along her collarbone, down into the hollow between her breasts, across her belly to her navel. She caught a whiff of sweetness, and then she understood. The orchids. The velvet of their petals left a tingling wake. Everywhere he touched her, her flesh came alive.

Now she felt the fronds brush the insides of her thighs. She spread them a little wider as she sensed that her companion was sinking to his knees. 'David,' she entreated, 'kiss me.'

The flowers continued their leisurely dance over her flesh, but now she felt a new, sharper pleasure. David gently pushed his tongue through the curly thicket hiding her sex and flicked at her swollen clit. Kate moaned and pressed herself against his mouth. Still without using his hands, he burrowed into her, lapping and probing, hungry for her woman-flesh, thirsty for her juices. She buried her fingers in his wonderful hair and pulled his head deeper into her groin, urging him to consume her completely.

David felt her urgency. He became less gentle. He used his teeth to nip at her lips, sucked her clit into his mouth and pulled on it until she screamed. 'Oh, David!' Kate cried, forgetting her audience, forgetting everything except the frantic storm of sensations between her legs. 'Fuck me, David. Give me your beautiful cock.'

'Only too happy to oblige, my love,' said David, his voice muffled by her hair. 'Why don't you get down on your hands and knees?'

Kate scrambled into position, thrusting her rear into his face. David spread her wide and gave her one last hard lick, starting at her clit and ending at her anus. Then, before she could catch her breath, he slipped inside her. Her passage was so wet with her lust and his saliva that she felt no resistance at all, just the smooth slide of his hardness and then the delight of being full of him.

He grasped her hips and began pumping. It was so familiar, so right. Kate felt his scratchy pubic hair rubbing against her arse, smelt the muskiness of his sweat. Yes, she thought, yes, as he plunged deeper, already swelling towards climax. She could feel every motion he made, sense the blood pulsing in his flesh. She breathed in time with him, letting go of the taut, strained climb to orgasm, focusing instead on him. She loved him, she knew it within her heart and within the hot depths of her sex.

He came quickly, and then her own climax took her unexpectedly. Sweet fullness surged and burst inside her, inevitable rather than explosive. Waves of bliss washed through her. She lay on her stomach, enjoying the soft nap of the carpet on her skin and the precious weight of her lover lying on top of her.

'I'm sorry, Kate,' David murmured. 'I couldn't hold back. It's been so long, and I wanted you so much.' He rolled off her, and she twisted until she was on her knees facing him. She stroked his face and kissed him.

'Don't worry, David. You were wonderful. You made me realise how very much I've missed you.'

Playfully, she picked up the discarded stem of orchids. She ran the blossoms up and down his still-tumescent cock, noting how it jerked and thickened at the contact. 'Of course, you know that flowers are the way to a woman's heart.'

Suddenly, Kate remembered her other guests. Somtow sat on the couch, leaning forward with his hands on his knees, lips parted in a half-smile. Gregory leant against the wall, his muscular arms folded over his chest, his eyes smouldering. Kate had the fleeting notion that he might be jealous. Nonsense, she thought, he is just impatient at having to wait.

Somtow stood up as she turned her eyes to him. 'Katherine, my dear. Have you recovered sufficiently from this young man's excellent attentions?'

He extended a friendly hand to David, helping him to rise. 'If so,' continued the Thai, 'I am eager to take my turn.' As David returned to lounge on the divan, Somtow knelt in front of her. With his slender, artists hands, he began to knead her breasts, tugging gently on the nipples to lengthen them. He spoke seriously, but that playful twinkle was there in his eyes.

'Katherine, what can I do to please you? How can I prove to you how totally devoted I am?' He reached behind her to retrieve a pillow from the other sofa.

'Why don't you lie down and make yourself comfortable?'

Curious to see what he would do, she lay on her back as he indicated. Instead of placing the pillow beneath her head, he arranged it under her hips, so that her sex was elevated and open. The position alone made her horny. What was her decadent prince up to?

'Relax, my dear, and give yourself up to pleasure.' He placed one elegant finger directly on her clitoris, just in contact, with barely any pressure. It drove her crazy, but she held still, allowing the sensation to build. Now he was rubbing her there, still with only one finger. Looking up at him between her knees, she saw that with the other hand he was fondling himself, massaging his cock with slow, sensual strokes. The sight of his smooth, pale shaft swelling in his hand made her ache inside.

He captured her clit between forefinger and thumb, rolling and pulling on the sensitive flesh as if it were another nipple. Meanwhile, he inserted his middle finger into her soaked cunt, sliding it up and down against the inner walls.

'You certainly are very wet, Katherine.' He added a second finger, then a third; he rubbed her clit and his cock a little faster. She twisted her hips, pushing against his hand, wanting him deep inside.

'I know I do not have enough fingers to fill you the way you want, Katherine. Even my cock is not enough.'

'Oh, no, Somtow. I want you. I want your cock.'

'I have a better idea,' he said, with an angelic smile. He reached for the bowl of fruit, and selected a ripe mango. He rolled the egg-shaped fruit in one hand, the fingers of his other hand still busy in her cunt. The mango was about the size of his fist. As it lay in his palm, he couldn't close his fingers around it. 'As you probably know, Thailand is famous for its mangoes. They are the sweetest and most succulent in the world.' He removed his hand from her sex. It was gleaming and wet with her juices. 'Excuse me for just a moment.'

Kate held her breath, watching as he lubricated the smooth rind of the fruit with the moisture from her cunt. He licked the mango. 'Delicious,' he said.

He parted her lower lips with one hand. With the other, he brought the slippery fruit close to her opening. 'Relax now, Kate. Relax and enjoy.'

He pressed the mango against her, trying to work it into her. 'Think how good it will feel,' he murmured, 'once it is inside.' Impossible, thought Kate, but the narrow end was already through the gateway.

Somtow returned his attentions to her tingling, throbbing clit, trying to make her hornier, wetter. She tried to open herself, spread her legs as wide as she could. It seemed that the smooth oval was stuck. Then Somtow pushed, hard and sudden. There was a brief moment of pain, then the mango was completely inside her cunt.

Kate was reminded of Noi's bulging dildo. There was the same feeling of being stretched beyond her limits, full beyond belief. The dildo had felt foreign, though, lifeless and artificial. The mango inside her was alive, organic, warm and slick with her juices. The fruit-flesh was firm, but resilient.

Somtow began working her clit in a new way. He rubbed it against the object inside her, using the friction to build new sensations. Meanwhile, the mango pressed against her, stimulating every nerve in the flesh that enclosed it. She felt a little twinge as the mango came in contact with her cervix. Then this discomfort was erased by the first, far-off rumblings of orgasm.

Somtow was using both hands on her. He squeezed her swollen labia between thumbs and forefingers and ran them along the length of the lips from front to back, tracing the opening where the mango had disappeared. He placed his palm over her sex and used the heel of his hand to gently push against the rounded solidity that lay beneath the wet surface. Kate moaned under his touch, pulled her knees to her chest and offered him better access to all her folds and openings. He responded by mashing her clit hard against the mango. At the same time, he slid one slender, wet finger deep into her rear passage.

The climax began deep inside her. She had never felt anything like it. The muscles of her inner walls started to tremble. Her body seemed to be swelling inside. The mango felt tighter and tighter. Wave after wave of contractions shook her, intense, violent, ecstatic. She screamed and clutched at the carpet, the pressure inside almost unbearable. Suddenly, she felt a tearing pain, then openness. Hot liquid streamed from her gaping cunt. The damp, sticky mango lay between her legs, expelled by the force of her orgasm.

When Kate regained her senses, she saw Somtow still kneeling between her legs, a delighted smile on his face. He was peeling and eating the mango. 'Absolutely the best mango I ever tasted,' he told her, placing a morsel on her tongue. The fruit practically melted in her mouth. Its sweet, spicy flavor lingered long after she had swallowed.

'Ah, Somtow!' She kissed him lightly. 'You never cease to amaze me.' She saw that his cock was still painfully hard. 'But what about your pleasure? I don't want to leave you unsatisfied.'

Gregory interrupted. 'I'm sure that Somtow will tell you that giving you pleasure is all that he needs for satisfaction. And perhaps that is true.' He strode across the room and stood looming over them. 'In any case, he has had his chance. It's my turn now.'

He held out his hand. Kate took it, and he pulled her

roughly to her feet. 'Now then, Kate,' he said, pinning her hands behind her and searching her face with steely eyes. 'What should I do, to please you?'

Kate stared back at him bravely. Beat me, she found herself thinking, bugger me, use me however you wish. The solicitous attentions of her other lovers, much as they had pleased her, left her longing for something darker.

At the same time, she realised, she did not want Somtow and David to see her degraded and humiliated at Gregory's hands. Especially David. After her stay in Bangkok, he seemed so innocent to her. She did not want to shock him by showing him her true perversity.

So, she was silent, hoping that Gregory would understand her mixed emotions, that he would find some way to satisfy her without revealing the depths of her depravity.

'I know,' Gregory said finally. He brushed her lips with gentle fingers. 'I know exactly what you would really like.

'Stay where you are, Somtow,' he said to the Thai, who was just starting to move back to the couch. 'I will need your assistance with this. And yours too, David.'

Kate tingled all over as she guessed what he planned.

'Somtow, lie down on those pillows. Let's put that cock of yours to some use.'

'Straddle him, Kate. Settle that greedy cunt of yours down on that very impressive erection.'

Somtow closed his eyes and gave a sigh of delight as Kate followed instructions. He began to move inside her. 'Stay still,' said Gregory sharply.

'Now, get over here, David, in front of our little Kate. Lean forward and put your weight on your hands, Kate. Now open your mouth, wide. David, stick your cock in her mouth. Deeper, all the way in. She can take it. She likes it, don't you, Kate?'

'Now, stay still.'

Gregory strolled around them, his own erection bobbing. Kate could feel his appreciative gaze. Neither

Somtow nor David moved, but she could feel their cocks pulsing, aching to fuck her.

'Now for the *pièce de résistance*. Of course, you won't offer any resistance, will you, my horny little piece?' Gregory knelt behind her, between Somtow's spread legs, and pulled her arse-cheeks apart. Without any preparation or lubrication, he plunged into her.

'Ah . . .' Kate cried out, her mouth full of David's flesh, and sank down on Somtow's cock. Somtow moaned with pleasure. He pulled back his hips then thrust as deep as he could, just as Gregory impaled her with another stroke.

It was unbelievable. Kate sucked hard on David as she rode Somtow, clenching her cunt muscles around his smooth shaft. Meanwhile, Gregory reamed her, burying his cock up to the root in her quivering hole. He was rough and abrupt. It hurt, but she found she couldn't distinguish the pain from all the other pleasures that assaulted her.

He worked smoothly, steadily, and soon the other two men caught his rhythm. Three cocks moved in unison, filling her until she thought she couldn't bear it, then pulling back to leave her holes empty and hungry.

She heard Gregory speaking softly. 'Oh, you like this, don't you, Kate? My little slut. If you had more orifices, you would want them all full of cocks, wouldn't you? Cocks and fingers, dildos and butt plugs, you want it all, don't you, Kate?'

David forced his cock deep into her throat, nearly choking her. Somtow ground into her, the head of his cock banging against the top of her womb. Gregory withdrew, then rammed her so hard it brought tears to her eyes. More, she thought. Fuck me harder.

Even as she relished it, Kate was surprised by David's and Somtow's roughness, so atypical. Then she understood. Gregory was simply using her other lovers as extensions of his own will. They were his toys, no less than she was.

The extent of Gregory's power thrilled and frightened her.

'You see, Kate. I told you the truth. I know what you want, and what you need.' Was he speaking aloud, or did she only hear his words in her mind? 'You're drawn to me because you know I can tame you. Only I can give you what you crave – love and discipline.'

She bucked and moaned, overwhelmed by sensation and emotion. Gregory pulled halfway out, then pushed a thick finger into her, next to his cock. Her flesh, already stretched beyond endurance, screamed in protest, even while her heart repeated, yes, yes, my master.

Her mind clouded with pain and desire, she realised only gradually that David's cock was no longer in her mouth. She opened her eyes to find that Somtow was sucking eagerly on David's member, while continuing to fuck her cunt. David's moans echoed sweetly in her ears.

Gregory had released them from his thrall. As this thought crossed her mind, the man behind her put his hands around her waist, and lifted her off Somtow. His cock still embedded in her arse, Gregory carried her towards the bathroom.

Kate looked back to see Somtow kissing David's neck and gently mounting him from behind. Her intuitions had been correct. She smiled to herself at the strange ways of fate.

The bath was huge and luxurious, with a sunken tub and twin removable showerheads. Gregory set her on her feet in the tub, facing the tiled wall. She whimpered with disappointment as he slipped out of her.

'Don't worry, my pretty,' he said softly, nibbling on her earlobe. 'You will be full again soon enough.'

He came back with her discarded dress in hand. 'I need something to bind you with,' he said. 'Do you mind if I use this?'

He was serious in his question, she could see. If she refused, he would find something else. She shook her head. 'Whatever you wish,' she said, feeling a thrill at her own submission.

As she watched, he tore two strips off the hem, the muscles in his arms bulging as he attacked the tough material. 'As I told you that first night, silk is ideal for this purpose.' He smiled warmly, drawing the gossamer fabric across her shoulders and down her back so that she shivered. 'As are you, my soft, strong slave.'

He wrapped the strips around her wrists, then fastened them to the shower pipes protruding from the tiled side walls. Her arms were spread wide, as if in an embrace. She was comfortable, but had very little freedom of movement.

Gregory stood behind her, cupped her breasts in his big hands and whispered in her ear. 'What I am going to do now will hurt. It may hurt a lot. But I know that you can bear it, that you will bear it, for me. Won't you?'

'Yes,' said Kate quietly.

'Yes what?'

'Yes, master.'

'Good girl. Now bend over a little.'

He spread her cheeks again. She wondered if he would resume sodomising her. She was sore from his previous ploughing; she felt loose and open. Nevertheless, she wanted him to touch her there, and he did, inserting one hot finger and wiggling it deliciously.

'Oh, you do like that, Kate, don't you? You like me to play with your ass?'

'Yes, master,' she whispered, blushing despite herself at the obscene way he spoke.

'Do you like this?' he asked. He pushed two more fingers in and spread them apart. Kate moaned and said nothing.

'You're not sure? Well, I like it. I like to use your body. I like to see you give in to me, despite the pain, in order to please me.'

He pushed in his fourth finger. Her sphincter was a ring of fire. She bit her lip and fought back tears.

'I know that hurts, Kate. But you like to be full. I know you do.'

Then he did it. He balled his hand into a fist and pushed the whole thing into her. Kate screamed and tried to pull away. He stroked her hair, calming her, all the while with his hand buried in her rectum.

'Relax, Kate. Open yourself to me. Let me take you.'

His voice soothed her, despite her pain and panic. He moved his impossibly huge hand inside her.

'You know I love you, Kate. Don't you?'

The question seemed so absurd, posed by this fearsome stranger with his fist in her arse, and yet she knew it was true. Through these long weeks, even as he mocked and abused her, he had supported her, assisted her, avenged her. Never had he taken her further than she was willing to go. At his cruellest, he never lost touch with her. She had thought that his main interest was in satisfying his perverse lusts. Now she saw, in the clarity of her pain, that his first concern had always been her – challenging her, guiding her, satisfying her.

She nodded, unable to speak.

'I love you and I want you, Kate, to be my slave and my partner. I want you to be my wife.'

An odd moment for a proposal, she thought dreamily, floating above the agony in a haze of pleasure. Not a story we can really tell our children.

His voice was husky, and his fist inside her was vibrating. She realised he was jerking himself off with his other hand.

'There's so much I can give you, Kate.' His breath was coming faster. 'So much I can teach you.' Kate's cunt was drenched; she was close to coming herself.

'So many ways that I can fuck you,' he gasped and then he ground his fist deeper into her bowels as his spurting come spattered her rear.

Pain, pleasure, it was all blurred as Kate followed him over the edge. Her body convulsed. She would have collapsed if not for the bonds. From a long way away, she felt him pull his hand out of her, felt herself gaping, the tender flesh twitching and raw.

'Ah, Kate, you're mine. You will be mine, won't you?' She caught the hint of worry in his voice and understood, in triumph, that even now he was not really sure of her.

She nodded weakly. 'Yes, Gregory. Yes, master.'

His powerful arms held her for moment. Then he turned on one of the showers, took the head in one hand and aimed it at her buttocks, washing off the come and the sweat. The hot stream played in her open arsehole: degrading, delightful. Next he aimed it at her sex. The warm liquid dripped deliciously down her thighs.

'Someday,' he said quietly, 'I might decide to bathe you in my urine instead.' Kate's heart jumped. 'Would you like that, Kate?'

'I don't know, master,' she said, her voice barely above a whisper. She knew the real answer, and so did he.

Turning off the shower, he began to untie her. 'Well, we will see, won't we, Kate.' He chafed her wrists to get the blood flowing, then placed her hands gently behind her head. 'We have plenty of time, Kate, you and me – time to explore what you really enjoy.' He kissed her lips tenderly. 'Now, where did you leave your collar?'

Chapter Twelve
Opening

*I*t was only nine o'clock and already there was quite a crowd. Some of the patrons were quite remarkable, too. There was that pale, fragile-looking woman in the motorcycle jacket, for example, leading the huge black man by his leash. Across from her, a skinny man in red leather trousers lounged on the couch. His corset-clad slave knelt before him, licking his bare toes. A pair of androgynous twins strolled arm and arm, platinum blondes sheathed in black spandex jumpsuits. They stopped every now and then to kiss, their tongues twining like serpents.

Leather, rubber, velvet, silk. Spike-heeled boots and jingling chains. Soft voices as the synthesiser melodies swelled and faded. It was opening night at Justine's.

Kate wore latex: thigh-high leggings, elbow-length gloves, a tight bodice that pinched her nipples, a mini-skirt that scarcely hid her bare sex. She was masked. Her red-gold hair curled luxuriously above her latex-covered forehead. Her lips were painted scarlet.

They had worked hard over the last six months, and she was proud of the result. The club had a high-tech ambience: recessed lighting, black velour couches and shiny, stainless-steel pipes criss-crossing the space. There were many levels: sunken wells strewn with cushions, platforms, stages and stairways. In some places, the shiny bars gathered into structures reminiscent of a cage, but one could never be sure that was the intent.

The room was spacious, almost cavernous. Here and there, though, it was divided by curtains of translucent black silk, lending an air of privacy, intimacy.

On raised pillars around the room, three-dimensional scenes and images flickered and faded – mysterious, erotic, obscene. Here a stern governess in Victorian garb was lashing at a young woman's bare bottom with a birch switch. There, two hooded men in black knelt in chains before their mistress, servicing her with their eager mouths. Across the room, Kate saw the naked form of a woman, struggling in the coils of a gigantic snake. Her mouth was open in ecstasy as the serpent penetrated her, front and rear, with its tail and tongue.

The images seemed solid and real, but if you looked at them steadily, they would shift, mutate, transform themselves like dreams. Kate was amazed at her own creations. Her work had come a long way, a long way indeed under Gregory's tutelage.

Scattered around the fringes of the room, private booths provided virtual-reality experiences, or, for the bolder ones, the opportunity for trysts in the flesh. One could don gloves and a headset and feel the whip in one's hand, watch your victim's skin redden, hear his or her cries for mercy. A full cybersuit allowed you to feel the lash yourself, to hear the jibes or praises in your master's or mistress's voice.

Kate stood by the curtained doorway, welcoming newcomers. Outside, a discreet sign, silver on black, was the only indication of the club's existence. Entrance to tonight's festivities was by invitation only, or through the virtue of being the friend of a friend. Later, they would advertise, but only in select locations. Based on this evening's turnout, Kate felt assured that the club would be popular.

Her costume was hot. Sweat trickled between her

breasts. The salt stung her buttocks. Last night, Gregory had caned her for the first time. She had wondered why it had taken him so long to get to that point, when he had threatened it so many times and she had almost begged for the experience. Now she knew. The pain had been beyond anything she had known, excruciating, unbearable, white-hot, luminous. Afterwards, Gregory had cradled her in his arms and whispered endearments, licked the tears from her eyelids. She smiled to herself, savouring the knowledge that she pleased him as no other did. She was learning more about him every day, the tenderness and the insecurity that he masked with his dominant persona, his loyalty and honesty, his unfailing respect even as he abused and degraded her.

She sighed to herself. It was hard to understand. But still she felt she had made the right decision.

Gregory's ring was heavy on her middle finger. It was iron, lined with gold. Not a wedding ring, at least not yet. She had asked for six months to consider his proposal. The time was nearly up, and she was fairly sure what her answer would be.

A familiar figure, lithe and graceful, entered through the curtained doorway. 'Somtow!' Kate exclaimed, rushing to take his hand in welcome. 'I never expected to see you here.'

'Gregory sent me an invitation,' he said with his old mischievous grin. 'I could not resist the temptation. I had to find out more about the dark side of my Managing Director.'

Somtow bent and kissed her lightly. She looked around, nervous. Gregory did tend to be jealous. Had he invited Somtow to test her?

But Somtow was merely teasing her. Since the contest, he had respected her choice. He had never tried to seduce her again, though they saw each other frequently in the course of DigiThai's day-to-day operations. Did she regret this, she asked herself, looking at Somtow with a critical eye? He was as handsome and elegant as ever. Her heart still beat faster when she remembered some of their outrageous encounters. But she had realised months ago that her most exciting moments with Somtow had been those that echoed the power dynamics of her relationship with Gregory.

As for David, Kate sensed that he had expected her choice. Furthermore, he had found consolation in Somtow, who was only too happy to sooth his frustrations. After his two weeks in Bangkok, much of which, she suspected, had been spent in Somtow's company, he had returned to Boston. They still wrote and talked frequently. He had a boyfriend now, a stockbroker named Jason. 'You warned me about Bangkok,' he had remarked during their last phone conversation. 'But I never expected to discover that I was bisexual! I guess I have you to thank for opening up this new dimension in my life.' They had both laughed, but then he said seriously, 'I expect that it may be quite a while, though, before I find another girlfriend. Gregory is very, very lucky.'

Speaking of her master, she caught a glimpse of him across the room, watching her with her former lover. He wore a leather hood that hid his eyes, but she could see that he was smiling. He beckoned to her.

'Excuse me, Somtow. Duty calls.'

'Have a good time, Katherine,' he said softly. 'And I will try to do the same.'

In a moment she stood before Gregory. He towered over her. He was bare-chested save for a wide strap of leather that stretched over his left shoulder and fastened to his belt. Below, he wore tight black leather pants and boots with pointed toes. Her eyes strayed, as they often did, to the flames that decorated his flesh. They always seemed to change. She had traced the lines a hundred times with her fingers and her tongue, but each time she found new patterns. Her heart beat hard as it always did when she stood this way in the heat of his gaze. Even after all these months, she thought, in wonder, all these hours and days together.

'What do you think, Kate?' he asked with a mocking smile. 'What do you think of Justine's?'

'A dream fulfilled,' she answered sincerely. 'A small miracle.'

'Not exactly the word I would have chosen – miracle.' He laughed. 'There's not much that's holy here. But a dream, yes; the first of many dreams that we will chase together.'

Kate was silent. She wanted to believe this was true.

'How are your stripes?' he asked suddenly.

'Sore,' she said simply.

'Let me see.'

Though they were essentially in public, Kate didn't hesitate. She turned her back to him and hiked up the skirt, baring her buttocks to him and her sex to anyone in the club who cared to look. No one seemed to notice. The guests were all intent on their own games.

He knelt down behind her and ran his tongue along one of the welts. His hot saliva stung, yet it soothed at the same time. 'Inflamed,' he said, licking another one. 'Lovely. The bright shameful badges of your love for me.'

'Yes,' she said. 'Exactly.'

He stood up and crossed his arms over her chest, holding her against him and nuzzling her neck. The leather of his pants scraped against her raw skin. 'I had thought to put you on the block tonight, at the auction.' Her heart skipped a beat. One of the evening's planned attractions, Kate knew, was a slave auction where guests might volunteer to sell themselves to the highest bidder. 'But now, I think I want to keep you to myself. I just want to show everyone how much I love you, and how you love me.'

Kate wondered nervously what he had in mind, then pushed her fear away. She didn't care. She trusted him, would do whatever it took to show him that.

'Come with me, little Kate.' He led her by the hand up a short set of stairs to one of the elevated platforms. Her skirt was still rolled up; she knew better than to pull it down. Their movement attracted the attention of some of the guests. They watched curiously.

A network of bars decorated the top of the platform. There was a horizontal one a little below waist height, flanked by two verticals.

'Bend over,' Gregory said. She understood. He wanted to display her wounded backside to the assembled company. She knew by their demeanour and their attire that many would recognise the marks of the cane.

She rested her hips against the bar and bent over, spreading her thighs as she knew he wanted. 'Good,' said her master. 'Very good. Now hold the vertical poles.' She complied. He began to tie her wrists to the poles with silky nylon rope. 'Just in case you change your mind,' he jested.

'You know that I won't, Gregory.'

'Well, I like seeing you bound, anyway. As you know. And so do our clientele.'

Kate could see a little through her legs. Sure enough, most of the customers were standing watching the tableau on the platform.

Gregory stroked her buttocks, so proudly displayed, while every eye in the room followed his movements. He traced one of the welts with his fingers, then pinched it so that she cried out. The audience was silent, holding its breath in excitement.

'Hush, my sweet one. Hush.' He took a butt-plug from his pocket, and twisted it into her. She could imagine how it looked, bulging out between her cane-striped cheeks. Then from his other pocket he retrieved a silvery clamp. Kate gasped as he caught her clit in its jaws.

'There, my love. That's perfect.' He came around in front of her and kissed her tear-stained face.

'Now wait here, for me; wait while our customers admire your beauty and your obedience.'

Kate breathed deeply. She felt the throbbing in her clit changing from pain to desire. She felt the plug stretched her hind hole, and she wanted more. She imagined herself given over to the crowd. He would do that someday, she knew.

She looked into the fierce, proud eyes of her master, her lover, and smiled through her tears.

'I will, my love. I will.'

BLACK LACE NEW BOOKS

Published in February

MIXED DOUBLES
Zoe le Verdier
£5.99

Natalie takes over the running of an exclusive tennis club in the wealthy suburbs of Surrey, England. When she poaches tennis coach Chris from a rival sports club, women come flocking to Natalie's new business. Chris is skilled in more than tennis, and the female clients are soon booking up for extra tuition.

ISBN 0 352 33312 X

SHADOWPLAY
Portia Da Costa
£5.99

Daniel Woodforde-Ranelagh lives a reclusive but privileged existence, obsessed with mysticism and the paranormal. When the wayward and sensual Christabel Sutherland walks into his life, they find they have a lot in common. Despite their numerous responsibilities, they immerse themselves in a fantasy world where sexual experimentation takes pride of place.

ISBN 0 352 33313 8

Published in March

RAW SILK
Lisabet Sarai
£5.99

When software engineer Kate O'Neill leaves her lover David to take a job in Bangkok, she becomes sexually involved with two very different men: a handsome member of the Thai aristocracy, and the charismatic proprietor of a sex bar. When David arrives in Thailand, Kate realises she must choose between them. She invites all three to join her in a sexual adventure that finally makes clear to her what she really wants and needs.

ISBN 0 352 33336 7

THE TOP OF HER GAME
Emma Holly
£5.99

Successful businesswoman and dominatrix Julia Mueller has been searching all her life for a man who won't be mastered too easily. When she locks horns with a no-nonsense Montana rancher, will he be the man that's too tough to tame? Will she find the balance between domination and surrender, or will her dark side win out?

ISBN 0 352 33337 5

To be published in April

HAUNTED
Laura Thornton
£5.99

A modern-day Gothic story set in both England and New York. Sasha Hayward is an American woman whose erotic obsession with a long-dead pair of lovers leads her on a steamy and evocative search. Seeking out descendants of the enigmatic pair, Sasha consummates her obsession in a series of sexy encounters related to this haunting mystery.

ISBN 0 352 33341 3

STAND AND DELIVER
Helena Ravenscroft
£5.99

In eighteenth-century England, Lydia Hawkesworth finds herself helplessly drawn to Drummond, a handsome highwayman. This occurs despite the fact that she is the ward of his brother, Valerian, who controls the Hawkesworth estate. There, Valerian and his beautiful mistress initiate Lydia's seduction and, although she is in love with Drummond, Lydia is unable to resist the experimentation they offer.

ISBN 0 352 33340 5

If you would like a complete list of plot summaries of Black Lace titles, or would like to receive information on other publications available, please send a stamped addressed envelope to:

Black Lace, Thames Wharf Studios,
Rainville Road, London W6 9HT

BLACK LACE BOOKLIST

All books are priced £4.99 unless another price is given.

Black Lace books with a contemporary setting

ODALISQUE	Fleur Reynolds ISBN 0 352 32887 8	☐
WICKED WORK	Pamela Kyle ISBN 0 352 32958 0	☐
UNFINISHED BUSINESS	Sarah Hope-Walker ISBN 0 352 32983 1	☐
HEALING PASSION	Sylvie Ouellette ISBN 0 352 32998 X	☐
PALAZZO	Jan Smith ISBN 0 352 33156 9	☐
THE GALLERY	Fredrica Alleyn ISBN 0 352 33148 8	☐
AVENGING ANGELS	Roxanne Carr ISBN 0 352 33147 X	☐
COUNTRY MATTERS	Tesni Morgan ISBN 0 352 33174 7	☐
GINGER ROOT	Robyn Russell ISBN 0 352 33152 6	☐
DANGEROUS CONSEQUENCES	Pamela Rochford ISBN 0 352 33185 2	☐
THE NAME OF AN ANGEL £6.99	Laura Thornton ISBN 0 352 33205 0	☐
SILENT SEDUCTION	Tanya Bishop ISBN 0 352 33193 3	☐
BONDED	Fleur Reynolds ISBN 0 352 33192 5	☐
THE STRANGER	Portia Da Costa ISBN 0 352 33211 5	☐
CONTEST OF WILLS £5.99	Louisa Francis ISBN 0 352 33223 9	☐
BY ANY MEANS £5.99	Cheryl Mildenhall ISBN 0 352 33221 2	☐
MÉNAGE £5.99	Emma Holly ISBN 0 352 33231 X	☐

THE SUCCUBUS £5.99	Zoe le Verdier ISBN 0 352 33230 1	☐
FEMININE WILES £7.99	Karina Moore ISBN 0 352 33235 2	☐
AN ACT OF LOVE £5.99	Ella Broussard ISBN 0 352 33240 9	☐
THE SEVEN-YEAR LIST £5.99	Zoe le Verdier ISBN 0 352 33254 9	☐
MASQUE OF PASSION £5.99	Tesni Morgan ISBN 0 352 33259 X	☐
DRAWN TOGETHER £5.99	Robyn Russell ISBN 0 352 33269 7	☐
DRAMATIC AFFAIRS £5.99	Fredrica Alleyn ISBN 0 352 33289 1	☐
RISKY BUSINESS £5.99	Lisette Allen ISBN 0 352 33280 8	☐
DARK OBSESSION £7.99	Fredrica Alleyn ISBN 0 352 33281 6	☐
SEARCHING FOR VENUS £5.99	Ella Broussard ISBN 0 352 33284 0	☐
UNDERCOVER SECRETS £5.99	Zoe le Verdier ISBN 0 352 33285 9	☐
FORBIDDEN FRUIT £5.99	Susie Raymond ISBN 0 352 33306 5	☐
A PRIVATE VIEW £5.99	Crystalle Valentino ISBN 0 352 33308 1	☐
A SECRET PLACE £5.99	Ella Broussard ISBN 0 352 33307 3	☐
THE TRANSFORMATION £5.99	Natasha Rostova ISBN 0 352 33311 1	☐

Black Lace books with an historical setting

THE SENSES BEJEWELLED	Cleo Cordell ISBN 0 352 32904 1	☐
HANDMAIDEN OF PALMYRA	Fleur Reynolds ISBN 0 352 32919 X	☐
JULIET RISING	Cleo Cordell ISBN 0 352 32938 6	☐
THE INTIMATE EYE	Georgia Angelis ISBN 0 352 33004 X	☐
CONQUERED	Fleur Reynolds ISBN 0 352 33025 2	☐
JEWEL OF XANADU	Roxanne Carr ISBN 0 352 33037 6	☐
FORBIDDEN CRUSADE	Juliet Hastings ISBN 0 352 33079 1	☐

Black Lace non-fiction

------- ✂ -------------------

Please send me the books I have ticked above.

Name ....

Address ....

....

....

.... Post Code ....

Send to: **Cash Sales, Black Lace Books, Thames Wharf Studios, Rainville Road, London W6 9HT.**

US customers: for prices and details of how to order books for delivery by mail, call 1-800-805-1083.

Please enclose a cheque or postal order, made payable to **Virgin Publishing Ltd**, to the value of the books you have ordered plus postage and packing costs as follows:

UK and BFPO – £1.00 for the first book, 50p for each subsequent book.

Overseas (including Republic of Ireland) – £2.00 for the first book, £1.00 for each subsequent book.

If you would prefer to pay by VISA or ACCESS/ MASTERCARD, please write your card number and expiry date here:

....

Please allow up to 28 days for delivery.

Signature ....

------- ✂ -------------------